THE

Indigo

NOTEBOOK

OTHER BOOKS BY
LAURA RESAU

The Ruby Notebook

Star in the Forest

Red Glass

What the Moon Saw

THE *Indigo* NOTEBOOK

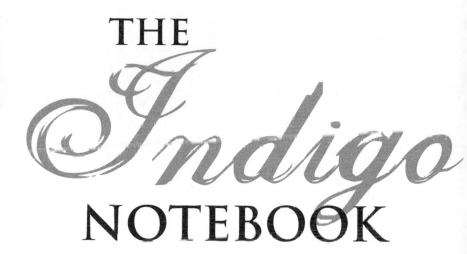

LAURA RESAU

EMBER

All rights reserved. Published in the United States by Ember, an imprint of Random House Children's Books, a division of Random House, Inc., New York. Originally published in hardcover in the United States by Delacorte Press, an imprint of Random House Children's Books, New York, in 2009.

Ember and the colophon are trademarks of Random House, Inc.

Grateful acknowledgment is made to Coleman Barks for permission to reprint Rumi excerpts from *The Essential Rumi*, translated by Coleman Barks, copyright © 1995 by Coleman Barks (HarperSanFrancisco, an imprint of HarperCollins Publishers).

Visit us on the Web! randomhouse.com/teens

Educators and librarians, for a variety of teaching tools, visit us at randomhouse.com/teachers

The Library of Congress has cataloged the hardcover edition of this work as follows:
Resau, Laura.
The indigo notebook / Laura Resau. — 1st ed.
p. cm.
Summary: Fifteen-year-old Zeeta comes to terms with her flighty mother and their itinerant life when, soon after moving to Ecuador, she helps an American teenager find his birth father in a nearby village.
ISBN 978-0-385-73652-7 (hc) — ISBN 978-0-385-90614-2 (lib. bdg.)
ISBN 978-0-375-89384-1 (ebook)
[1. Mothers and daughters—Fiction. 2. Single-parent families—Fiction. 3. Fathers—Fiction. 4. Ecuador—Fiction.] I. Title.
PZ7.R2978In 2009
[Fic]—dc22
2008040519

ISBN 978-0-375-84524-6 (tr. pbk.)

RL: 6.0

Printed in the United States of America

13 12 11 10 9 8 7

First Ember Edition 2011

For Bran and Ian,
the loves of my life

Acknowledgments

Writing a book is a huge group effort! I am eternally grateful to my editor, Stephanie Lane Elliott, for her brilliance; to my agent, Erin Murphy, for her amazing energy; and to the people at Delacorte Press for their behind-the-scenes magic. You are all phenomenal at what you do.

Old Town Writers' Group—Laura Katers, Leslie Patterson, Sarah Ryan, Lauren Sabel, and Carrie Visintainer—continues to be my lifeboat in the tumultuous sea of writing. Thank you for your friendship and fabulous critiques. My mother, Chris, is a genius for knowing where a manuscript-in-progress needs to go. She loves the characters so much that she will stop at nothing to defend their story (no matter how many revisions it takes me!). Thanks, Mom.

I couldn't have written this book without inspiration, research assistance, and hospitality from my close friends María Virginia and Laurentino. I also thank their relatives for giving me a warm welcome into indigenous communities near Otavalo. Thanks also to Alecssandra and her generous family for sharing their home with me on my Ecuador trips. Conversations with the fairy godmother librarian of my childhood, Selma Levi, her son, Adam Klein, and Tim Baird enabled me to deepen the emotional resonance of this story.

My brother, Mike, has helped me understand feelings about adoption throughout our lives—an experience that I drew on in writing this book. Thanks to my father, Jim, for always believing in me, and for mailing me odd little newspaper clippings and trinkets to spark my creativity. My son, Bran, and husband, Ian, have let me leave their world for hours every day and disappear into the world inside my little trailer (with only a little bit of screaming and crying and moaning, *"Maaaamáááááá . . ."*). Ian, thank you for giving me the support that lets me dream and fly—I suspect that's why my books tend to involve true love and happy endings.

Chapter 1

It's always the same, no matter where in the world we happen to be. Just when I get used to noodle soup for breakfast in Laos, or endless glasses of supersweet mint tea in Morocco, or crazy little *tuk tuk* taxis in Thailand, Layla gets that look in her eyes, that faraway, wistful look, as though she's squinting at a movie in the distance, and on the screen is a place more exotic, more dazzling, more spiritual than wherever we are.

On rainy hills, she dreams of parched desert drum rituals. On windswept islands, she yearns for ancient jungle secrets. On palm-treed beaches, she imagines sacred mountain waterfalls. When her mind starts drifting off, our bodies and suitcases soon follow.

And here we are, Layla and me, on the last leg of a journey from Southeast Asia, our plane swimming in clouds above the Andes, hovering, once again, between homes.

The plane lurches like a spooked elephant. My hands clench my notebook, and my eyes flick back to the flight attendants to see if they're in emergency mode. No, they're stuffing sugar packets into a metal container, their faces calm under thick masks of makeup. In the window seat beside me, Layla sits cross-legged, flirting with the middle-aged guy in the aisle seat, both of them leaning across me.

Turbulence doesn't faze Layla. She loves it, like a roller-coaster ride thrown in for free, that flutter in the stomach, that rush of adrenaline pulling her into the moment.

I click my seat belt shut and elbow her. "Hey, Layla, the seat belt light's on."

She shrugs. "Don't worry so much, Zeeta, love."

I reach across and fasten her seat belt. She kisses my temple and leans toward the flight attendant, her blond hair hanging like a curtain over my lap. "Red wine, please."

Of course, the man insists on paying for her wine, pulling a few bills from a silver money clip with manicured fingers. He's wearing khaki pants, a neatly tucked-in white cotton shirt, the sleeves carefully rolled up to reveal muscular forearms, and a silver watch. He looks like he stepped out of a magazine ad for something domestic. He's the quintessential Handsome Magazine Dad, metallic blue eyes and a touch of distinguished gray at his temples. He'd be posed in a shiny stainless-steel kitchen, casually flipping a pancake while his younger wife and daughter smile at the table, as if they've been caught midjoke.

I wonder what he thinks of Layla: a cute, disheveled hippie chick in a slightly see-through cotton wraparound skirt tucked over her knees, with her bare toes peeking out. She's almost thirty-five but looks twenty-five. She always smells of sweet sweat and essential oils, whatever scent addresses her chakra deficiency that day. Today she's chosen a citrusy smell, something bright and tart.

I used to wish for a Handsome Magazine Dad, but I've pretty much given up by this point. Every year in a different country. Fifteen years, fifteen countries, well over fifteen boyfriends for Layla. Fifteen *dozen* maybe, one for each month. It's way too late now for a normal home, normal family, normal childhood.

I open my latest notebook, indigo-colored, and ask the man, "What's your full name?"

"Jeff Ryan."

I jot that down and then write, *Efficiency Consultant for Financial Institutions,* which is apparently his job, whatever that is. "Jeff, if you had one wish, what would it be?"

Usually people ask why I'm asking, and usually I say, "So I can remember you," which is true, and flatters them. But the real reason I've filled all these notebooks—a different color in every country—is deeper, buried inside me. It has something to do with wanting to figure out this thing called life, hoping that by sifting through other people's wishes and

memories and dreams, I can find the pieces I need to understand it.

"One wish?" he says, looking amused. His voice is warm
and gravelly. "Honestly? To settle down." He sips his wine,
maybe deciding how much more to tell. "My girls are grown.
My wife left me three years ago." He lets out a breath. "I'm
tired of the online dating scene in Virginia. I just want my
life back to normal."

I jot down his answer, feeling wistful. *To settle down. Normal.*

Before I can move on to more questions, he shrugs off the
sadness that's crept into his voice. "So"—he grins at Layla—
"you lovely ladies on vacation?"

"Our life is a vacation!" Layla's extra-giddy since we're between places. "Phuket last year. Off the coast of Thailand.
Now I'll be teaching English in Otavalo." She clicks her
plastic cup against his and sips. "Cheers!"

Just hearing her mention Phuket makes me ache. In Thailand, I'd woven myself into life in our beach town. I savored
my routines—walking through the noisy market, riding my
bike down a jungly dirt road, taking morning swims with
friends, eating coconut sticky rice wrapped in banana leaves.

I glance across the aisle, out the window, where there's
nothing but pure white mist. And a boy staring into it. He
looks about my age, maybe a year or two older. Sixteen? Seven-
teen? His skin is just a shade darker than mine, tea without
any milk swirled in, and his hair the same as mine, long and
black and pulled into a braid. He could be an Otavaleño

Indian, a descendent of the Inca. I've seen them on street corners all over the world in ponchos, playing pan flutes.

The flight attendant leans toward him, a mauve, lip-lined smile pasted on her face. *"¿Señor, algo para tomar?"*

He knits his eyebrows. Finally, he speaks, stumbling over his words. *"Quiero—quiero—"* he says with a heavy accent and an edge of desperation.

Strange. Maybe he only speaks Quichua.

"Orange juice, please," he finishes in American English. Reaching for the juice, he catches my eye and blushes.

Layla, meanwhile, is on a roll with her captive audience. "This whole region is overflowing with sacred waters. There's a waterfall that grants your wishes. . . ." She has that look in her eyes now, the mouthwatery look that some people get over chocolate cake.

Jeff nods, looking enraptured. When Layla pauses, he jumps in. "You know, you're refreshing. Different." He pulls out a business card from another silver clip. "Let me take you out to dinner. I'm based at banks in Quito for a month, but I'll be making some visits to a branch in Otavalo."

Without glancing at the card, Layla tucks it into the waist of her skirt, showing a peek of hips tanned caramel on Phi Phi Island, a short boat ride from our home in Phuket. "Thanks."

She'll never call him, and not just because she's against phones. He's just someone to charm for a few hours. For a sustained effort of a few weeks or even days, the guy has to be young, unshaven, shaggy-haired, and extremely irresponsible—like her most recent ex-boyfriend, a wandering, dreadlocked artist clown who sold shell jewelry on the beach.

Jeff flashes me his model smile, his teeth unearthly white, probably from a fresh tooth-bleaching strip. "You could come along too. Are you two traveling buddies?"

I smile, trying to swallow the jaded been-there-done-that feeling. "I'm Layla's daughter."

"Oh." He blinks, rearranging his assumptions.

Layla grins. "She's always called me Layla."

"Oh," he says again. "And she's yours?" he blurts out. "You look so young. And you two don't look alike. I mean, you're both really pretty—" He's wishing he could take his foot out of his mouth.

I don't hold it against him. I press my lips together and stare at a point beyond his head, to the boy across the aisle. Now the boy's holding up something to the window's white light—an ice cube? A clear stone?

Layla strokes my arm. "I know. Isn't her skin magnificent? I'd kill for that color. Never burns."

Soon the conversation will take a turn to how "mixed-race" kids always turn out beautiful—in the same way that mutts are tougher than purebreds—and then he'll ask, *Where is her father from, anyway?*

"She gets her color from her father," Layla says.

I give her a look.

She twitches her nose, a silent apology.

I put on the headphones without bothering to change the

channel from Muzak. Anything to block her out. Across the aisle, white light oozes through the plastic window. No contours of a landscape, no glimpse of what's ahead. Again, I watch the boy, his forehead pressed against the window, peering into the mist like he's looking for something.

And then he turns and stares right at me. The corner of his mouth lifts in a half-smile. A smile that for some reason gives me a tiny speck of hope. Maybe this time will be different.

Chapter 2

Normally, Layla and I take rickety, cheap, old third-class buses wherever we go, but at the baggage claim, Jeff insists on paying for our cab with his company's expense account. "It's too late at night," he says firmly. "Dangerous for two young women on their own."

Layla accepts with a shrug and a smile, even though this is a tea party compared to the truly dangerous late-night situations we've found ourselves in. Before heading to his rental-car agency, Jeff makes sure we're safely in our authorized taxi, and says, "Call me, Layla, all right?" Through the rolled-down window, she shakes his hand absently, thanking him and jumping into a conversation with the taxi driver. Already moving on.

"Bye, Zeeta," Jeff says as the taxi pulls away.

I wave goodbye, a little sorry for him, wondering if one day Layla might ever choose a responsible, stable man like him. On the ride to Otavalo, she rambles on to the driver about Pachamama, the Andean version of Mother Earth, as I expertly tune her out, slipping into my magazine fantasy family. In my favorite ad, which I cut out and taped into a notebook a couple of years ago, the Handsome Magazine Dad and younger mom and daughter are lounging on bright white sofas, barefoot, in matching cotton pajamas, reading the newspaper and smiling. And you know that later they'll do Normal Family things together, like riding bikes to the park or hopping into their new SUV to go to the mall, where they'll run into neighbors they've known all their lives.

An hour and a half later, around midnight, I snap out of my fantasy when we reach downtown Otavalo, mostly deserted at this hour. The streets are narrow, made of interlocking gray stones, and the buildings just a few stories high, a mix of Colonial and new. Streetlamps cast pools of light on the sidewalks, onto shadowy squares filled with neat little gardens and trees, their trunks painted white. We pass a few people, some staggering, maybe walking home from bars.

Around the next corner, our new home comes into view. Layla found this apartment online, fell in love with the old facade of peeling white paint, the blue iron gate in front, the flowered courtyard inside. Once the cab stops, she steps onto the sidewalk, into the yellow lamplight. She spreads her arms wide, like wings, beneath the swarm of moths fluttering above her. "Zeeta, love, this is it!"

"For a year," I mutter. "What's the point?"

"Lighten up, Z!" Layla heaves her giant backpack over her shoulders. "You're amazingly, extraordinarily, phenomenally lucky!"

"I'm tired, Layla." I pull my green cloak from my backpack and wrap it around myself, breathing in its familiar wool smell. We stand in the chilly night air, waiting for the landlady to answer the buzzer as the cabdriver unloads our remaining bags.

Layla's eyes are dancing, her arms flailing, her bangles jingling. "You know, most kids would do anything to live your life."

I nod sleepily. What kids have told me is they'd do anything for a mom like Layla. A mom who, when I was little and scribbled all over the wall with an orange crayon, whipped out a purple one and joined me. But when your mother is that weird, you can never be as weird as her. So you become the responsible one, the practical one. Even if that's not who you are. You become the one who says, *Maybe you should get a job with health benefits this time. Maybe we should stay here another year now that we're settled in. Maybe it's time to register me at a school.*

But yin and yang is what it's all about. That's what one of Layla's ex-boyfriends told me in Brazil, two countries ago. There must be a tension, a kind of tug-of-war that keeps us both from falling over the edge.

. . .

In the middle of the night, I wake up with my heart pounding, my insides on fire. This is life. I'm in it. Am I where I'm supposed to be? Is this right? Of all the places in the world, I am here. In Ecuador. Of all the ages, I am fifteen.

I unzip my sleeping bag, sweating. The clock says three-thirty a.m., the worst time to wake up drowning in panic. I feel raw, like my skin's just been peeled off. I take long, slow yoga breaths, letting my belly expand. The floor's hard beneath my body, just a foam roll-up mat and the sleeping bag. Bluish light seeps through the small window, maybe from the moon. My two ancient suitcases and overstuffed backpack loom like phantoms. Other than that, the room's empty. And it smells strange. Not like sand and salt like our Thai beach house.

Empty apartments terrify me.

I give myself a desperate pep talk. *Remember, Z, it's always like this. Hang in there. In a few days it'll feel okay.*

I do more deep breathing and glance again at the red light of the clock. Almost four a.m. now. In Thailand it's midafternoon. But this is more than just jet lag. These middle-of-the-night panics have haunted me for years now.

This is where you belong now, Z. Soon Ecuador will be your home.

As I drift back to sleep, I think ahead a year, to when I'll have to tear myself away from here, and already my chest aches.

. . .

The next morning I discover that the landlady has kindly stocked our refrigerator with a big container of blackberry yogurt and left a ripe papaya on the counter beside two sets of silverware. It makes me feel better that someone is looking out for us.

I eat breakfast at a tiny table on our balcony that overlooks the enclosed courtyard. My notebook is open and balanced on my knees. From time to time I put down my spoon and pick up my pen and jot down notes on this new home.

I started writing in my notebooks when I was eight. The first one was purple and lasted for our whole year in Guatemala. After that, I filled more and more notebooks every year, but I made sure they were the same color in each country, a small way of imposing order on my chaotic life. Just before we left for Ecuador, Layla and I stopped in a Thai stationery store to pick out my next notebook, a new color. I'd gone through purple, orange, blue, green, yellow, red, and white, and was wondering if I'd have to move to gray or brown, when Layla held up a deep purple-blue notebook and shouted, "Indigo!" I rolled my eyes and said, "It's just dark purple," but she insisted, "Indigo! It's an official color of the rainbow! The color of the third-eye chakra! The sky at dawn! And twilight!"

Writing in my notebooks always makes me notice more things. Now I'm taking in details like the birds hiding in the trees, singing and twittering, and throngs of cheery potted plants lining the walls. The balcony wraps around the courtyard, shared, I guess, by other tenants. Our apartment is tiny, on the third floor, up a treacherous, winding metal staircase. It took forever to drag our bags up here last night. The two bedrooms are more like closets, barely big enough to fit a bed.

The bathroom is even tinier, and not for the claustrophobic—sitting on the toilet, your knees press against the wall, which is just inches from your face. The landlady left a note: *Don't touch the shower faucet with wet hands or you might get shocked.* A small towel was hung up for that purpose, I assume, beside the shower, over the toilet paper. The toilet paper makes me sneeze. It's scented and embossed with tiny bears, and after use, has to be thrown into a minuscule pink trash can wedged beneath the sink. Each country has its different set of dangers, different set of quirks.

Layla's still sleeping, so I eat some yogurt and fruit alone in the cool air, the bowl balanced on my knees. My seat is a wooden crate covered with a scrap of foam. The rusted nails sticking out have already scraped my calves, made pink criss-crossing lines. I make a note to borrow a hammer and pound them in. I have to be on the lookout for safety hazards.

In a new place, Layla's priority is hanging up crystals of cut glass to catch the light and cast tiny rainbows everywhere. "It's not just decoration, Z," she says, if I point out that it might be wiser to address a gas leak or a broken toilet first. "It's to help with chi flow."

I finish the last of my yogurt, then wash my dishes and lay

them neatly on a towel to dry. Layla emerges from her bedroom, her hair a tangled, glowing mess in the sunlight streaming through the window.

"Morning, love."

"Morning." And then I decide, *This time will be different.*

This time will be different!

This time my life will change!

In a voice that sounds more like a command than a question, I say, "Why don't you call Jeff?"

"Huh?" She lights a match and starts a burner for tea, coming this close to setting her hair on fire.

"The guy from the plane." I lean against the small refrigerator. "For once, can you date a man who's not an artist or a clown?"

"What about that poet in India?"

"Call Jeff."

"Why, love?" She cuts moon-shaped slices of soft papaya and arranges them in a star on her plate, with a dollop of yogurt in the center. She smiles at it, pleased.

"Listen," I say. "I have three years left before college and I want them to be normal years. Normal."

"Give up wanting what other people have." She's quoting Rumi. This line in particular always makes me gnash my teeth.

"Will you call him?" I push.

"Mmmm. This papaya is at the pinnacle of ripeness."

I wipe the yogurt dripping from her chin. "Call him, okay?"

"I have no idea where his number is."

I search her things for the business card as she drinks tea and eats her moon-star food on the balcony and marvels at the courtyard. "Look at those flowers! This is paradise! *Every object, every being, is a jar full of delight.*"

"Including Jeff," I say under my breath. And then, in frustration, "Layla, I can't find the card anywhere."

"Then set me up with someone else, love. You pick." The steam from her tea swirls around her face. She half-closes her eyes like a sleepy cat and recites in a murmur, *"I should be suspicious of what I want."*

Rumi again. I roll my eyes. How can you argue with a mystic who's been dead for seven hundred years? I grab my bag—a woven red one from Guatemala—and stuff my indigo notebook in the side pocket, then head out, on a mission to find what I want more than anything: a normal life.

Chapter 3

At nine a.m., the cobblestoned streets are bustling with people, many of them Otavaleño Indians. The women wear long dark skirts and shiny blouses and thick shawls with hundreds of tiny gold beads wound around their necks. The indigenous men have long single braids, and are dressed in regular jeans and shirts. And some people—who must be mestizos, according to my guidebook—look like they could be from anywhere in the world, wearing pants, shirts, blouses, and skirts that have probably been imported from China.

My guidebook says that the difference between being indigenous or mestizo doesn't have to do as much with your skin color as it does with how you dress and wear your hair and what language you speak and your last name. I could probably pass for indigenous if I dressed right, if I walked in that tall, proud way.

Strange how with a little thought and effort, you can change who you've been forever. If Layla made an effort, could she change? I keep my eyes open for Dad-like men to set her up with.

This town feels almost cozy, in its valley surrounded by towering mountains, all shades of dazzling green rising into gray stone peaks. The sun's starting to heat up the morning air, reflecting off the cement buildings, some painted pastels, some bright blues and yellows. The stores look welcoming and cheery with their doors propped open—Internet cafés, bakeries, narrow restaurants with whole chickens roasting in the windows, little pharmacies, travel agencies.

It feels good to hear the musical rhythms of Spanish again. I'm finding I understand the language effortlessly, even though the last Latino country we lived in was Chile, five years ago. Of course, Spanish has always been one of my favorites.

I zigzag down streets, cutting across a big flower-filled square with a fountain and trees, past a whitewashed church, trying to follow my guidebook's route to the daily craft market at Plaza de Ponchos.

The first local I talk to is a blind man in a blue chair with a small orange plastic bowl on his knees. "I like your blue chair," I say, realizing as I say it that he might not know it's blue, might not even know what blue is. Feeling stupid, I drop a few coins into his bowl and keep walking.

"Gracias, señorita," he calls after me.

Soon I turn a corner, and there it is, Plaza de Ponchos, a sea of tarps and tables spread with fuzzy scarves and sweaters and bags, flower-embroidered shirts, sparkly silver jewelry, woven rugs, heaps and heaps of colors spilling out everywhere. I weave through the tunnels of stalls that smell of wool fresh off llamas and sheep and alpaca, an earthy animal smell mixing with the exhaust of passing cars. Tourists are chatting with vendors, reaching out to test the itchiness level of a poncho, or holding up a brown sweater beside a gray sweater to decide which color looks best. Meanwhile, the vendors are cajoling in singsong voices, a mix of Spanish and heavily accented English, "All-natural dye, special deal for you, three for twenty dollars, come on, buy, buy, buy . . ."

And then, at the end of a row of scarves and sweaters, seated behind a table, I spot a great big woman with a million gold beads winding up her neck and coral beads snaking up her arms, all the way from her wrists to her elbows. She sits like a queen on a throne, her blouse shining with hundreds of tiny blue flowers and wide, soft lace at her forearms. But the thing that sets her apart from the other ladies is her smile. A smile that's one hundred percent real, not the half-hearted smile of vendors just trying to sell you something. If you know you'll only live a year in a place, you want to start being around a smile like that right away.

I'm not a naturally outgoing person, but I've learned to be. I've learned to walk right up to people who look interesting and introduce myself—it's the only way to make friends when you move around so much.

You make yourself bigger than life. You walk with your head high and your shoulders relaxed and a little swagger in your hips. You act like you never wake up at three-thirty a.m. in a nervous sweat. You exude a confidence you don't have.

I smile at her and hold out my hand and say in Spanish, "*Buenos días.* I'm Zeeta."

Without skipping a beat, her hand meets mine. "*Mucho gusto,* Zeeta. I'm Gaby."

I forget my Dad-candidate search for the moment and say, "Gaby, what matters most to you in life?" because another thing I've learned is that you have to dive straight into the important questions, the kind that pierce through small talk and jump right into a person's core. The kind that would otherwise take years to figure out.

"Breathing," she says. "If I weren't breathing, I wouldn't be alive, would I?" She closes her eyes and takes a long, deep breath that looks as if it tastes like lemon sherbet.

"If you had one wish, Gaby, what would it be?" And after a moment, I add, "Except world peace or something noble like that," because she seems like the type who would wish a selfless wish. "And besides more wishes," I add, because she also seems the clever type.

"Happiness," she says matter-of-factly.

"But I mean specifically, what would bring you happiness?"

She shrugs her big shoulders. "The way I see it, people

think they know what they want, and it turns out they don't have a clue."

She answers a few more questions, which I record in my notebook, and then she interrupts herself to call out to a passerby. His hand just barely grazed the soft alpaca scarves on her table, and she must have noticed. "Five dollars, *señor!* But I'll give you a discount since I like your eyes!"

The guy smiles, and after a few moments of teasing and bargaining, he buys three for ten dollars. "I really do like your eyes!" she calls after him, giggling at him as he leaves, looking pleased.

She turns to me and says out of the blue, "Wishing is tricky, Zeeta."

"Tricky?"

"When I was a girl, my *ñaña*—"

"*Ñaña?*" I ask. I'm fluent in Spanish from living in Chile and Nicaragua and Guatemala, but each country has its own slang. It always gives me a little thrill to discover new slang, like finding a coin or jewelry on the ground and slipping it into my pocket.

"My *ñaña*," she repeats. "My sister. She wanted nothing more than to be mestiza. For her, that meant being rich and beautiful. So she refused to speak Quichua and stopped wearing her *anacos* and blouses and got a perm and highlights."

"Is your *ñaña* happy now?" I ask.

"She's been a maid for a mestizo family for thirty years. No family of her own, no business of her own, no passion in her life." She clucks. "And look at my two sons. They live in Spain, play music there. When they're in Spain, they want to be here. When they're here, they want to be in Spain." She laughs and tilts her head at me, curious. "Well, what about you, Zeeta? What would you wish for?"

"A home," I say. "A normal home. With a normal family." I raise my eyebrow at her defiantly. "And I know for a fact that would make me happy."

She nods, obviously unconvinced.

I change the subject. "So, Gaby, you probably meet lots of eligible bachelors here at the market, right?"

She raises an eyebrow.

"If you come across anyone who might make a nice, boring dad, let me know."

She shakes her head and gives a deep belly laugh and I feel very grateful for my first friend in Otavalo. I suspect that when I wake up at three a.m. tonight, my room won't feel quite so empty or strange-smelling or terrifying.

Chapter 4

B ack at the apartment, jet lag hits me like a sledge-
hammer. I have a sudden, desperate urge to take a nap. It's
three a.m. back in Thailand. Layla's looking amazingly bright-
eyed, sitting on the balcony next to a twenty-something guy
in superbaggy pants with orange patches on the knees and a
faded, threadbare shirt that says SOMEONE IN RHODE ISLAND
LOVES ME.

"Zeeta, love! This is Giovanni. From Venezuela."

I'd bet my life he doesn't have a retirement account. "What
do you do, Giovanni?"

"Teach surfing. Travel all over the coasts, stay a while in
each town." He pulls something out of his pocket. Balloons.
He blows up three, twists them into a flower, and presents it
to me, grinning. "And in the off-seasons, I'm a clown."

Layla gives me a sheepish look and the tiniest shrug of a shoulder.

The flower balloons dangle from my hands. "A clown?"

"A clown."

After he leaves, I scream, "Another clown?"

"Well, this one's not an artist clown. He's a surfer clown. And he's Taoist."

It turns out he lives in the apartment next to ours, but he'll have to leave unless he can scrounge up rent with a new clowning job. I'm secretly hoping the clown market is satu rated here.

Over the next week, I take lots of naps, slowly recovering from jet lag. Layla hangs out with me and the clown on the balcony after her English classes. He's nice enough, but when I ask if he's saving for retirement, he says, "*Amiga*, I don't plan on living that long."

Gaby's found a few possible suitors for Layla, mostly other vendors at the market, some of whom are saving for retirement. There's the friendly, tubby antique trader who knows so much about the sixteenth-century Spanish conquest you'd think he'd lived through it himself. When I bring Layla by the market to casually check him out, she chats with him about his antique Virgin Mary statues, and then, after five minutes, drags me away, whispering, "Notice how spittle collects at the corners of his mouth? No way could I date someone like that!"

My favorite candidate is the Beatles-obsessed twenty-something jewelry seller with the handsome chiseled face (which I feel makes up for the male pattern baldness). Their conversation lasts for a full half hour, but in the end, she murmurs to me, "I just can't get past the hair."

"What? Not scraggly enough for you?"

She shrugs. "My new clown is much cuter. And more soulful."

Apart from the failed setups, I spend my days gathering basic necessities—mattresses, a mop, shampoo—and writing in my indigo notebook and exploring. Already, I've gotten to know a bunch of locals—the sisters at the bakery where I buy my midafternoon pastry snack, the elderly landlady who's always bringing us food, the blind man in the blue chair with the orange plastic bowl.

The blind man interests me. He's already filled seven pages in my notebook. He sits in one place for a few hours, and then, when he feels like it, he picks up his little blue chair, walks a few blocks, finds a new place, sets down his blue chair, gets comfortable, and puts the bowl back on his knees. I watch him from a distance sometimes. I wish he could see how comfortable and cheerful and perfectly at home he looks sitting there.

A week after our arrival, I'm heading toward Gaby's booth in Plaza de Ponchos. I'm all tropical orange today: wrapped in a papaya sarong from Thailand with tangerine flip-flops, licking a mango ice cream cone, starting to like this town. The sun's beating down on the cement and cobblestones, so bright I'm squinting. My guidebook says Otavalo is less than twenty-five miles from the equator at an altitude of eight thousand feet—much closer to the sun than most places on earth, which explains how, when the sun shows itself, it feels almost blinding.

When Gaby catches my eye, she motions excitedly for me to hurry, which isn't easy to do in a sarong and flip-flops.

"What's up, Gaby?"

"*Mire.* Look at that guy." She points across the square toward the rug section. "The gringo." I scan the crowd for an American—someone decked out in a fleece jacket and khaki shorts and Tevas, his skin and clothes bland next to the rainbow colors of wool and the locals' warm, brown skin. But there is no pale tourist in the direction Gaby's pointed.

"Where?" I ask.

"There. By Alfonso's carpets, by the blue tarp. He looks like us Otavaleños but I think he's really a gringo."

And I spot him, a teenage guy about five and a half feet tall, my height, short for an American guy but average around here. He's wearing shorts and a white raw cotton shirt, embroidered with white zigzags, the kind they sell at the market. Local guys, on the other hand, seem to prefer long pants and store-bought clothes. Now that I'm focusing on him, this guy seems American except for one thing: apart from his clothes and his gestures, he looks like any other Otavaleño. He has their strong cheekbones and the same cinnamon shade of skin. And like most Otavaleño guys, from boys to old men, his black hair is long and braided.

But he walks like a bumbling American, taking long

strides without finesse, his backpack knocking sweaters off tables, and then, as he bends down to pick them up, knocking off some scarves. If you live in a different country every year, you notice that each culture has its own way of walking, moving, standing, sitting, talking, looking. It's hard to put your finger on what exactly the differences are. With Americans, it's a kind of klutzy confidence, hovering between endearing and annoying. Looking at this guy, I agree with Gaby; he must be a gringo.

"What's he doing here?" I ask.

"Who knows. He can't speak any Spanish, poor boy." She shakes her head. "We think he's lost. All morning, he's gone from booth to booth, saying, *'Mamá, Papá.'*" She grabs my arm. "Look, Zeeta, he's coming this way!" She waves her arms, trying to get his attention. Finally, she catches Alfonso's eye and yells in Quichua across the square. Quichua is the language of the Otavaleños, apparently what they use at the market when they don't want you to understand them. I imagine she's saying something like, "Hey! Tell that clueless kid to get his butt over here!"

Alfonso laughs, shouts back to her, and points our way. He gives the boy a friendly shove in our direction.

The boy stumbles toward us, politely stepping aside for people, only to get even more jostled by the crowds. Those Americans. People assume I'm American because *Layla* is technically American. And although my accent is hard for people to pin down, most say it sounds more-or-less

American. But the truth is I have no country. I was born in Italy but left before I was a year old. I am nationless.

Finally the guy reaches Gaby's booth and shrugs off his backpack. Little beads of moisture cling to his face. He wipes his forehead with his sleeve and takes a sip from his plastic water bottle. That's another telltale American thing, the ever-present water bottle.

"Hi," he says in English. "I'm Wendell." He smiles a hopeful smile, and that's what makes me recognize him, the way the corner of his mouth turns up. The boy from the plane who had problems ordering orange juice.

"Zeeta here." I shake his hand, which is damp with sweat. "And this is Gaby."

Gaby nods and shakes his hand, discreetly wiping it on her skirt afterward. *"Mucho gusto."*

He turns back to me. "You were on the plane, weren't you?"

I nod. "Across the aisle."

"In between your parents, right?"

"Layla's my mom. But that was just some guy we'll never see again." And then, before he can ask why Layla and I look nothing alike, I say, "Wendell, what do you want more than anything?"

"To find my birth parents," he answers without a pause. And before I can move on to ask his favorite place in the world, he says in a voice so sincere it sounds naked, "Will you help me, Zeeta?"

. . .

We find a nearby café, and as he reads the menu, his eyebrows scrunched together, I study him. What is he like on his own turf? My guess is that in school he teeters on the edge of popular, enough to make him self-assured, yet not cocky. Judging by the muscles in his calves, he probably plays some school sports, track maybe, or cross-country.

He looks pretty clean-cut, no tattoos or piercings, yet no name brands flaunted in your face either. His long braid is striking, the most alternative thing about him, and I wonder if kids at school consider it hippieish or elfin or exotic or what. His grades in school? Hard to say, but he's definitely smart—alert eyes, observant, curious. And his way of talking— at least based on our brief conversation on the way to the café—includes no "dudes" or "f-in' " as a universal adjective.

His eyes plod over the menu, his lips moving.

"Need me to translate?" I ask.

"No thanks. I took two years of Spanish, so I can read it okay. It's the listening and talking part that gets me. All the words run together, you know?" The corner of his mouth turns up. Endearing.

When the waitress comes, we order pastries and coffee with lots of milk and sugar. I haven't said I'd help him yet. First I want to find out what I'd be getting myself into. I open my indigo notebook, pen poised, and ask, "So, what do you know about your birth parents?"

"Hardly anything." He pauses, then says quickly, as though he's just mustered up the nerve to jump into ice-cold water,

"I think they're alive, at least my birth mother, because she relinquished me." His eyes flicker to the TV blaring a comedy show in the corner. "I hate talking about this."

I nod, trying to look professional. "Names?"

He shakes his head. "Spent all week trying to find records. No luck."

I twirl my pen like a baton, a skill I picked up years ago in my school's parade practice in Chile. "Pictures?"

Again, he shakes his head.

I stare. "How do you think you'll find them, Wendell?"

He puts his face in his hands.

Immediately, I wish I'd softened my words. I've caught him in an in-between place. A time when emotions are raw and unclothed. I can relate.

He takes a breath. "I thought this was a smaller town. And I figured they'd look like me." He glances at the other people in the café, most grinning at the TV. Several of the men have long black hair and fine, sculpted faces and tea-colored skin, just like Wendell. "Everyone here looks like me." He looks disoriented, like when you wake up to a sudden, bright light.

"Don't worry." I keep my voice airy. "By the time you go home, all white Americans will look the same."

He laughs. "My mom and dad—I mean, my real mom and dad—my adoptive ones, that is"—he taps his spoon on the table, a nervous rhythm—"they think my birth mom came from a village just west of Otavalo. But they don't know the name."

I want to take the spoon from him and press his hands together.

He pulls something from his pocket: a small crystal, the size of his thumb. The thing he was looking at on the plane. Carefully, as though it's an eggshell, he places it in my hand. "They told me this was wrapped in my blankets."

I examine the crystal. It's a translucent, five-sided cylinder, coming to an uneven point. Parts are cloudy, parts clear.

Crystal, I scribble in my notebook, surrounding the word with question marks. A pretty feeble clue.

"Let's let our unconscious minds ponder this a bit," I say, echoing one of Layla's ex-boyfriends in Phuket, a self-pronounced psychotherapist who lived in a tent on a beach and offered free advice like a hermit sage.

Wendell and I sip our coffee and munch on flaky pastries layered with sweetened goats' milk and he asks about the places I've lived. I recite the laundry list of fifteen countries. He asks me about each one, about the food and the people and the landscape, and when I get to Thailand, I linger on how Layla and I used to catch a *tuk tuk* to the market and eat coconut ice cream doused with condensed milk and sprinkled with crushed peanuts.

Now he's pulling out an old-fashioned camera and screwing on a lens and filter. "I'm listening," he says. "It's just that your face is all lit up. And the sun's hitting your hair at the perfect angle. You can see these reddish highlights."

I keep talking, asking him more indigo-notebook questions, a little self-consciously now that he's clicking the camera at me. After we finish our third cup of supercreamy sweet coffee—which leaves me wound up—we stand, stretching.

Again, he smiles that halfway smile. "So."

"So," I say.

"Are you in?"

I make a mental list of pros and cons.

The cons are obvious. The task seems fairly hopeless: wandering around villages searching for people who may not want to be found, based on a crystal and vague directions. He can't even pay me. I'll have less time to give English lessons to the market vendors to make money. Less time to get our apartment in shape. Less time to make sure Layla gets her visa and other necessities. I could be wasting mountains of time on this boy. And even if by some miracle we succeed, he'll leave and I'll never see him again.

He's staring at me, waiting, looking earnest and hopeful.

I move on to the pros. He notices things like red highlights in my hair. His funny little half-smile makes me happy. I like being near him.

Is that enough?

There's more. He could tell me tales of his normal life, which is probably the closest I'll get to living one myself.

And even more. He understands how it feels to be pelted with questions you can't answer—like what you are, or where you're from—questions that chip away at you little by little until you feel like a pile of tiny pieces that could blow away in a breeze. How it feels to be always searching for some magical glue that will hold your self together.

The deciding factor comes straight from my gut or my heart or somewhere very irrational. It is this: If we find his parents, maybe one day, as utterly impossible as it seems, I'll find my own father.

"I'll do it," I say.

"Thanks!" He looks truly grateful. "So, what next?"

"I'll ask around and see if I can figure something out. Meet you back here tomorrow? At ten?"

"Sure." He puts his camera strap over his shoulder. "I guess I'll head back to the hotel."

I want to draw out the conversation. "Which hotel?"

"Hotel Otavalo."

"That's fancy." I've passed it on the way to the ATM. It even has a doorman.

"The owner's giving me a major discount. Friend of a friend of my mom kind of thing. I couldn't afford it otherwise. My parents paid for the plane ride and I emptied out half my savings account for the lodging and food."

"Oh." I always feel wistful when people mention savings accounts. Layla's and mine disappears every year when we fly to a new place, a major contributing factor to my middle-of-the-night panics.

I feel like I should hug Wendell goodbye, or at least shake his hand or make some parting physical contact. For a few moments we stare at each other, and right when it seems on the verge of too long, I notice he's started looking *through* me, at something faraway behind my eyes. A strange look has come over his face. "Zeeta—" He stops.

"What?"

"Nothing." He rubs his hands over his face. "See you to-morrow." He tosses a five-dollar bill on the table. "Be careful tomorrow morning." His voice is falsely casual.

"Careful?"

"In the water."

And before I can say, *What water?*, he half-runs out the door.

Chapter 5

I weave through the crowds already milling around the market, toward Gaby's booth. All the coffee and sunshine is making me sweat like crazy. Early mornings here are usually cool, but once the sun reaches a certain point overhead, if there are no clouds, it suddenly becomes blazing hot. Pan-flute music floats from the booths, notes mixing together in wavy melodies over excited voices of vendors and tourists. Markets always make me feel like I'm in the middle of a party, the perfect place for my happiness to spiral out when I'm in a good mood.

And I *am* in a good mood, a very, very good mood, for the first time since leaving Thailand. But doesn't it seem like even when you're in a very, very good mood, there's always one little nagging thing, like a tiny stain on a brand-new shirt? In this case, it's Wendell's strange look and his parting words about water.

Did I mention water to him? I fast-forward through our conversation. No, nothing about water. Finally, I decide to ignore the water thing and rewind to the part about the reddish highlights.

I'm practically skipping, when I pass the blind man in the blue chair. His name, I've discovered, is Don Celestino. As usual, I drop some coins into his orange plastic bowl. He knows my name by now, and somehow always recognizes me, even before I say a word. By my smell? The sound of my footsteps? The way I drop the coins in his bowl?

"Thank you, Señorita Zeeta," he says. *"Que Dios te bendiga."*

We chat a bit, and I ask him if he's run across any eligible bachelors for Layla (he hasn't), then I make my way through the crowd to Plaza de Ponchos. I spot Gaby, one eye on the sewing in her lap and one eye on the crowd, searching for customers to charm.

"What happened to the lost boy, Zeeta?" she asks eagerly.

I plop down onto a wooden chair and fill her in.

As I talk, she makes tiny, fine stitches on a white blouse, an elaborate blue flower pattern laced with silver thread. "A crystal, eh?" She nods, lost in thought. "You should go to Agua Santa first. Just west of here. Famous for its *curanderos*." She knots a strand of blue thread and surveys her work. "There they use special rocks to heal. They say each of their rocks has its own powers and personality." She raises her eyebrows and lets her needle hover in the air like the point of a question mark. "But Zeeta, what does this boy hope to find?"

"His birth parents."

"Yes, but I mean really, what does he hope to find?"

At home, Layla's lying on her back in the middle of the living room with her arms and legs outstretched like a snow angel.

"Hey, Layla. What's up?"

"Waiting for a seed to be dropped."

"Being a sheet of paper?" I ask. "A spot of ground?" We have fifteen years' worth of inside jokes. I learned this Rumi verse by heart when other kids were chanting patty-cake:

> Try and be a sheet of paper with nothing
>   on it.
> Be a spot of ground where nothing is
>   growing,
> Where something might be planted,
> A seed, possibly, from the Absolute.

I'm grateful she's doing this in the privacy of our home. One afternoon in India she climbed up a tree in a public square. It was an especially sweltering day, and as she put it, "It looked all cool and sacred and dappled up in the branches." A policeman found her, told her it was forbidden, and demanded she come down. She tried to charm him into letting her stay.

It didn't work.

He slapped her with a huge fine. Until her next paycheck, we lived on the random scraps in our cupboard. One night, over a meal of onions and rice and weak tea, I exploded, "Why, Layla? Why couldn't you just think, *Oh, what a nice tree,* and keep on walking?"

She touched my hair. *"Let the beauty we love be what we do. There are hundreds of ways to kneel and kiss the ground."*

I pulled away. "Then do it in our own living room!"

Now, here she is, rolling onto her stomach, extending her body into yoga boat pose—in our own living room, as requested.

I reward her with a smile. "I met a guy today, Layla."

"¡Que pleno!" she says, which we've discovered means "Cool!" in Ecuadorian Spanish. We usually speak in English but throw in bits of slang from wherever we happen to be. I particularly like *que pleno.* It literally means *how full,* which makes perfect sense. When something's cool, you feel full, like you can temporarily forget about the missing piece of yourself.

She stands up, stretching. "What's he like? Do tell!"

"He's American, kind of clueless, but cute. He was adopted from here. I'm helping him find his birth parents."

"Que pleno." She winks.

My face grows warm. "I'm just helping the guy."

Layla leans over and ruffles my hair, a gesture that might incorrectly lead you to believe she's maternal.

"So did any seeds from the Absolute fall?" I ask, changing the subject.

"One of these days," she says. "Someday soon."

Layla always lights candles for regular dinners. She says they bring us into the present moment, but I think it just makes it harder to see our food. Tonight, after she twirls her first forkful of spaghetti, she says, "So, Zeeta, love. I figured we could go to the sacred waterfall tomorrow for my birthday. I got directions and everything."

"A waterfall?"

"The one that fulfills your wishes, remember?"

I nod, remembering Wendell's comment. The hair on my arms stands up. How did he know? And he said to be careful. What did that mean? If I tell Layla, she'll make us burn incense and lug along her bag of protective amulets: green jade, red jasper, a handful of crystals, and a trusty head of garlic.

Instead, I make an excuse. "I already told Wendell I'd hang out with him tomorrow morning." I take a bite of salad.

"No problem. We're leaving at four. Back by eight a.m. at the latest."

"Why so early?" I moan.

"It's an hour's walk to the waterfall. We have to do it at dawn."

"What'll we do there exactly?" I already feel tired just thinking about it.

"Bathe in the waters to purify our spirits." Her eyes widen into an otherworldly look. "Clear our minds, focus on what we truly want. Let the universe manifest it."

"I think I'll just watch."

Layla ignores that. "And something our landlady told me," she says, leaning in, waving her fork, excited. "If you bathe with rose petals, you can make your ideal man fall in love with you."

"Can I choose your ideal man?"

"Ha! Dream on!" She drains her last sip of beer. "Your turn to do the dishes, love," she says, and whizzes past me into the bathroom, swishing her skirt.

"It's always my turn to do the dishes." If we ever let it be her turn, the sink would be filled with a mountain of cockroach-infested plates coated with crusty, moldy stuff.

"Mystics are experts in laziness." She's quoting Rumi again. *"They rely on it, because they continually see God working all around them."*

"More like because you continually see *me* working all around you."

I fill the sink with soapy water, plunge in my hands, start scrubbing a pot. We fall so easily into this banter. We've been doing it for years, playing these roles. Zeeta, the Down-to-Earth One. Layla, the Dreamy One. But isn't real life trickier and stickier? In real life, beliefs ooze like honey from one shape to another. Of course, I never admit this to Layla.

Despite my cynicism, like it or not, she's formed my sense of reality. So I do my own secret rituals, carry hidden talismans. I practice restraint, flowing into the social norms of our current town. Still, bits of Layla in me burst through here and there: tangerine outfits, silk scarves in my hair. At least they're clean and ironed, I tell myself.

I rinse the soap from the dishes, set them in the drying rack, wipe the counter.

"Hey!" Layla calls out from the bathroom. "You can wish for that Wendell guy."

"I'm just his translator, Layla! It's purely professional."

"Whatever. So, are you coming to the waterfall?"

At the mention of water, my insides tighten again. I'm not telling her about Wendell's mysterious warning. It worries me, though. I'm definitely not letting her go alone in the middle of the night to swim around naked without someone to watch out for her.

I roll my eyes. "Fine."

Layla's a kite and I hold the string. I'm the heavy one, the one stuck to earth. I wonder if she resents that I keep her earthbound, knowing that if one day I let go, she could fly away. Which is maybe another reason why I say I'll go to the waterfall, to keep hold of that string.

Chapter 6

"Psst." Layla's voice rips into my sleep. "Wake up, Zeeta."

My eyelids creak open. I've just had my usual three-thirty a.m. panic and finally gotten back to sleep, only to be woken up again. The clock's red light blares 4:11 a.m. I groan.

"Come on, Z," Layla says, shaking me. "Get dressed! The sacred waters await!"

"Ten more minutes," I mumble.

The breeze at dawn has secrets to tell you," she whispers.

"Don't go back to sleep.
You must ask for what you
    really want.
Don't go back to sleep.

People are going back and forth across the
  doorsill
Where the two worlds touch.
The door is round and open.
Don't go back to sleep."

"It's too early for Rumi, Layla."

But by now my grogginess is fading, and I toss back my covers and drag myself from bed. Twenty minutes later we're walking through the cold night, black except for a sliver of moon. I'm wearing my cloak with a hood and toting a bag of extra clothes in case Layla gets cold. She's wearing a thin cotton T-shirt and a long, gauzy skirt—underprepared, as always. At least she thought to pack a towel and flip-flops in her bag for after the ritual.

"Sure you know where we're going, Layla?"

"Of course. It's just outside the city." She tucks her hands under her armpits, shivering.

I toss her a jacket.

She kisses my cheek. "Oh, love, this is why I bring you along."

I wonder at what precise moment in our past Layla became the child and I became the grown-up. When did I start bringing a coat in case she got cold or crackers in case she got hungry? As long as I can remember, it's been me. And before that? Maybe we were just cold and hungry more often, which Layla probably felt was adventurous since it made us extra-appreciative of our next meal and snuggling under warm covers at night.

We turn onto the dirt shoulder of the highway that circles downtown Otavalo in a kind of asphalt moat. Occasional trucks barrel by at top speed, their headlights emerging from the darkness like passing comets.

I think of Wendell. He smelled good yesterday, all sweat and sunshine and that boy smell, fresh, like laundry detergent and cotton.

I met lots of gloriously average American kids on our last trip to my grandparents' house in Maryland. I envied them, secure in suburbia. They didn't think twice about having a real living-room sofa and an actual bed and two family cars. Some had even kept the same best friend since kindergarten. Why couldn't my life be small and neat and contained like a single-serving pack of Frosted Flakes?

I wonder if being with Wendell will make me feel part of this world, if I can get absorbed in it, the way you do in certain movies. I want to turn his life around in my hands, examine its textures and colors, breathe it in, imagine it's mine.

After an hour of walking, the faintest indigo light of dawn illuminates the horizon. Layla and I turn up a cobbled street to a small village. "Look! Roses!" she cries. "I forgot to bring them, but the universe put them in our path." She plucks some salmony pink blossoms from the roadside and tucks them in my bag.

The sky's growing lighter and lighter, the stars disappearing, the moon fading. "Hurry, Zeeta! We have to do this exactly at dawn." We half-run through the center of town, a little cement-slab plaza, and then through a gate and into the woods. A big wooden sign reads CASCADA DE PEGUCHE. Peguche Waterfall. The woods are dark, all green shadows, full of birds waking up and starting their songs. Water's rushing somewhere below the path.

The tree shadows seem a little ominous, and again I remember Wendell's warning. I glance at Layla, wondering whether I should mention it. No, she'll just make us come back tomorrow loaded with amulets and charms. Another day of waking at four a.m. seems entirely unappealing.

"So, Zeeta," Layla says, breathless. "Tell me. What are the qualities of my ideal man?"

"A homebody who saves for retirement. And lives in the same place for years. And whose idea of excitement is barbecuing with neighbors. And whose expertise is *not* making flower balloons."

"Hmmm," she says. "Sounds excruciatingly boring."

The running water's growing louder and louder, drowning out our words, and I try to let it drown out Wendell's warning, which keeps running through my head. We make our way along the path, the moon barely lighting the way, as Layla whispers Rumi in rhythm with our steps.

"Who gets up early to discover the moment
    light begins?
Who finds us here circling, bewildered,
    like atoms?
Who comes to a spring thirsty
and sees the moon reflected in it?"

The trail curves, and we emerge into a huge clearing. There it is, water tumbling down a towering cliff, shooting its spray everywhere, fine droplets of mist wrapping around us. It's the kind of sight that really does take your breath away. Otherworldly, straight from the set of a fantasy film— *The Chronicles of Narnia* or one of the Lord of the Rings movies. A shower of liquid diamonds. We stand on the wooden bridge spanning the river and stare. The water's falling from a height of a ten story building, straight down the side of a cliff, pounding the pool below. It makes me feel very small and very fragile.

"Wow!" Layla says. *"Que pleno."*

"Que pleno," I agree.

"All right, let's do this."

I squint through the mist, at the white water churning, violent and relentless. "Layla, I don't know if this is a good idea."

She kisses my hair. "Oh, my little worrywart." She crosses over the bridge and makes a left, along a steep embankment, toward the base of the waterfall, where huge rocks glisten between the path and the water's edge.

I follow, feeling nervous and giddy. Later, I'll complain about being woken up in the middle of the night, but secretly, I'll relish the memory. You hardly ever remember the normal days where you get up at the normal time and do the normal things. No, what you remember are the times you got up in the middle of the night to see an eclipse or a meteor shower or a sunrise or to bathe in a wishing waterfall. Especially when it's tinged with a sense of danger.

Layla tears off her clothes and drops them in a heap on a rock. I pick them up after her and fold them neatly, tucking them inside the plastic bag. I drape the towel over my arm, ready. Barefoot, she creeps across the rocks, clutching a handful of rose blossoms, toward the pool beneath the waterfall. She clings to the slick crags, half-crawling toward the water's edge. I've seen her naked countless times before, cleaning the apartment or lounging on the sofa, idly sketching ink doodles on her arm or leg or belly as though she were a blank canvas. To her, life is the ultimate artistic masterpiece, and it's up to you, the creator, to make it as wildly dazzling as possible.

She's chanting now, her voice mingling with the waterfall, and I catch a few words here and there, easily filling in the rest.

> "Soul of my soul of the soul of a
>   hundred universes,
> Be water in this now-river . . ."

I watch her, my muscles tense. The center of the pool looks deep, with more rocks hidden underwater and strong, whirling currents.

She makes it to the water's edge.

And then, she disappears.

At certain rare moments, time loses meaning. A second becomes a lifetime. Or a day becomes the blink of an eye. Layla's time underwater feels like years. It feels like I've been crying and mourning her for decades. Like I've lived a lifetime without her, with her drowning and dying and leaving me alone to live a bland, beige, tasteless existence.

But all of that's happened in the course of a few breaths, because I haven't moved and the moon hasn't budged in the sky and the morning light hasn't come, and everything is still half-draped in darkness when her scream rips through the waterfall's rush.

"Layla!" I call out.

No response, only the pounding water.

Hot panic shoots through me. "Layla!" I scramble across the rocks on my hands and knees. "Layla!"

I strain to see through the darkness and spray, looking for any sign of her—an arm, a leg, a lock of blond hair. Nothing. Only the white foam and mist and relentless beating of water on water. The waterfall is nearly deafening, a world of rushing water. I wonder if the scream I heard was my own. "Layla!"

I crawl closer, climbing over the stones, grasping at their

jagged edges that dig into my palms. Vaguely I notice the rocks tearing into the soles of my feet, the flesh on my knees. I move closer and closer, wiping the mist and water and tears from my eyes, scanning the water for a glimpse of her skin.

When I'm a few feet from the edge, I see it, her hand flying up from the dark water. Her face appears next, terrified, only to be sucked back under. I grab a fallen branch with one hand and hold on to a sharp rock with the other, and lean over as far as I can, extending the branch.

Her arms thrash through the chaos of spewing water, her fingers clutching at the slippery stone. "Layla!" I shout. "Grab on!"

Her hands reach out and, yes, thank God, they grasp the branch.

I pull her in, straining with all my might. Once she's close enough, I reach out my hand and hang on to her. My fingers dig into her flesh as she climbs weakly up the rock. She lies on the stone, gasping and coughing and gagging.

I put a towel over her and wait for my heartbeat to calm, my shaking to stop. I'm soaked from the waterfall, my clothes stuck to me and my face damp with mist and tears. I lick the blood from my palms.

Layla's whole body is trembling, heaving. She's crying, too, a raw, animal crying.

I hug her, rocking her like a small child. After a while, she says, "I'm so sorry, Z. I'm so sorry."

"Shhh, it's okay, Layla." I hold her close.

"No, it's not. I'm going to change, Zeeta. I swear to you, I'm going to change."

Of course, she won't change. We've had near-death experiences before, and after the initial freak-out, she's back to her usual self before long. Last year, off the coast of Java, her boyfriend of the month had made a sailboat with salvaged parts and taken us on a three-day cruise. On the second day, at dusk, a tropical storm started brewing. The wind and rain blew with terrifying force. I'd never felt that humans were so flimsy and insubstantial. It seemed inevitable we'd be swept away.

Below the deck, Layla and I cowered, holding each other. Layla was moaning nonstop. "Oh God, Z, what have I done? What have I gotten us into? Oh God, I'd give anything to be in Maryland now. To be with Mom and Dad and you at the kitchen table. Playing Monopoly. Or Chinese checkers. Boggle. Scrabble. Backgammon. Oh God . . ."

The boat broke in half, and miraculously, we didn't die. Sometime after midnight, the storm ended, and we found ourselves floating in a tiny lifeboat in shark-infested waters. For a while, I sat there, soaked and shivering, stunned at the regular rhythm of my heart, still beating. Then I started warming up and thinking about Maryland, and how we'd be going there, and how we'd spend heavenly evenings playing Chinese checkers.

As the lifeboat rocked, the boyfriend fell asleep, but Layla and I stayed awake, watching the clouds clear little by little, revealing more stars than I'd ever seen before in one place. She said,

"When the ocean surges,
don't let me just hear it.
Let it splash inside my chest!"

I resisted snapping that the last thing we needed was a chest full of ocean water. Instead I said, "When are we leaving for Maryland?"

For some reason, Layla was sticking her head over the side, tempting whatever toothed creatures lived under the water. "Look!"

I peered out, cautious. Lights glowed far below the surface. It was a strange sensation, like looking out the window of an airplane at night and seeing points of city lights.

"Luminescent squid," she whispered reverently. "What a rare, beautiful thing has happened to us, Zeeta! How many people on this planet get to see glow-in-the-dark squid?"

I fixed my eyes on hers. "Last I heard, death by starvation and dehydration isn't pleasant."

"Don't worry, love," she assured me. "We'll be saved."

Sure enough, by sunrise, some fishermen came across us and brought us to shore and fed us fresh fish and papaya juice for breakfast on a little wooden table. Layla pronounced it the best meal ever and whispered in a kind of prayer,

"Some nights stay up till dawn,
as the moon sometimes does for
    the sun.
Be a full bucket pulled up the
    dark way
of a well, then lifted out into light."

Needless to say, we didn't go to Maryland.

On the way back from the waterfall, I can't bear how Layla's limping down the path like an old lady with her shoulders hunched over, her wet hair plastered to her face, as if the water beat the life force out of her.

Halfway down the path, I say, "Hey, why don't we both bathe with the rose petals off the trail here, where the river's calmer?"

"Really?" Her voice is hoarse.

"Yeah. You can wish for a nice, boring guy and a nice, boring life where you don't get sucked under waterfalls at dawn."

She doesn't laugh. She gives me a long, serious look. "That's what I'm going to wish for, love. That's my gift to you."

We veer off the path, through scratchy bushes, which don't bother us since our flesh is already torn up.

The river's still flowing strong here, but we find a nook behind a tree root where the water swirls in a gentle pool. By now it's light, a fresh light, slanted and misty and dappled through the leaves. Layla takes off her clothes, exposing red scratches crisscrossing her legs, and bruises and welts starting to form over her torso. Five beet-pink spots mark her forearm where my fingers clung to her.

She dips into the water, hanging on to the tree roots with one arm. She rubs rose petals over herself with the other, her lips moving in a silent prayer, some petals clinging to her, others floating down the river.

Once she comes out, I take off my clothes and lower myself into the icy water. I gasp as I completely submerge myself. Then I straighten up, the water waist-high, and rub the petals over my goose-bumped skin. I focus on my own wish, as much as I can with my shivering.

I wish for a home, a real home, a home that we live in for years, a normal home with a normal father and a normal mother.

The petals eddy in the current and float downstream. As I climb out, teeth chattering, I hear the echoes of two warnings—the first, Wendell's voice, *Be careful.* And the second, Gaby's—*We don't know what we want.* The first has, oddly enough, proven itself true. And the second? The second I try to let go downstream with the petals.

Chapter 7

As we leave the forest, Layla announces, "That was one of the scariest moments of my life."

Supposedly, her number-one scariest moment happened in an airport. "Being scared," she always says, "drops you to a deeper place, where you make life-changing decisions." In this case, the life-changing decision was to raise me alone. She was nineteen, and had been traveling for a year on her own before college, and it made her feel more alive than she'd thought possible. She was in Italy when she discovered she was pregnant with me. She hadn't realized she was pregnant until four months in. She'd never had regular periods, and she didn't have any morning sickness, until she began to notice that she'd developed a strong aversion to blue cheese.

Plus, her belly was starting to bulge. My father was not in the picture.

But that wasn't what she found scariest.

Her parents bought her a plane ticket and told her to come home to Maryland and move in with them. At the airport, she was almost to the front of the line with her giant backpack when she had a flash of what her life would be like raising a baby with her parents in suburban Maryland.

That was her scariest moment, imagining that future.

It was as though all the months of no morning sickness hit her full force. She ran to the bathroom and threw up.

Then, feeling better, she returned to the line. Again, just as she reached the front of the line, a wave of nausea overtook her and she ran to the bathroom. This happened five times, until she missed her flight.

She returned to her pensione in Florence, and felt fine except for the blue-cheese aversion. Over the next month, she rebooked her flight three times, and every time she was overcome with nausea at the airport.

"The universe was redirecting my path, Zeeta," she says solemnly whenever she tells me the story. "Sometimes it has to resort to painful things to put you on the right path." She called her parents and told them she was going to travel the world with her baby. "And then, I felt happy," she says, triumphant.

She gave birth to me in Italy. And then we moved to Nepal, where she hired a nanny to watch me while she taught English. Supposedly, I was an incredibly easy baby. When I needed something—a diaper change or a feeding—instead of crying, I politely called out, "Agoo? Agoo?" Within a year Layla was ready to leave again, and she chose Tunisia. And thus began our wandering life.

All thanks to the vomit that wouldn't quit.

"There's something pink stuck to you," Wendell says, pointing to my chest, right above my shirt's neckline.

I look down and peel it off. "Oh. A rose petal."

He tilts his head, eyeing me curiously. The morning's cool, and he's wearing a cream alpaca sweater with brown llamas encircling the neck. Gaby probably flattered him into buying three sweaters for twenty dollars. Light's pouring through the café window, lighting up a patch of dust motes and settling on his sweater's soft fuzz. "How'd a rose petal get there?"

"Long story," I say.

"You're mysterious, Zeeta." Steam from his coffee is rising and swirling near his face before dissipating. I'm extra-appreciative of these details after the brush with death this morning.

I sip my coffee, my red bead bracelets clicking with the movement. Today I'm wearing all red and pink silk, inspired by the rose-petal ritual, feeling lucky that Layla's still alive. After a moment, I say, "Okay, the long story involves hiking to a waterfall. And a near-death experience." I raise an eyebrow significantly. "In *water*."

Wendell looks alarmed. "Are you okay?"

"It wasn't me. It was Layla. She nearly drowned. But then I helped her find her true love with rose petals. All before six this morning." I stop there, trying to keep my tone light. A description of nude river bathing seems too much. And most of all, I just want to forget those horrible images of Layla helpless in the churning water. Even thinking about it gives me that same choking feeling as my middle-of-the-night panics.

"Wow. I'm glad your mom's all right."

I stare at him. "How'd you know?"

"Know what?" he stalls.

"You told me to be careful in the water."

He studies a spot above my head. "I guess you mentioned it to me yesterday, and it sounded kind of dangerous."

"I didn't know about it then."

"I bet I overheard your mom talking about it on the plane." He shifts in his seat, uncrossing one leg and crossing the other. "So, what about our quest for my birth parents?"

I stare at him another moment, then give in for now and tell him Gaby's advice about going to Agua Santa.

His eyes widen. "Sweet. A real lead. Let's go tomorrow morning."

"Wendell," I say, opening my notebook, "what are you really looking for?"

"My birth parents," he says, confused.

"I mean, deeper than that. Like, what made you come here now, at this moment?"

He shrugs. "School's out and I had enough money saved up from my after-school job."

I push harder. "But Wendell, there's something, I know there is. What's the precise thing that made you throw up your hands and say, 'That's it, I'm going to Ecuador'?"

He laughs. "You're psychic, aren't you?"

"I think you're the psychic one."

He shifts his eyes.

I tilt back in my chair and wait.

"Well, there's lots of reasons," he says finally. "Layers of reasons, you know?"

"So what's one layer then?"

"Well, for example, there's this girl," he says.

"Oh."

"She's my ex-girlfriend, but I think we'll get back together."

"Oh."

"Well, She—" There's a certain way guys talk about girls they're completely smitten with. *She*, infused with awe. *She*, with a capital S. "See," he continues. "She said I was—I can't believe I'm telling you this—She said I was too—"

"What?"

"She broke up with me because I was always afraid She'd break up with me. She got sick of it. She said I had abandonment issues. So I decided to come here and find my birth parents and go back home and be a brand-new person and She'd be so impressed She'd want me back." He stares at a deep scratch in the table. "I'm an idiot."

"Hmmm," I say. That's the best response when you don't know what to say. Other people assume you're having deep thoughts. And usually they just keep talking until you can swallow your disappointment and compose yourself.

"Okay, Zeeta, now that I spilled my guts, give me more details about this rose-petal thing."

I look him straight in the eye. "I stripped off my clothes and rubbed rose petals over my wet, nude body in magical waters." I raise an eyebrow. "And made a wish."

As expected, he flushes and looks away, at the mountains. But then he asks, in a low voice, "Think it works?"

"Our landlady says it does."

He moves his head closer across the table. "Will you take me there, Zeeta?"

"Why?"

"I want to wish for Her back."

"Maybe next week," I say, a little meanly. "I don't feel like getting up before dawn again this week."

"Thanks, Zeeta." He pulls the sweater over his head and wraps it around his waist. That's another thing about Americans—they don't wrap sweaters around their shoulders like most people in the world do. But the around-the-waist way shows off Wendell's broad shoulders under a snug white T-shirt. I try to ignore it. The shoulders are off-limits. They belong to Her.

Outside the café, we stand looking at each other for an awkward moment. He takes out his camera and moves the knobs around and snaps a picture of me. "There's another one," he says, squinting at a place on my neck. And this time, now that we've forged a friends-only bond from the ex-girlfriend talk, he takes the liberty of reaching his hand to the tender space on my neck behind my earlobe and plucking off the rose petal himself.

I swallow hard. "Is the ex-girlfriend thing the deepest layer?"

"What?"

"The deepest reason for coming? What you're really searching for?"

He looks at the sky and at the sidewalk and everywhere but my face. "I guess. Well, *hasta mañana,*" he says quickly, with a terrible accent.

"*Hasta mañana,* Wendell," I call after him.

I spend the afternoon at the food market, buying ingredients for a pot of hearty soup for Layla's birthday dinner. Thirty-five years old. She says she's officially old now that she has to round up to forty. Supposedly she's found three white hairs, although when she plucked one out and showed it to me, it just looked light blond. "Look!" she insisted. "It's a different consistency!" I've decided that cooking together will cheer us up, peeling and chopping and frying and letting the sizzling smoke wrap around us like a cocoon. She'll forget about the waterfall and the alleged white hairs and I'll forget about Wendell's sort-of-ex-girlfriend.

She's spending the day with the Taoist surfer clown in Quito to apply for her work visa, but she plans to be back in time for dinner. "It's not a date," she promised this morning. "It just so happens he needs to renew his visa. But don't you think it's pretty responsible of him to renew his visa?"

I head home, into the setting sun, one bag full of tomatoes, cucumbers, cilantro, potatoes, dried lentils, quinoa, and onions. And in the other bag, inside knotted, doubled plastic, is a raw, bloody chicken, just chopped into four parts by a market lady's enthusiastic butcher knife.

Wherever we live, Layla and I try to cook the local food, most of the time at least. When we're lazy or just settling into a new place, we fall back on spaghetti, the old standby. Here in Ecuador, potato-chicken soup seems to be the staple, with heaps of fresh cilantro. People eat plenty of *canguil*—popcorn—as a side dish, but I can't seem to cook it without either burning it or having kernels pop out all over the kitchen. Yesterday, our landlady smelled the charred popcorn and, out of pity, brought us over a bowl she'd made herself.

I'm walking past the Internet café, the bag handles digging into my palms, when I spot Layla. Her flowing white dress is what jumps out from the crowd first. The dress is thin cotton, backlit by the evening sun, a little see-through. She refuses to wear a slip, even though I beg.

And then I notice she's walking next to someone.

Very close. Maybe even touching.

And it's not an elderly person or a little kid or a clown.

It's a middle-aged guy.

A few paces closer, I recognize him. The man from the plane. Handsome Magazine Dad.

He's nodding and listening to Layla, who's telling him a story, her arms spiraling in flamboyant gestures. He's tall, stooping down to listen to her. He's dressed in a tasteful light blue button-down with tan leather shoes and pants as white as his teeth. Today he's stepped out of an ad for a family vacation at a giant, international hotel, like a Marriott or a Hilton.

Now Layla's waving her hand and bouncing toward me, as he jogs to keep up with her. "Zeeta! It's Jeff. On the way to the bus stop, the universe stuck him right in my path!" She gives me a meaningful look.

"Hi, Zeeta," he says, holding out his hand, giving me a firm-yet-warm shake. "Nice to see you again."

"Likewise," I say, suddenly tongue-tied, as though he really is a magazine model or some other celebrity. Which he is, in a way, for me at least. He could easily be the star of any Normal Family fantasy. It's strangely thrilling and a little nerve-racking to see him standing so close to Layla.

She beams. "We spent the day together. I know I said I'd go to Quito for my visa, love, but I'll do it another day." She looks so proud, about to burst. "And you'll be happy to know I ditched the surfer clown."

I'm practically speechless. "Great, Layla!"

"What serendipity!" she says, turning her face up to Jeff's. "Did you know that the word *serendipity* comes from *Serendip*? An old name for Sri Lanka. These traveling princes of Serendip went on a quest, but they kept stumbling across marvelous discoveries. And their discoveries turned out even better than what they'd been looking for."

She's starting to sound flaky and weird and soon she'll start quoting Rumi. I bring the conversation back to earth, mustering up my most normal smile for Jeff, hoping Layla will seem less zany by association. "So," I sum up, "Layla was looking for a bus and she found you instead. That's great."

"It's serendipitous for me, too," he says, looking fondly at Layla, as though he's barely restraining himself from tucking a stray piece of blond hair behind her ear. "I was on a dating quest." He grins. "For a quiet homebody type. And instead I meet this gorgeous world traveler. And I'll tell you something"—he drops his voice, letting me in on a secret— "we've been having the best conversation I've had in years."

Unbelievable. I silently thank Layla for not scaring him. For refraining from suggesting they find a grassy hill to roll down, which she's been known to do with men she's just met. She really is trying. I wonder how long it can last.

Jeff touches her bare shoulder. "Listen, I need to get back to the bank and do a little work tonight." He turns to me, flashing his white smile. "Zeeta, I'm coming back to Otavalo for the weekend. How about on Saturday we all have lunch together? *Restaurante Americano.* One o'clock. My treat. Bring a friend if you'd like."

It takes them ten minutes to say goodbye, with all the blushing and smiling and tittering. Finally, Layla and I walk home, her carrying the bag of veggies and grains, me carrying the raw chicken.

She talks the whole way home, giving a Why Jeff Would Be a Good Boyfriend monologue, even though she doesn't need to convince me of anything. I'm sold.

"You know, Z, he'll be good for me. Nutritious, like quinoa." She pulls out the small plastic bag of tiny, light brown, doughnut-shaped grains. Studying them, she says, "Quinoa's the only grain that has all the essential amino acids, that's what our landlady told me."

She drops the quinoa back in the market bag. "It'll feel strange at first, trying to be a new person and being with a different kind of man. But I'll do it for you, and for us, because the waterfall this morning was a wake-up call. I need to change. It's time. And Jeff will be my guide in the realm of responsible grown-up stuff, don't you think? I'm excited about it. I really am. He's good-looking, isn't he? In a conservative way. You know, I really think he'd look great nude. He's muscular, have you noticed? Apparently his big thing is working out at the gym. I'd love to paint him. Don't worry. I won't ask him to model for me right away . . ."

As she goes on and on, I nod periodically and try to wrap my mind around the significance of all this.

Maybe the near-death experience really has changed her.

Maybe the sacred waters really have worked.

Maybe my life has, miraculously, just veered onto the normal course.

For years, I imagined this moment, the moment my life would turn off the twisty, mountainous, forested, pebbled road to the wide, clean, SUV-filled highway. And now it's actually happening. My stomach is jumping around and I'm picturing me and Layla laughing at a kitchen table in Virginia, and Jeff serving us pancakes and saying, *What shall we do today, ladies? The neighborhood pool? A barbecue on the deck?*

"So what do you think about this Jeff thing?" she asks. "Aren't you happy?"

"Of course." Gently, I add, "And please try to be normal with him."

"How?"

"For starters, lay off the Rumi quotes. Tone down your outfits. Just be normal."

In silence, we walk toward our apartment, contemplating our possible new life, squinting into the setting sun, Layla swinging the bag of veggies and quinoa, me swinging the bag of bloody chicken.

Chapter 8

The bus to Agua Santa looks as though it might have been elegant thirty years ago—faded red velvet seats, ragged gold curtains with fraying tassels. The smell of diesel and damp wool fills the close space. A few other passengers sit scattered on the bus, mostly indigenous Otavaleños. The women are dazzling, sitting straight and elegant in their shiny, white embroidered blouses with lace sleeves, and cream wool shawls. These are everyday clothes, what they wear to work the fields and feed pigs and butcher chickens and wash dishes.

"These ladies should star in a laundry detergent commercial," I whisper to Wendell.

He gives a half-smile, not moving his gaze from the raindrops meandering down the clouded windowpane.

"What are you thinking about?" I ask, hoping he won't say his ex-girlfriend.

"Wondering if they'll be happy to see me. I mean, maybe I'm someone's dark secret." He turns to me. "What about your father?"

"What about him?"

"Where is he?"

"Who knows. We never met."

"What do you know about him?"

"Two letters. J.C."

"Initials?"

I nod. "But I don't know if they're his first and last initials or first and middle or what."

Wendell gives an encouraging half-smile. "At least it's something."

"I'd rather have a crystal. Something to hold on to. To sleep with under my pillow."

He looks down. I bet he's slept with that crystal under his pillow. "Think you'll find him someday?" he asks.

I consider how much to tell him. "I've made up plenty of fantasies over the years," I say finally, twisting my rings. "In Laos, I went through this phase where I convinced myself I'd run into him on the street. So I looked at every face that passed for some man who looked like half of me. I tried as hard as I could not to blink, because what if I blinked and I missed him? Soon my friends started asking me why I bugged out my eyes all the time, and then Layla started saving up money to get my thyroid tested, so I stopped. I let it go."

I glance up, a little embarrassed.

His voice comes out low. "And now what do you think about him?"

"I'll probably never meet him. Layla doesn't know anything about him. But I think he must be a mix of all the parts of me that she doesn't get."

Wendell nods, poking at the torn seat fabric in front of him. "When I meet my birth parents, I think my weirdness will make sense."

"What weirdness?"

"You'll think I'm crazy."

"No I won't."

"Forget it." And he turns back to the raindrops.

When I was little and asked Layla about my father, she'd say something like, "Oh, my darling Zeeta, he's a creature of the sea. A man of the moon. When he plays guitar, you fall into the place where everything is music." It felt like a game, a quirky version of a bedtime story, but once I was older, it drove me crazy. On my thirteenth birthday, over the strawberry shortcake she'd made, I interrogated her.

"What's J.C. stand for?"

She played with the whipped cream. "I don't know."

"How can you not know?" I jabbed my fork into a strawberry.

She sighed. "I was nineteen, on a Greek island, drunk on a jug of red wine. There were a bunch of us on the beach that night—ragtag backpackers around a bonfire. I was looking at the sea, feeling lonely, wondering what I was going to do with my life, when he emerged from the water. Like some sea creature turned human."

I stabbed another strawberry. "Layla. Give me the truth. No fairy-tale crap."

"This is it, I mean it. He sat in the sand next to me and talked about the ocean and sea turtle eggs and the moon."

"Where was he from?"

She reached across the table, touched my cheek. "Love, I know it's hard for you to accept. But I just don't know."

I leaned back, my stare icy. There had to be something, some key. It was just a matter of sifting through Layla's infuriatingly vague, flaky memory.

"Well, did he have an accent?"

She rubbed her forehead. "He spoke English well. I couldn't put my finger on his accent." She was starting to crack. "Honestly, Z, I was young and I hadn't traveled that much yet and I don't know." Her voice shook, her lip quivered, tears seeped out.

It made me happy. "Slut," I whispered.

Layla was quiet for a long, long time. Finally, she wiped her face and said, "If I hadn't had that night, you wouldn't be here. And you're everything, Z. The light of my existence."

Later that night, I started feeling bad. I took the cake from the fridge and cut two pieces. I even lit a candle. "Hey, maybe J.C. was a college kid on summer break," I said as a kind of peace offering. "Maybe he was a marine biology major with a minor in music."

"Well," she said, picking at the cake, "I guess it's possible."

So that's what I decided. By now he must be director of a giant city aquarium, maybe even SeaWorld. He probably had kids—maybe my half brother and half sister. That Greek island trip was a little blip in the landscape of his wonderfully normal existence. And tragically, he was oblivious to its consequences.

The bus slows at the base of a steep, cobbled road that meanders up into the mountains. Far above, the gray peaks wear long, green robes, swirling into valleys, rippling into smooth mounds. Patches of leaves and grass and dark soil form a haphazard pattern, like scraps of velvet and suede and silk stitched together. White houses with tiled roofs spread in clusters across the hillsides. I spot a candy-pink house at the turnoff, which Gaby described as a landmark. She instructed us to walk up the hill for a kilometer or two, then turn left toward the houses.

"Let's go," I say to Wendell, slinging my pack over my shoulder. It's heavy with fruit I picked up at the market to offer the locals as gifts. He follows me, bumping into people and saying *"perdón, perdón"* with his American accent. I'll have to teach him to roll his R's sometime.

We head uphill on the muddy road flecked with worn stones, bits of grass poking through here and there. The rain falls in tiny droplets, cold and silver, carrying the smell of wet earth. I whip out my hooded emerald cloak from Morocco and wrap it around my shoulders.

Through the mist, a woman in a black shawl passes, carrying a bundle of firewood on her back, followed by two men, water dripping from the edges of their hats. I say good morning in Quichua, as Gaby taught me. *"Alli punlla."*

"Alli punlla," they answer, surprised.

After they pass, Wendell makes a low whistle. "How many languages do you speak, Zeeta?"

"Over a dozen, but only well enough for pleasantries. Deep discussions about politics and the universe and long-lost fathers? Maybe seven."

"You scare me," he says.

He's not the first guy to say that. I've given up on trying to figure out exactly what they're scared of and how seriously they mean it. In every country we've lived in, boys my age—and girls, too, for that matter—have hung out with me because I'm exotic. Sometimes they confess their deep, dark secrets (which I promptly record in my notebook), but only because I'm an outsider and won't judge them. And I'm always leaving again soon anyway. Most kids keep a friendly distance, as though I'm a fascinating yet unpredictable animal. Certain older people, like Gaby, seem to take it all in stride, and embrace me like a temporary granddaughter or niece.

We cross old, weed-filled train tracks, and Wendell whips out his camera and snaps a picture. "Perspective shots turn out great." He turns to me, clicks, and carefully tucks the camera back inside his shirt. I wonder what his sort-of-ex-girlfriend will say when she sees me in his pictures. I wonder what he'll say about me. *Oh, she's just this girl I'll never see again. Just my translator.*

I've had my flings with tourist boys. The first one was when I was thirteen, in Brazil, and spent a blissful week body-boarding and holding hands with adorable French Olivier. Last year, on Phi Phi Island, I met an Australian, Patrick, with ice-blue eyes and freckles. For two weeks, we surfed and snorkeled and swam and kissed and went on long walks. Both times, for months afterward, I wrote them e-mails and listened to our music and mooned over their pictures and reread their notebook pages. Then their e-mails stopped. After the Australian, I finally faced the truth. For them, I was nothing more than a vacation-girl hookup, an exciting break from real life.

But this *is* my real life, this endless vacation.

I glance at Wendell. His lips are tender and curved like a Buddha's lotus-flower mouth, and purplish-blue in the cold. I will not be his fling. Especially knowing he's in love with a sort-of-ex-girlfriend.

Kids' voices drift toward us, muffled through the damp air, squeals and laughter and shouts. Through the fog, I can just make out three girls running from a house to a pigpen and back again, playing chase. In their paths, chickens squawk as the kids barrel through.

I stride up to the girls. They look about four, six, and nine years old. The oldest one's wearing a white embroidered blouse, gold beads, a cardigan, and an *anaco*—a straight, wraparound skirt—while the littler ones have on jeans and Disney polar fleece sweatshirts with hoods. They have round, pretty faces, glistening eyes, cheeks pink with cold. At first they look about to run at the sight of us, but instead, on second thought, they giggle.

"Buenos días," I say.

"Buenos días," they reply shyly.

"I'm Zeeta. And this is Wendell."

The oldest one says, "I'm Eva. This little one's my *ñaña* Odelia, and she's my other *ñaña*, Isabel."

"Well, *chicas,* we're looking for Wendell's birth parents. He was adopted by an American family as a baby. Want to be our guides? Introduce us to the people in your town?"

The girls stare at Wendell and titter and confer in Quichua, and then Eva says, "Come with us. There aren't that many houses. We'll just take you to all of them." The littlest, Odelia, takes one of my hands, and Isabel takes the other, and we set off down the road. They don't seem to notice the drizzle, and soon they're shooting off questions like fireworks. *Where are you from? Do you have animals? Are you two married?* I burst out laughing at the married one, but then remember that Gaby got married when she was fifteen. It isn't so far-fetched to them.

They chatter and tell stories that I translate in snatches to Wendell—a rich man on the hill who made a pact with the devil, a greedy man whose hacienda was magically drowned in a lake, a woman named Mamita Luz who sounds like everyone's fairy godmother. Mother Luz. Mother Light. They particularly love talking about her. She's the mother of all the children of the village, they say. She gives all children fresh-baked still-warm bread so that not a single child will ever go hungry. Her husband is Silvio, but everyone calls him Taita Silvio. Father Silvio. "We'll go there after we finish," Eva says, "to eat bread."

Timidly, Odelia takes Wendell's hand. "If you don't find your mother, Mamita Luz will be your mother."

After I translate, Wendell gives me a look full of questions. I shrug, mystified.

The houses are spaced far apart, each with its pens of pigs, its slew of dogs, its cow or horse or donkey, and the occasional beat-up truck. Some buildings are cement, some adobe, some put together with an assortment of scrap wood. At the first house, three round, pretty women are working under a shelter that lets a little drizzle through. They're taking hardened corn kernels off cobs, but they stop and smile when we approach. "Sit down, sit down," they insist, pulling up extra plastic lawn chairs.

They're pleased with the peaches I give them and amused that we offer to help them strip the corn kernels. We talk for a while, going over the same questions the girls asked us. *Wendell's from Colorado. I'm from nowhere. No, we're not married.* (I can't help blushing at that one.) *The only animals in the picture are Wendell's corgi-Lab mix and his ancient goldfish. No, not a single pig or sheep.*

Soon our fingertips are growing sore from the kernel

stripping. When we get to the part about Wendell's birth parents, the women turn their palms faceup. "Only God knows." The oldest woman gives us two eggs fresh from under her hen as a goodbye present.

At the next house, a family invites us inside. They're eating around a long table, about ten of them, ranging in age from three to seventy, with the TV blaring a singing talent show. They accept a bag of strawberries and make us have a bowl of potato soup with them as we shout over the TV about Wendell's search.

They speak among themselves in Quichua and, finally, shake their heads. "Sorry, we don't know. Only God knows."

Wendell doesn't seem too disappointed, probably because everyone's nice and feeds us and acts concerned. They're all amazed that Wendell doesn't speak Quichua, much less Spanish. "But you have our face!" they exclaim. "And you even wear your hair long, like us!"

All afternoon, we go from house to house. It's the same with the next seven houses. People share food, talk, and ultimately claim that only God knows.

And now it's sunset and for the past hour, little Odelia's been pleading, "Now can we go to Mamita Luz's? Now? How much longer till Mamita Luz's?"

It's almost dark, and we have to go back soon. "Okay, *chica.* Just for a few minutes."

She claps her hands and does a little dance.

On the way there, I ask Eva, "What about your parents? They might know something."

A cloud passes over her face. "Our *mamá* is out," she says, her voice suddenly quiet. "She works as a maid in Otavalo all day."

"What about your father?"

The girls look at one another.

"He's sick," Eva says.

"Yes, sick," Isabel says.

Solemnly, Odelia adds, "Very sick."

Chapter 9

The girls lead us through a misty maze of paths and corn rows. Odelia's a little hummingbird of darting energy, chatting nearly nonstop, her eyes impossibly wide. Isabel walks and talks a little slower, but somehow manages to get a word in edgewise here and there. Eva's observant and protective like a mother wolf, warning us to watch our step over holes and rocks, her eyes flicking around, always on the lookout for unseen dangers.

We walk on a path by an irrigation ditch, a two-foot-wide channel of water with corn plants on either side reaching higher than our heads, making a tunnel over us, sheltering us from the drizzle. To our left, the cornfield ends in a backyard. From the wall of the house, a clay mound protrudes, a giant bump in the adobe.

Odelia points and jumps up and down. "Mamita Luz's bread oven!" And then she and Isabel are running, unable to contain their excitement, pulling me along, with Wendell and Eva right on our heels. And sure enough, as we come closer, the rich, warm smell of baking bread surrounds the house in a sweet cloud. Smoke's rising from the chimney, swirling into the raindrops. In front, sprays of pink bougainvillea are climbing the walls, emerging from tangles of blackberry bushes heavy with shiny berries. A few chickens peck around in the mud among red and orange potted flowers in old tin cans. The house is a cheerful oasis in the rain.

The girls knock on the heavy wooden door, Odelia bouncing in anticipation.

As we wait, Wendell turns to me, shivering. It's grown colder now that the sun's setting. "Ever feel extra alive?"

I think of how Layla felt more alive than ever the first time she traveled. "When we move," I say slowly. "The first month or two, there's that time when I notice everything—all the colors and sounds and smells—they seem magnified." I don't mention that this in-between time is also the time my middle-of-the-night panics are worst.

"Yeah," he says. "That's how I feel now. Freezing my butt off, but alive."

The door opens, and there stands a woman, middle-aged, round as a soft roll. The girls rush into her arms and she wraps all three of them up like a blanket. She reaches out for my hand and Wendell's, and holds them for a moment, beaming. *"Mis hijos!"* My children!

She ushers us inside, to a room on the left—a kitchen—where three other children, two boys and a toddler girl, are sitting by the fire, pulling apart pieces of steaming bread and munching with delight.

They stare at us, curious, until finally a brave boy says, *"Buenas tardes."*

As we introduce ourselves, the girls put their hands in mine and Wendell's, firmly, claiming first dibs on their new friends.

For a moment, Wendell and I stand, savoring the heat, gazing around the room. The ceiling is high, with exposed beams, and covered in straw. There's hardly any furniture in here, just two large wood pillars with spoons and pans and ladles hanging from nails. The walls are rough, pink clay with bits of straw and old corncobs poking out. Small benches and stools line the walls, ready and waiting for more kids to come. An old guitar leans in the corner, with reed flutes of different sizes on a stool beside it.

In the center of the room, a hearth fire pit holds hot coals beneath a bubbling pot of tea, something lemony. The woman dips a steaming cupful for each of us, and motions for us to sit on a bench. In one sweeping motion, without a fuss, she takes a blue wool poncho from a nail on the wall and drapes it over Wendell's shivering shoulders.

Then she floats over to a hole in the wall that's hiding an orange fire glow and an iron rack. Inside, on a giant metal pan, are little balls of dough, just beginning to turn golden. And farther back, I glimpse the blackened wall of the inside of the bump we'd seen from the outside. She feeds more wood into the oven and then plucks some rolls from a pan beside it. Smiling, she drops one in each of our hands, and sits down with us. After we've eaten our rolls—which are so otherworldly delicious I'm sure we've stumbled straight into a fairy tale—she drops second rolls into our hands and announces, "I am Mamita Luz."

She's staring at Wendell, maybe sensing he doesn't speak Spanish or come from here.

"Nice to meet you," I say, sipping my tea. Lemon balm, it tastes like. With tons of sugar. "Thank you for the bread. I'm Zeeta and this is Wendell. He's American."

Wendell pipes in with *"Gracias, gracias,"* in his rough accent.

She smiles appreciatively, and stares at him, curious.

Wendell says, "Zeeta, thank her. Tell her that this is the best bread I've ever eaten. Ever."

What he really means: *Please, please, be my birth mother.*

When I translate the bread compliment, she laughs and crinkles her eyes. "How could I not share bread with you? You are my son."

I blink. It can't possibly be this easy.

But then Mamita Luz motions to me. "And she is my daughter." And to the girls. "And they are my daughters." And to the boys. "And they are my sons."

Once I translate, Wendell's quiet for a moment, then says, "Zeeta, can you ask her if she's had any kids by birth?"

Mamita Luz shakes her head slowly in response. "My breasts

have never fed milk to a baby." She pats her great bosom with no self-consciousness. "Instead, I am blessed with all these children, the children of the village, and more, like you two. And instead of mother's milk, I feed my children bread."

Wendell's face falls.

I want to reach out and hold his hand. Instead, I open my indigo notebook. "When is the moment you felt most alive, Mamita Luz?"

She looks around the room, at the children eating, stuffing their cheeks like chipmunks and talking and laughing with their mouths full. "I wanted children with all my heart. But God did not give me any. For years I felt half dead. Then, my husband built me this oven, just like the one my grand-mother had. I started baking bread. And children started coming. Soon, every day my kitchen was full of children, happy and full. One day I looked around and realized I was no longer half dead. No, I was more alive than ever." From the huge, steaming pot, she ladles more tea into our cups. "Now," she says, "what brings you two all the way out here?"

I'm speechless. It's true, this woman has stepped straight out of a fairy tale. Finally, I say, "Mamita Luz, Wendell was adopted sixteen years ago. Do you know who his birth parents might be?"

She smiles wistfully. "Who are the people who nourish you and love you?"

After I translate, he says, without hesitation, *"Mi mamá y papá."*

"And now you have another mother, me, Mamita Luz. And you have Pachamama, Mother Earth, always below your feet. So many mothers. If you don't find what you think you're looking for, don't be sad. There are ties stronger than blood, *hijo*."

And then, as though an internal alarm clock has buzzed, triggered by a certain golden bread smell, she whisks over to the oven. With a long wooden paddle like a flat oar, she pulls out the next batch of bread as the kids gather around her, eagerly watching.

I note that she's evaded our question, but there's no time to push her for more information. It will be dark soon and Layla will be wondering where I am. We down the last drops of tea and say goodbye to the kids. Mamita Luz ushers us to the door, where it's dusky blue outside, just the faintest light silhouetting the mountains.

"Come back tomorrow when my husband is here. He will want to meet you." Wendell starts taking off the poncho, but she firmly pats it back on his shoulders. "Wear it home and bring it back tomorrow, *hijo*."

Mamita Luz walks us to the end of the path, to the road, a shawl draped over her head. She holds Wendell's hand for a moment and tilts his face, studying it from all angles. Rain droplets lace her eyelashes, like tiny crystals in the streetlamp's glow. She wipes the water from her cheeks. "Go now, children."

. . .

Wendell and the girls and I walk down the path through the corn, over the irrigation ditch, to the main street. A few streetlamps spot the darkness with flickering pools of light. Odelia clings fiercely to her sisters' hands, telling us about a monster who lives in the shadows. As we near the intersection with the road that leads downhill to the bus stop, I notice someone at the edge of the road in a weedy ditch. A man, talking and singing to himself and clutching a nearly empty bottle.

Odelia stops in her tracks, refuses to budge.

Eva and Isabel have stopped too. The girls whisper in Quichua. Odelia starts crying.

In a slurred voice, the man calls out, "Is that you, daughters?"

Isabel bites her lip.

"Come here," he yells. "Who are you with?"

Holding hands, the girls move closer to him the way you might approach a vicious dog.

"What are you doing with my daughters?" Spit flies from his mouth. "You trying to steal them?"

I take a step back. "They're helping us look for my friend's birth parents. He was adopted from this town."

He nods, squints at Wendell. "How old are you, boy?"

"Sixteen."

He grunts. "There was a woman." He takes a swig. "She had a baby. No one ever knew what happened to the boy."

"And the woman?" I ask.

He coughs and spits out a shiny clump of mucus. "After a while, she disappeared too."

As I translate for Wendell, I resist the overwhelming urge to hold his hand or touch his shoulder.

"What's the woman's name?" I ask the man.

"Who knows. She wasn't from here."

I translate for Wendell. He says nothing, only licks the rain from his lips.

"What about his father?" I ask.

Suddenly, the man stands up and waves his fists in the air. "You're trying to steal my daughters, aren't you?"

The girls back up. Isabel's crying now too. Their father's moving toward them, staggering, punching the air.

Wendell steps between him and the girls.

Eva whispers to me, "I'm taking my *ñañas* to spend the night with Mamita Luz. Come back tomorrow." The girls run down the street, their father shouting after them.

Wendell and I stay still for a moment, hearts pounding, unsure what to do.

Meanwhile, the man is stumbling after the girls, but they have a big head start that keeps widening. Finally, the man falls down at the roadside and sucks the remaining liquor from his bottle.

Wendell takes my hand and we walk quickly to the intersection and turn right. Once we reach the hill, we run.

Chapter 10

We sit, not talking, as the bus moves down the dark highway, following its headlights. Romantic ballads blast from the speakers.

Finally, Wendell says, "Think the girls are okay?"

His breath is warm. It still smells like sweet, lemony tea.

"They'll be safe at Mamita Luz's," I say.

"I was sure she was my birth mom. From the second she opened the door." He presses his lips together. "Like I'd *seen* her before."

The blaring music forces our heads close, so that my eyes are just inches from his. "Maybe you just *want* her to be your birth mother."

Wendell plays with a loose thread at his shirt hem. "I bet we'll find something out when we come back tomorrow."

I'm doubtful. "We could just try another village."

"I have to give back the poncho. And there's that mystery woman."

Right. Let's not forget the ranting of an incoherent drunk man. Carefully, I say, "Remember, we have limited time and lots more villages."

"I have a feeling about this place, Zeeta. A few more days. If nothing shows up by then, we'll move on."

Although this whole thing is rapidly turning into a waste of time, we did have a fun day together in this village, and the girls are very cute, and I wouldn't mind some more of Mamita Luz's bread, so I say, "All right."

We stay silent for another song, and then he says, "Zeeta, I have some letters." He hesitates. "Can you translate them into Spanish?"

I get the feeling this is something big he's asking me. "Sure."

"No one's ever seen them before."

"What are they?"

"Since I was eight years old, I've been writing letters to my birth parents. Mostly on birthdays and holidays. I have about twenty now. I want to give them to my birth parents."

A large woman toting huge bags squeezes past us in the aisle. I lean close to Wendell to avoid being bumped. Ever notice how the touch of certain people, even accidental, can send tingles through your whole body? For a second, Wendell's arm grazes mine, and a warmth floods into me. Layla would probably boil it down to chi. She went through a phase a few years back in Morocco where all she wanted to do was sit around holding hands and sending chi back and forth.

After the woman passes, I say, "It would be an honor to translate your letters," and I keep my head close to his, nearly touching, feeling the chi flow in the dark, lemony-sweet air.

We stop at Wendell's hotel room for the letters. It's Colonial, painted buttery yellow with white trim around tall French windows. A doorman with a gold tooth greets Wendell by name on the way in. Inside, from behind a desk, a pudgy middle-aged woman in a suit shoots him a giant smile. "Wendell! Good to see you!"

"Hey, Dalia." He gives a quick wave and keeps walking.

"You're popular here," I say as we enter the lobby, a huge pillared space with an indoor garden bursting with orange bird-of-paradise flowers. The wooden floors shine with pine wax and smell like a forest.

"She's the owner. The friend of a friend of my mom I told you about."

"*Que pleno.* You're lucky."

"Not really. She's basically my babysitter."

I raise an eyebrow.

"When I told my parents I was going to Ecuador, they were excited. They thought they'd come along, too. Then I said I wanted to go alone. At first they said no, but then my mom e-mailed all their old Peace Corps friends and found someone who knew someone who ran a hotel here. And here

I am. On the condition that I tell Dalia the babysitter everywhere I go. That and call home every day. A little oppressive."

"I still say you're lucky."

While he runs up the polished marble stairs to his room, I wait in the lobby on a worn velvet chair, watching a tiny bird flit around the garden. I try to imagine Layla going to all that trouble to make me safe.

During my childhood, regardless of the country, I ran wild after school. The only rule—recommendation, really—was that I had to be home by dark. In the evenings, when Layla was feeling too mellow for dancing under the full moon or forming an impromptu drum circle, she read me her favorite books of poetry over and over. Mostly Rumi, but also Thich Nhat Hanh and Khalil Gibran. One night, I asked her why I didn't have rules like the other kids. Why didn't I have to do my homework right when I came home from school? Why didn't I have to change out of my school uniform to keep it clean? She kissed my cheek. "That's why we read together, Z. So that you get chock-full of wisdom. So you know for yourself how to live." She gave me another jasmine-scented kiss, her hair tickling my face. "Rules are an illusion."

Wendell's coming back downstairs now, breathless, holding a pack of folded-up letters tied with a red ribbon. He pulls them out of the ribbon and hands them to me quickly, before he can change his mind.

"Here they are," he says, tucking the ribbon into his pocket and folding his arms across his chest.

"Okay."

"They're embarrassing," he warns.

"That's okay."

"They're the only copies I have." He looks as though he wants to take them back.

"I'll be careful."

He rocks on his heels. "Well, good night."

"Hey," I say, slipping the letters into my bag, "want to come to lunch with me and Jeff and Layla tomorrow? Jeff's treat."

"Okay."

It's almost like he's my boyfriend and he's about to meet my parents. I wonder how he'll react to Layla's nonstop Rumi quoting. I wonder if Jeff will like him. If he'll like Jeff. Of course, Wendell's in love with his sort-of-ex-girlfriend and Jeff is a man I barely know.

Still, it feels almost normal.

All through tonight's leftover potato–chicken soup dinner with Layla, she talks about Jeff, how his retirement money is diversified in money market accounts and mutual funds and IRAs. "I talked to him for an hour today at the phone booth down the street. Me, on the phone for an hour! I told him about how I almost drowned. How it made me realize that the most important thing is to give you and me a safe life."

"Hmmm." The waterfall incident seems like the absolute wrong thing to tell a guy you're starting to date. It's the perfect example of emotional instability—clear evidence that she's crazy enough to wake up in the middle of the night and get naked in a raging waterfall to make a wish. "And how did he react to that?" I ask.

"He said, 'Listen, Layla, my whole job is transforming hopeless messes into efficient systems.' And then he told me all these ideas for ways I can change. He has a whole Power-Point presentation on this topic! He says it's hard at first, leaving your comfort zone, and that you'll naturally come up with a million reasons why you should go back to the old way, but if you stick with it, it's worth it in the end." She smiles and sips her bottle of Pilsener.

I sprinkle extra cilantro into my soup, watching the green bits float around like tiny lily pads. "So you didn't scare him off?"

"No! He says I'm a breath of fresh air. He loves hearing about everywhere we've lived. He says I open his mind. And don't worry, I left Rumi out of the conversations." She tilts her head. "You know, I think Jeff sees me as the ultimate efficiency-consultant project." She scoops the last chunk of potato into her mouth. "He says I should start small. Organize my clothes drawers."

"Good luck with that," I say skeptically. Layla tends to just jam whatever into the nearest drawer and then spends ages looking for things. When her crown chakra's weak, she desperately needs to find that purple head scarf, or when her heart chakra's blocked, that pink silk tank is the only thing that will fix it.

Layla downs her last sip of beer and disappears into her room, leaving me with the dishes as usual. I don't complain.

I'm curious to see if she'll actually organize her clothes or if she'll get distracted and paint murals all over the drawers instead.

In my room, I open my notebook to a fresh sheet. My hands are pink and wrinkled from washing the pile of dishes. From down the hall in Layla's bedroom, I hear drawers opening and closing, cabinets creaking and slamming, the sounds of efficiency. I realize that with all the excitement over Jeff, I didn't fill Layla in on the Agua Santa trip.

Usually we hang out and talk for hours and manage, in a mellow, meandering way, to eventually cover all the events of our day. Tonight, though, Layla's energy has seemed somewhat hyper and jumpy. I remind myself of what Jeff said, that transformation involves leaving your comfort zone.

I pull one of Wendell's letters from my bag and smooth it out beside my notebook. It looks old, written on wide-lined notebook paper, in pencil, in awkward, uneven letters.

Dear birth mom and dad,
    Did you come to colorado in july? Because we went to a fair and there were these four guys playing flutes and mom said there from ecuador and they looked like me and I thougth one of them was you. Were you looking for me? Did you see me? Why din't you say hi? I felt too embarissed to say hi and I was wurried mom

and dad might feel sad or maybe scarred you'll take me away so I din't say anything. Wich one were you? The one with the black boots right? I asked for black boots for cristmas. May be I look like you. Mom and dad said you were probly poor and that's why you couldn't take care of me. But you din't look poor.

Bye,
Wendell B. Connelly,
age 8

I lie on my mattress and close my eyes. I wish this eight-year-old Wendell had known the seven-year-old Zeeta who walked around bug-eyed for weeks because she was afraid to blink. They would have made good friends.

Restaurante Americano is five-star, with starched white tablecloths and two stemmed glasses and three forks per setting. Most tables are empty, except for three with tourists talking softly as a Muzak version of an Andean folk song plays. I've always watched these kinds of places from afar, as though I were at the zoo, observing creatures of a completely different species. Sometimes I've tried to imagine myself talking and laughing with them. Layla likes to make fun of places like this, where she claims the food is extra-bland and extra-expensive. I hope she doesn't crack any jokes about it, since Jeff's the one who picked this restaurant.

She's sitting across from me, wearing a straight skirt and button-down white blouse she bought for a job interview in Morocco—her lone set of respectable clothing. We joke that she tricked them into hiring her by pretending she was normal. And then, when she started the job, she went back to her see-through skirts and peasant blouses, but by then it was too late because the students were all half in love with her.

We introduce everyone, then Layla orders a seven-dollar appetizer of soggy fried plantains that cost fifty cents at the market. It's a good thing she doesn't comment on what a rip-off it is, because we soon learn that Jeff has eaten every meal in Otavalo here, chicken and boiled vegetables. "I'm a creature of habit," he says apologetically. Luckily, Layla seems to find this cute.

When the waiter comes back, I order two daily specials, one for Layla and one for me.

"What's the daily special?" Wendell asks.

I shrug and pop a mushy plaintain in my mouth. "We always get the daily special wherever we go. It's usually the best thing. And the freshest. Least likely to make you sick."

Wendell orders the special too. "When in Rome . . . ," he says with his half-smile.

"Heck," Jeff says. "I'll take it too." He twirls a strand of Layla's hair around his finger. "You bring out the free spirit in me, Layla."

"So where are you from, Jeff?" Wendell asks.

"Virginia." He leans back, as though the very mention of home sets him at ease. "A D.C. suburb. Just off the beltway."

I've heard of this state. It borders the squiggly Atlantic state of Maryland where my grandparents live, the only state in the United States I've been to.

"What's it like in Virginia?" I ask.

"My neighborhood's really safe. Lots of open space. Bike paths to jog on. Just a mile run to the gym from my house." He goes on and on, and I listen intently. It sounds like Maryland, deliciously normal.

"And some really great golf courses!" A dreamy look has come into his eyes. "I have to admit, I miss it already." He laughs. "After what, a week?"

Layla smooths her hair, which is brushed into a neat ponytail. "Jeff's a man of routine."

He nods. "Good routines are key. To raising kids, to making the workplace efficient, you name it." He says this so convincingly, it must be part of his PowerPoint presentation. I imagine him in a sleek suit, talking to a room full of important bankers. He's bathed in the glow of the projector's light, an organizational savior in a halo of dust motes.

He cuts a plantain slice in half and nibbles. "You ladies are amazing, traveling all over the place, routines changing all the time. I'm trying my best to get used to it—the lack of water pressure in the showers, brushing my teeth with bottled water, dealing with a different language. It's good for me. Expands my horizons." He dabs the napkin at the corners of his mouth. He is, by far, the most polite and meticulously groomed man I've ever seen seated next to Layla. Not even a stray ear hair.

Layla smiles. "And he's expanding my horizons." She rubs her lips together. She's wearing mauve lipstick. The last time she wore lipstick was at that job interview in Morocco.

Wendell eats another plantain slice. "Traveling's totally worth the hassle. It makes your mind go down completely unexpected pathways, you know?"

I smile. "Serendipity, some would call it."

The daily special arrives. It's a skinny, furless creature, complete with claws and teeth, nestled between a side of salad and two boiled potatoes. "Your *cuy*," the waiter announces.

Jeff studies the charred animal. "A rat?" he says finally.

"Guinea pig," I say, taking a bite.

Wendell stares. "I had a guinea pig named Thomas. A really cute little guy."

Layla digs in. "Chickens are cute too," she says, waving her fork. "Especially the babies. I bet you don't think twice about eating chicken, do you?"

"It's good," I say, taking another bite. "A little dry, but good."

Layla adds, "Better than snake or iguana."

"Oh my," Jeff says, cutting his potato.

I love that this man says things like "Oh my." And I love that he's not entirely freaked out by the guinea pig. Well, at least he's trying not to be.

Wendell takes a bite, twisting up his face. "I can't stop thinking about Thomas." He hides the carcass under some lettuce and chows the plaintains and potatoes.

Layla holds a forkful of meat to Jeff's mouth. "Come on, it tastes like chicken!"

He takes a minuscule bite, the size of a pea, swallows it whole, and downs it with an entire glass of water. He blinks rapidly. For a minute I'm afraid he's going to run to the bathroom. Then, to my relief, he laughs and says, "Wait till the guys at my golf club hear about this."

An observer might think we look like a magazine ad for a fun family-dining experience, if, of course, you can overlook the dead rodent.

After dessert, Wendell pours a long, steady stream of sugar in his coffee. Layla and Jeff have just headed off for a guided walking tour of the city, leaving Wendell and me lingering at the table. "Layla's nice," he says, swirling in an entire mini-pitcher of cream.

My eyes widen. "That's the first time in the history of the universe that anyone's used that adjective to describe Layla."

"Really?" He sips his coffee. "What do they usually say?"

"Eccentric, exotic, zany, wild, creative, flighty, weird, stunning, dazzling, bizarre . . ."

He grins. "Well, she seems like a regular, nice person to me."

Once Layla and I went skiing in Chile, my first time skiing, and as I built up momentum, going faster and faster, I suddenly felt out of control. I didn't know how to slow down or change direction or make myself stop. So I kept barreling down the hill, telling myself that skiing was fun and it was what regular families did for vacation and I should be enjoying it. Just before I slammed into a tree, I let myself fall.

Now, this barreling-downhill feeling has come back to me. I'm not sure why. And I'm not sure what to do about it. So, for some reason, I impulsively reach my hand under the table, find Wendell's hand, and hang on.

Chapter 11

The next morning, on the bus on the way to Agua Santa, I tell Wendell, "Sorry I held your hand. I know you're obsessed with that ex-girlfriend, and I respect that. I just felt—I don't know how I felt. Scared maybe. For no good reason."

"It's okay." He smiles. "Good reason or not, my hand's here for you."

"Okay." I feel pathetic. This morning a large zit appeared on my chin, which I can't stop picking at. And I slept terribly, woke up with bruised crescents hanging below my bloodshot eyes.

"Are you freaked out that your mom's seeing a new guy?" He's looking at me with concern.

"No! Jeff's the type I've been begging her to date for

forever. You should have met some of Layla's old flames." I ramble on about all her slightly crazy former boyfriends, surprised at the fondness I have for each irresponsible one.

"They sound pretty cool," he says.

"They were, I guess." And I'm quiet for a while, staring at the torn fabric seat in front of me.

Last night Layla stayed out late with Jeff. I was in bed, half asleep, when she came home, and I waited for her to bound into my room, like she usually did after outings with new men, feeding me ice cream and giving me details. But she tiptoed into the apartment and I heard the subdued sounds of her brushing her teeth, running water as she washed her face, and then the click of her bedroom door closing. At that point I was wide awake, and it took me ages to fall asleep again.

In a couple of hours, I had my three-thirty a.m. panic, and managed to sleep for maybe another hour, until Layla started clattering around in the kitchen. I assumed she was cooking her favorite Thai street-food treat, *pa tong go,* which she sometimes gets middle-of-the-night urges to make. I waited for the yummy, greasy smell to seep under my door, expecting her to burst into my room with a plate of steaming, chromosome-shaped fried dough. Eventually, I fell back asleep. This morning she said she'd gotten a bout of insomnia and was just making chamomile tea to help her sleep.

The crisp breezes and sunshine are coming in through the bus window, cheering me up a little. Outside, the mountains loom high overhead. Each of the mountains has its own personality. Some beam down at you, gently, like a big-bosomed grandma. Some are sexy, slinking around in the lacy clouds. Others shoot up, jagged and fierce, with a passionate energy. Some guard magical realms, their smiles silent and secret. No wonder the locals say that the mountains are gods.

At Agua Santa, we step off the bus, breathing in the blue-green freshness. On the way up the hill, corn leaves wave alongside us, and farther below, a sea of corn stalks ripples in the valleys. This time, Wendell has the blue poncho and a jacket and umbrella in his backpack, although he doesn't need them after all.

"I translated a letter," I say, pulling the original and translation from the front pocket of my bag.

"Thanks." He glances at it, cringing.

"It was sweet, Wendell. I could relate. If I was your birth mom, I'd be touched."

"Not after you read a few more." He switches the subject. "Help me conjugate?"

I chose the verb. *Aguantar. To bear. To bear going up this long hill. I bear, you bear, he, she, it bears, we bear* . . . Then we work on his *R* rolling. His accent and grammar are getting a little better. He can do basic greetings and ask questions and answer easy, slow questions.

He veers to the side to take photos of some tiny flowers growing near rocks, which involves switching to a macro lens. "My mom and dad speak Spanish," he says, lying on his stomach, his face inches from the flowers. "Learned it in their Peace Corps years in Guatemala." He snaps a few photos from different angles. "They were always trying to talk Spanish with me when I was younger. You know, as part of their plan to keep me in touch with my roots and all. It drove me crazy. I flat-out refused to speak Spanish. In middle school I rebelled and took French. Then, in high school, I was thinking about coming to Ecuador some day, so I switched to Spanish."

"You should talk with your parents. Once you get home. Keep in practice."

"My ex-girlfriend's in AP Spanish. She might help me out."

"Why didn't you ask her to translate the letters?" My question sounds more like an accusation.

He shrugs, puts on the lens cap, and slings the camera over his shoulder.

We walk for another minute in silence. My throat's getting tighter and tighter, and finally I say, "Because you'll never see me again?"

"No." He stops walking. "No, that's not it at all."

Suddenly, shrill kids' voices break the silence: "Zeetaaa! Oooendellll!" Eva and Isabel and Odelia are running toward us, waving their arms with abandon. "Let's go! He's waiting for you! Taita Silvio!"

At Mamita Luz's house, the door's propped wide open, letting smells of fresh bread and potato soup and popcorn drift out. Mamita Luz greets us at the door, the children trailing around her.

And there, on a small stool in the kitchen, playing a hand-clapping game, is a man. He looks about Mamita Luz's age, and wears a white button-down shirt, stained at the cuffs and collar. His tan pants and work boots are coated with mud. He's a small man, but a man with a presence, as though an invisible spotlight's shining on him. He turns to face us.

It's striking, his resemblance to Wendell. High cheekbones, full lips, square chin, protruding ears. Of course, the man's face is much more lined and weathered, his hands calloused. He stands up and steps toward us. He's a few inches shorter than Wendell. Looking up, he reaches out his hand. "Silvio Quimbo, *para servirle.*" Here to serve you.

Wendell echoes, "Wendell Connelly, *para servirle,*" even though I doubt he knows what it means. He hands Taita Silvio the blue poncho. *"Gracias."*

Taita Silvio looks at him for a while, then turns to me and introduces himself.

We all sit down with the children on low benches, and eat the potato soup and popcorn and fresh bread. The room fills with laughter and small talk, about where Wendell lives in the U.S. and what his parents do and what animals are raised and which plants grown in Colorado.

I open my notebook. "Taita Silvio, what do you do when you're feeling sad?"

He thinks for a moment. "I remember my star friend." When he was little, he says, he used to collect firewood with his aunt before dawn, in the shivery, shadowy woods, and he always noticed a special star that glowed brighter than any other, a star that shone red and blue and yellow. He believed that this star was his friend, coming out just to greet him. "Whenever I felt sad, wherever I was, I remembered my star friend."

"I want a star friend!" Odelia cries.

"You can have one, my daughter," he says. "Next time you're out at night, pay attention to which star is asking you to be its friend."

"And if my dad's running after me and yelling, it will be up there, right?"

Taita Silvio picks her up, puts her in his lap. "Yes, *mija*. Especially then."

Wendell watches them, his gaze intense.

For the rest of the time, Odelia keeps interrupting to ask how much longer until it's dark, poking her head outside the door every few minutes.

Taita Silvio veers the conversation back to Wendell, asking whether he's happy in Colorado, whether his family treats him well.

"Of course," Wendell assures him.

Mamita Luz has to have told Silvio about Wendell's search, but he stays silent on that topic.

Finally, Wendell says, "Ask him, Zeeta."

At a break in the conversation, I ask, "Taita Silvio, do you know anything about Wendell's birth parents?"

He smoothes Odelia's hair. "Son, it sounds like your parents in Colorado love you. They treat you well. Why would you come here?"

"I need to know my birth parents."

Taita Silvio studies Wendell's face. Finally, he says, "Even though it could be painful . . . or dangerous?"

Wendell matches his stare. "Even then."

After a pause, Taita Silvio looks down at Odelia's hair. "Some things aren't meant to be known, son."

There's something he isn't telling us.

Chapter 12

"Silvio looks like me." Wendell plays with the tassel on the bus curtain, lost in thought. "Doesn't he?"

"Yes," I admit. "Especially in the ears."

"Thanks." Half-smiling, he pulls some hair from his braid to fall over his ears.

"But," I say, "he's not exactly forthcoming with information." After a beat, I add, "You want to keep looking here? Even after what Silvio said about danger?"

"A few more days." Wendell looks hopeful. Or maybe desperate. "Please, Zeeta."

"This is based on what, now? A feeling?"

"A feeling." He gives me a wry look. "And the ears."

Over the next few days, we spend the mornings and early afternoons in Agua Santa. A bus from Otavalo to Agua

Santa passes about every fifteen minutes, so we never have to wait long. The girls are always there to greet us with so much enthusiasm you'd think it was years since they last saw us. In the mornings, they bring us around to more houses, and soon we know just about everyone in Agua Santa. Later in the afternoon, back in Otavalo, I teach English to Gaby and other vendors at the market while Wendell goes to the Internet café, presumably to send mushy e-mails to his sort-of-ex-girlfriend. I'm not making much money, and I'm a little worried about how I'll pay for school uniforms. Apart from that, and the mushy e-mails that aren't directed toward me, I have to admit I'm enjoying myself, quickly filling up my indigo notebook.

At night, I curl up with Wendell's letters. With every letter, I glimpse him at a different age, all the Wendells who make up the current Wendell like nested Russian dolls. In some ways, I feel as though I've known him for years. In one angry letter, he wrote, ". . . and it's all your fault I'll never, ever, ever turn white, no matter how hard I try." I remember asking Layla when my hair would turn blond like hers and scratching at my skin, searching for whiteness underneath.

In another letter, he wrote that one day, when he was in line at the grocery store with his mom, the cashier assumed he was with the Mexican family behind them. He bit his tongue hard to hold back tears. He would forget he was different until the reactions of strangers reminded him. This I can identify with too. I'd assumed my life was typical until I grew conscious of people's stares and bewildered questions.

Translating the letters makes me notice details about Wendell, like how enthusiastically he sings "Head, Shoulders, Knees, and Toes" with the girls, complete with gestures. They love it. Word must have spread, because soon, when any kid under twelve in Agua Santa catches sight of him, they start tapping their heads and shoulders, begging for the song. Odelia knows it by heart now and sometimes spontaneously stops to do a quick round at the roadside.

In the early afternoons, along with the girls, we help Taita Silvio and Mamita Luz with their chores: feeding the pigs and chickens and guinea pigs, clearing paths, weeding, chopping wood, washing dishes. Throughout the day, people trickle in and out of their home. Many are neighbors who come to buy bread. Others are their older "children" who come to visit, home for vacation from where they work in Spain, or Japan, or the United States. They come bearing gifts from afar: flashlights, boots, and hats for Taita Silvio, and shawls, kitchen gadgets, and jewelry for Mamita Luz. For hours they munch on bread and sip tea with dreamy eyes, reminiscing about coming to her house as children, flipping between Spanish and Quichua.

Other visitors are mysterious—small groups of three or four people who head straight for a small adobe hut with doves nesting in the corner. They take a seat on a wooden bench. They look solemn, strangely subdued. If they talk, it's only to murmur in low tones in Quichua. After a short wait, Taita Silvio shows up and discusses something in Quichua with them, and then they disappear into a windowless room across from the waiting hut. A half hour later, they reemerge, as though they're surfacing from a deep dive, sometimes shivering and soaking wet, but with a new spark in their eyes.

On the third morning, Wendell intercepts Mamita Luz on her way to the mystery room. She's carrying a glass goblet of water, a pair of ancient, heavy scissors, and a bunch of roses. "What does Silvio do inside there?" he asks.

"My husband is a *curandero*," she says proudly. A healer. "He tells people's fortunes, predicts their futures, diagnoses their problems, helps them heal." As I translate, she smiles and pushes the heavy door open, closing it behind her. I catch a glimpse of candles in the darkness.

Wendell is mesmerized. "You think he can really do all that stuff, Z? Like see the future?"

"Maybe. I've met healers all over the world, witnessed some amazing things. It's kind of an obsession of Layla's. Or was."

His eyes grow intense. "Is it something they're born with? Or something they learn? How does it work? How do they control it?"

"I don't know." I glance at the mountains beyond his head. I can't believe I have the urge to quote Rumi, but it slips out before I can stop it. "This ancient mystical guy named Rumi said there's another way of seeing, a backward-and-forward-at-once vision, something that's not rationally understandable. I guess they must learn how to use the vision."

When Taita Silvio emerges, I expect Wendell to drill him

with questions, but he stays quiet. For a few minutes, I chat with Silvio and ask whether it's all right if I ask his patients some indigo-notebook questions while they wait in the hut with the doves. "Of course, my daughter," he says, and heads out to chop firewood as Wendell stares after him.

Over the next few days, I talk with Silvio's patients about why they're here, what they're looking for, wishing for. By the light from the doorway, I jot down their answers. Many of them have come to find out if they'll have luck getting their U.S. visas, which they need for trips to the United States to play Andean flute music or sell Ecuadorian crafts. They say that traveling and working abroad is key to making enough money for a house, an education, their children's education. And apparently, their success in getting the visa depends mostly on whether the U.S. embassy person tending to them happens to be in a good mood or not. They tell me that having a *limpieza*—a spiritual cleaning—always raises your chances of getting a visa.

There are others who hope to find something else. One wants to cut emotional ties with his oppressive mother-in-law. One wants to figure out why she's been having trouble sleeping. Some want their babies to stop screaming at night. Some want love.

From my seat on the bench, I glance up from my indigo notebook to puzzle over Wendell. He seems to find excuses to watch the people coming in and out of the curing room. He sweeps the dirt patch outside the waiting hut. He scatters corn kernels for the chickens gathered there, his gaze fixed on the closed door, waiting for patients to come outside and blink in the bright light of day. I try to pinpoint his expression. It's an odd mix of longing, curiosity, and fear—a look nearly spilling over with questions that, for some reason, he won't venture to ask Silvio.

"Small and quiet," the old lady says. "With a timid smile." I jot down her words halfheartedly. *Small and quiet, with a timid smile* seems to be the vague consensus description when we ask people about the woman who disappeared sixteen years ago.

I translate for Wendell, who's taking pictures of the small, smoky kitchen with his camera balanced on his tripod. He's getting close-ups of the utensils hanging from her walls, blackened cast iron and worn wood speckled with burns. "*¿Algo más?*" he asks the woman. *Anything else?*

"She wasn't from here." The woman licks her lips, which curve over her toothless gums. She has a strong Quichua accent and I have to listen closely to catch her words. We almost passed right by her house without noticing it, a small one-room shack tucked away from the road, not far from Silvio and Luz's house.

"A name?" I ask hopelessly. Interview after interview of nothing can dampen your spirits. At this point, my stomach's growling and I just want to finish the interview and eat some of Mamita Luz's bread.

"I don't remember her name." The woman stirs a pot of potato soup with a long spoon. "She kept to herself."

"The baby's father?" The past ten times we've asked this, people have shrugged and look at the ground and mumbled, "Only God knows."

Instead she says, "Perhaps you should talk with the healer Silvio."

I glance up, shocked, my pen frozen in midair. "Why him, *señora*?"

She keeps stirring the bubbling soup. "I don't gossip."

When we interrogate Taita Silvio outside his house, he looks thoughtful but doesn't volunteer any information.

"But why would the woman tell us to ask you?" I push.

"Perhaps because my wife and I are considered the parents of the community." He stares intently at a pecking chicken.

Later, on the way to the bus stop, I say, "We've reached a dead end here, Wendell. It's been five days. Time to try some other villages."

"But I have this feeling."

I suck in a breath. "We're basing this whole fruitless search on a feeling?"

"Please."

"One more day."

That afternoon I don't have any English tutoring lined up, so while Wendell's at the Internet café, I wander over to Parque Bolívar. Don Celestino is sitting by the fountain in his blue chair, commenting on distant radio music and the feel of the breeze.

"Don Celestino," I say, opening my indigo notebook. "How do you know I'm me?"

"Because of the birdsongs in your voice."

"But you know it's me even before you hear me."

"There are birdsongs in your walk, too."

"Do you ever feel lonely with people coming and going all the time?"

"No. I feel happy."

"Do you ever feel scared not being able to see?"

"No. I have my chair."

It's Saturday, and Jeff's driving his black rental SUV, one hand on the steering wheel and the other wrapped around Layla's. Observing from the backseat, part of me wants to smile at this new development, but part of me dreads that this is the beginning of the end. When a man starts holding Layla's hand in that casual yet possessive way, she feels caged in. It's usually a matter of time before she dumps him. The boyfriends who've lasted longer than a few weeks are the ones who grab her hand only to run into the ocean or through a sudden rainstorm or down a hill with childish abandon.

Jeff's in town for the weekend, and we're headed to the Museum of Culture, which got two lines in the Ecuador guidebook. As a kid, I always begged Layla to take me to museums. In every country we've been to, I've longingly watched the happy families of foreigners streaming in and out of museums. Layla always waved her hand and said, "You want art and culture? Walk down the street with your eyes open. Talk to people. It's more fun. And it's free!"

The museum is just on the edge of town, but it takes a while to get there because Jeff drives about five miles an hour as buses and taxis whiz around us. "And I thought driving in D.C. at rush hour was crazy. That's nothing." He glances in the rearview mirror. "You've got your seat belt on, right, Zeeta?"

"Yep." I appreciate his concern for safety.

"We'll get there when we get there," he says. "I'm carrying precious cargo here." What a perfect Dad thing to say. Precious cargo. He pulls a crisp white handkerchief from his pocket and pats his forehead. Layla lowers the digital temperature from sixty-eight to sixty-five, then returns her hand to his.

I haven't seen much of Layla all week. She's been either at class, on the phone with Jeff, or holed away in her room, up to her elbows in manila folders and crates and ESL books and papers, attempting to file her teaching materials. This is part of Jeff's plan, an "up-front investment of time to create an efficient system of lesson planning," so that she won't be scrambling at the last minute to throw something together.

In the past, she's spent her hours between classes hanging out with the most eccentric expats or locals she can find, whiling away hours at cafés in conversations about Art and Existence, darting off on hikes to sacred mountains and lakes and caves. Then, a half hour before her next class starts, she whips into a whirlwind of activity, digging into her giant box of ESL stuff, cutting up flash cards and magazine pictures, jotting down ideas for wild grammar games and vocabulary skits. It's been strange to see her so calm and orderly.

I crane my head forward, between the front seats. "You're a superhero, Jeff. Layla's never been so organized in her life."

"She's making progress, isn't she?" he says. I notice he even has a little cleft in his chin, like Superman's.

Layla glances back at me. "Hey, Z, you know when I do visualization trips to other worlds? You know my animal spirit guides?"

I can't believe she's bringing them up in front of Jeff. "The stag and the puma?" I groan.

"Well, I was telling Jeff he's like my own personal guide to the regular world. It's like I lost the map a long time ago, and now Jeff's showing me around, making me feel at home here."

Jeff's eyes in the rearview mirror look earnest and surprisingly unfazed by the stag and puma comparison. "And Layla's my guide to the world of travel and adventure. Just at the time I needed it most."

This extreme sappiness is hard to swallow, but it's my dream come true, so I plant a big smile on my face and say, "Serendipity."

It takes us a while to locate the museum, which is hidden down a maze of unlabeled streets off the highway. Inside, it's musty and tiny and empty of people, only three dark rooms with a sixth-grade social studies–project feel. Homemade posters and little dioramas about local traditions are lined up behind locked glass cases. I can't imagine anyone trying to steal them.

Jeff stands gaping in front of a hand-drawn map of Ecuador. "It just hits me every once in a while. I'm on a whole different continent. The adventure of a lifetime! I wish my daughters were here."

It's touching that he considers a trip to a school-project-caliber museum the adventure of a lifetime. And it's sweet that he misses his daughters so much. I wonder if my father has other daughters and if he misses them the way Jeff misses his. I wonder if my father ever has some inexplicable primordial longing to see me, even though he has no reason to think I exist.

"Your daughters are lucky," I say.

"I'm the lucky one. And on my next trip, I'll take one of them along. You and Layla inspire me. All this parent-daughter globe-trotting. What a great bonding experience!"

I've always considered it more a burdening experience than a bonding one. I don't correct him. Instead, I say, "Tell me about your daughters."

He talks and talks, and Layla pipes in here and there—it's clear he's told her plenty about his daughters already. After an hour, I know about everything, from Chloe's first steps to Camille's volleyball team's championship. This is a man who adores the slightest flutter of his daughters' eyelashes. It's almost dizzying.

Finally, he turns his attention to the clay dioramas on display. "So, ladies, tell me, what have we here?" By now I'm hungry and ready to leave this place, but Layla translates each and every one of the informational signs into English for Jeff. He listens, captivated. She lingers on Inti Raymi, the festival of the sun, celebrated at the end of June, around the summer solstice. "We were supposed to be here for the procession to the waterfall, but I came down with the flu in Thailand." She sighs. "We didn't make it here till a few weeks later."

I remember this well. It was a big, traumatic thing for her, missing the summer solstice celebration. That's her all-time favorite part of the year, anywhere in the world.

"Good thing," Jeff murmurs. "Then we might not have met." He puts his arm around her shoulders, a careful, protective gesture. I expect to see Layla's shoulders stiffen in response, but no, they soften under his arm.

Layla translates more signs, about harvesting crops and exchanging food. Jeff's utterly fascinated, making ohs and ahs here and there.

I find myself yawning. It's uncontrollable, this yawning. I desperately want a nap. I never feel tired in Agua Santa, even in the middle of heavy labor. Maybe because in Agua Santa, I'm actually doing the harvesting of crops, not reading about it. I'm actually exchanging food with people, not just looking at a diorama of little dolls trading sacks of potatoes and corn.

I watch Layla carefully. She finishes reading a section on

the Yamor Festival, and then Jeff starts talking about Otavaleño wedding rituals. I find myself waiting for a slight parting of her mouth, the tiniest watering of her eyes, a hint of a suppressed yawn. But no, she seems inexplicably content.

Over the weekend, Jeff and Layla dine together each night at the Restaurante Americano, so I spend the evenings with Wendell. On Saturday, we cook together in the apartment— quinoa soup with heaps of cilantro. He's very good at dicing vegetables—he chops fast, creating tiny pieces. He cleans the dishes as we go along, too. I want to light candles for our dinners like Layla and I always do—it really does make the food taste better—but I worry he might get the wrong idea. So we eat on the balcony, under the light of an electric bulb.

Giovanni the surfer clown joins us, offering bits of Taoist wisdom in return for food. He talks about The Way, the flow of the universe, action without action, effortless doing. It sounds like yet another excuse not to wash the dishes, if you ask me. When I try to pin him down on the details, he twists three balloons into a rose, presents it to me, and says, "The Way that can be described is not the true Way."

Wendell and I smile at each other. After Giovanni leaves, Wendell says, "He's cool. I've never met anyone like him." A tiny part of me wishes he could have known the prewaterfall Layla.

On Sunday, Wendell and I make shrimp seviche from a recipe Gaby gave us. Giovanni's out, and Wendell and I are alone on the balcony. Even though no candles are lit, there's a certain feeling of intimacy in the pool of light beneath the bare lightbulb, the shadowy flowers and trees in the court-yard below us. From my back pocket, I pull out the next letter I've translated. "This one's my favorite so far," I say, and proceed to read it out loud.

"To the evil people who call themselfs my birth parents:
  I'm so mad at you!!!!!! Here's why:
1) it's all your fault no one will ever say to me, you look just like your dad, the way people say to Aiden. 2) you gave me away like you thought I was too ugly or dumb or something. well, I think your dumb and ugly. BUTT UGLY! Your so ugly PUKE looks nice next to you! 3) I bet you have kids locked in cages in a dunjon in your basement. Lucky thing my real mom and dad saved me from your cluches!
                    I HATE YOU,
                    wendell B. connelly,
                    age nine"

"There's no exact translation for *butt ugly*," I say.
He smiles and sucks on a piece of lime-soaked shrimp. "I thought about throwing that letter away."

"Whoever your birth parents are, they'll get a kick out of it."

We eat some more shrimp and popcorn and then he says, in a deliberately casual voice, "Hey, Z, you know how Taita Silvio looks like me?"

"It's uncanny," I admit.

"You think he's my birth dad? You think he had an affair with that mystery woman?"

I pick through my popcorn for an unburnt kernel, stalling. "It's possible. But he seems so devoted to his wife. Do you really want to go there? It could ruin his marriage. Is it worth it?"

Wendell's eyes harden. "I have a right to know." He finishes his last swig of papaya juice. "And if he won't tell us, we'll have to find the truth ourselves. Let's look around for clues."

"Snoop?"

"Snoop."

"That doesn't seem . . . devious?"

"What's devious is him hiding things from us." Wendell seems to be a generally mellow guy, the type who doesn't get angry easily. But spending all this time with him, I can see it. The coldness that's crept into his voice, the rigid set of his jaw.

"Okay, Wendell. Let's snoop."

Chapter 13

I blink, waiting for my eyes to adjust to the darkness, damp and cool as a cave's shadows. There's no electric light. The clay walls are blackened with smoke stains and hold the scent of candles and incense and earth. Candelabra encircle the room on a wooden ledge. Behind me, Wendell holds open the heavy wooden door to let in a sliver of light while I search for matches.

Here we are, in the curing room. Snooping. I feel terribly guilty about it. This morning we were helping Luz and Silvio in the fields, when, as planned, Wendell said he didn't feel well. He actually did look sick, probably his own angst over what we were about to do. I offered to come back with him while he rested. Unexpectedly, the house was locked, and we almost turned back, relieved. Then, on impulse,

Wendell suggested we try this room. I'm doubtful we'll find anything. It doesn't exactly seem like the place you'd store birth certificates or even illicit love letters.

Once I find matches and light a few candles, Wendell lets the door fall closed. My heart's pounding as I take in the room. In the corner, on the far end of the dirt floor, is a table that appears to be the altar. The entire wall behind it is a burst of color. Hung from the adobe are colorful plastic tablecloths with prints of yellow roses and sunflowers and bowls of honey and a blue teapot and cups—kind of an English garden pattern. Dozens of pictures of saints and Virgins and crosses and ribbons hang on the adjacent wall, along with fresh bundles of leaves and strings of Christmas lights and the Ecuadorian flag. Pushed against the side wall is a long bench that looks like it was painted blue years ago. Now, only a hint of blue remains.

An odd medley of objects covers the altar: plastic water bottles filled with colored liquids; roses; stones of all shapes and sizes, some as small as plums, others as heavy and big as melons; a shiny golden laughing Buddha with babies crawling on him, all of them bald with large round bellies. Next to the Buddha family sit scissors, a candle, a bundle of leaves, a glass goblet of water, and two worn pink towels.

"Look, Z." Wendell points to a neat row of crystals, four of them, by the Buddha babies. He holds his crystal next to them. They look similar, but I'm no geologist.

Then I see it, something that makes me break out in a shivery sweat.

Propped against a plastic bottle is an old photo, curled at the edges. It's in color, but faded and a little out of focus. A hugely pregnant woman stands in front of an adobe house, with muted green hills beyond. She has an early nineties hairstyle—bangs curled and hair sprayed high, hair glossed back in a ponytail. She's wearing the clothes of an Otavaleña woman, but with a red fleece jacket instead of a wool shawl. She looks about twenty years old, and stares into the camera with a reluctant, sad hint of a smile. A familiar half-smile.

At closer look, I notice a man's hand on her shoulder. The rest of him has been cut out of the photo in one uneven snip.

Wendell sees it too. He picks up the photo, and with absolute certainty says, "It's her."

Back in the cornfield, the corn leaves look like sponges, soaking up light. After spending all this time with Wendell, I notice the quality of light more. It's the key to a good photograph, he always says. The photo he holds carefully in his hands now is so blurred you can't even tell where the light's coming from. He keeps slowing down between the corn rows, pausing to study it.

In the distance, the girls are playing chase, screeching and laughing. Mamita Luz is working a few rows over from Taita Silvio, bent over with her machete. As we walk toward him. Mamita Luz stands up and stretches her back. "Feeling better, *hijo*?"

"*Sí,*" Wendell says, stopping in front of Taita Silvio.

Quietly, I say, "Tell us the truth. The straight truth."

He pauses, then nods, leaning on his machete.

Wendell holds up the picture. "*¿Mi mamá?*"

Silvio makes the faintest movement, a hint of a nod.

"Is she the woman who disappeared sixteen years ago?" I ask.

"*Sí.*" He sets down his machete.

"What's her name?"

"Lilia."

"What happened to her?"

He hesitates, then finally says, "She died. A car accident. I'm so sorry, Wendell."

Wendell's expression is unreadable. The photo trembles in his hand.

"And his birth father?" I ask.

He turns up his hands. "Who knows."

I study his face. He's lying. My voice drops. "You look a lot like Wendell. We know your wife can't have children, but—"

"Listen, son. I wish I were your father. But I'm not. We went to doctors in Quito. The problem is not only with my wife, but with me also. Perfect for each other, aren't we?" Avoiding our eyes, he picks up his machete and whacks at a weed.

Mamita Luz walks over, beads of moisture coating her round face. She puts one arm around each of us. Even her sweat smells like steaming bread. "Everything all right, *mis hijos?*"

Wendell shakes his head, his gaze fixed on Silvio. Using

the basic vocabulary of Spanish 1, he forms a question. Amazingly, it's grammatically correct, although the pronunciation leaves much to be desired. It's a desperate, last-ditch effort of a question. *"Taita Silvio, ¿tiene hermanos?"* Do you have brothers?

Taita Silvio freezes midswing. Lowering his machete, he whispers, "No."

"She's pretty, don't you think?" Wendell's sitting on a stool outside the curing room, staring at the picture of his birth mother. "I mean, if you overlook the hairstyle."

"Beautiful," I say, which is a bit of an exaggeration, especially since I can barely make out her blurry features. But there *is* something soft and kind about her expression, the way she holds herself, something I see in Wendell, too.

Mamita Luz is sitting next to me, taking kernels off corncobs, and the girls are gathering blackberries at the far end of the yard. Taita Silvio hasn't said anything for an hour. In the cornfield, he simply walked away, his machete at his side. Now he stands beside Wendell, looking at the photo and touching Wendell's shoulder, as though it might break. "Keep the picture, *hijo*. I should have given it to you sooner."

"Why do you have the picture?" I ask. "What happened sixteen years ago?"

Silvio shakes his head.

Mamita Luz frowns. "Tell him. He can handle it."

Taita Silvio sighs a few words in Quichua, then takes a

long breath. "She—Lilia—came to town one day with—a man"—and here he glances at his wife and unspoken words pass between them—"a man who didn't treat her well. She was poor and vulnerable. She kept to herself mostly. He didn't want her to have friends." Taita Silvio stops.

Mamita Luz continues. "And then her belly started swelling. She gave birth on November sixth."

"My birthday," Wendell murmurs.

Any lingering doubts about his birth mother's identity disappear.

"We helped her plan the baby's adoption while she was pregnant," Mamita Luz says, her eyes glistening. "Lilia left the man and came to live with us. We were with her at the hospital when she gave birth. We helped her say goodbye to the baby boy, and a few weeks later, we brought her to a safe place. Not long after that we got news that she was riding in the truck with—that man. He was drunk. He crashed. Lilia died."

Wendell listens closely as I translate. I can practically hear his thoughts. The only thing worse than a dead birth mother is a drunk jerk for a birth father. "And the man?"

Taita Silvio says something to his wife in Quichua. They're arguing about something. Finally, he shakes his head. "The man no longer exists."

Correction. The only thing worse than a dead birth mother is a *dead* drunk jerk for a birth father. I can feel Wendell's heart slowly falling.

"He was my father?" Wendell's voice cracks.

Again, Taita Silvio and Mamita Luz exchange looks and heated words in Quichua.

"What was his name?" Wendell pushes.

Taita Silvio stares at the ground. "I don't know."

"I need you to do a divination to find out," Wendell says.

Taita Silvio looks surprised. "I'm not—it doesn't always work."

"We have to try. I'll pay you."

Mamita Luz's apple cheeks are as stern as I've seen them. "The boy is strong enough to know the truth."

Taita Silvio squints at the sky, blue except for a few wispy clouds. "*Bueno*. My wife and I have to go to Quito for two days. I'll do the divination when we return."

Now the girls are running toward us in a flurry of excited shouts. "Look at all these blackberries!" Odelia shouts, her sisters trailing behind.

Taita Silvio and Wendell glance up with identical expressions. The bright sunlight illuminates their cheekbones, accentuating the shadows underneath. Their mouths are set and turned up a little at the left edge. Their ears, small and protruding, are echoes of each other.

Odelia holds her handful of berries over her head. "Look at all my berries!" she shouts to the sky. And to Taita Silvo, "Can my star see me? Even though I can't see my star?"

"Yes, *hija,* your star is always there," he says. "Your star watches you. Your star thinks about you every day and every night, even though you don't know it."

. . .

That evening at home, beyond all comprehension, Layla is sitting on the sofa, watching TV.

I'm speechless. TV? Layla's vehemently against TVs, calls them soul suckers. Once I find my voice, I squeak, "Where'd that come from?"

She glances at me, then back at the flickering screen. "Jeff bought it for us. There's a satellite dish on this building, did you know? We get a zillion channels."

I perch on the arm of the sofa. It's a rerun of *Friends,* which of course I've heard of, because some things you can't escape even in the tiny nooks and crannies of the planet.

She lays her hand on my knee. "Remember how you used to beg me for a TV when you were little?"

I nod. I gave up that dream long ago.

"It's more for Jeff than for me. He doesn't want to get behind on his sports viewing when he hangs out here. He keeps golf stats."

I wonder if this will be the kiss of death for him. For Layla, golf is the epitome of all things evil the world. She always observes that no matter what country we're in, whether jungly or desertic, the ritzy resorts have cleared a gigantic area and planted turf and dumped tons of water for irrigation, all because a certain portion of the world's population can't survive without this sport. I'm amazed she can even mention the golf-stat thing without a trace of sarcasm.

"So he's really into golf, huh?"

"It's actually an interesting sport if you give it a chance.

There's this whole golf subculture, you know? I've been so judgmental about it in the past, but there's something to it."

I can't think of anything to say.

"Anyway, he's entitled to his hobbies. He doesn't get my spiritual searching. In a grown-up relationship, differences can be healthy."

I fiddle with my rings. She sounds like an advice columnist in a women's magazine, the mainstream voice of reason. Since when did Layla call her spiritual-searching obsession a hobby? "Is he back in Quito now?"

She nods.

So I'll have her to myself tonight. That makes me secretly happy.

We watch *Friends* and *Frasier* and *Sex and the City* and *Desperate Housewives*. At first, it's fun. I see us from the outside, a bird's-eye view of a mother and a daughter side by side on a sofa, watching TV, laughing at the jokes, sharing a bowl of popcorn, worthy of a magazine ad. After two hours, I find myself waiting for Layla to say, *Let's paint the walls purple!* Or *Let's blast Moroccan music and belly dance on the porch!* Or *Let's have champagne and make crème brûlée!* But the only thing she says is, "Finally I'm getting it."

"What?"

"The appeal of TV." She hugs a pillow. "See, it's a necessary escape."

"Escape from what?"

"From life." She seems pleased with her analysis. "From a boring life, that is. A life you'd need to escape from." And she settles back into the couch and changes the channel.

Later, in my room, I unfold another letter. Wendell's warned me this one would be extra-embarrassing.

Dear birth mom and dad,
  I'm sorry that my last letter was mean. Let me tell you why I hate my FAKE mom. I was sick on Thursday with Stomach problems. STOMACH PROBLEMS. And mom wrote a note, wendell has diarea so he was not in School yesterday. And I gave it to mrs. woods and she read it and put it on her desk and then colin saw it and Said, wendell has diarea!
  I am So humeliated. I Said, mom why the hell didn't you write Stomach problems? I even Said that, hell. And She got mad at me. At ME! After She humeliated me! You wouldn't ever write that I had diarea, would you?
                    Sincerely,
                    wendell B. connelly,
                    age 10

P.S. an hour later. it's not like you have to come get me or anything. Mom came up here with brownies and said next time she'll write stomach problems. she promises.

I shuffle through all the times I've told Layla I hated her. Pretty much every time she's made us move to a new country, at least in the past few years. In each of my notebooks, there are solid pages with line after line of *I hate Layla. I hate Layla. I hate Layla.*

At the end of my tirades, after some sulking in my room, I could never resist coming out, lured by the sweet scent of rose petal tea and the peppermint and rosemary essential oils she heated to make me feel better. She'd say some Rumi quote like, "Oh, love, remember that sometimes, *what hurts you, blesses you. Darkness is your candle. Your boundaries are your quest.*" Then we'd drink rose tea with lots of honey and she'd pull me into whatever she was into at the time— playing the didgeridoo or dancing to African music.

Soon the hate faded. But in my notebook, I never crossed out the lines of *I hate Layla.* And I never filled a single page with lines of *I love Layla.*

Even though, of course, I did.

"Head, shoulders, knees, and toes, knees and toes!" Odelia belts out the song in the sweet, damp air, still fresh from dew. Wendell and I are touching our heads, shoulders, knees, and toes for the tenth time today. It's as though Agua Santa has a magnetic pull, won't let us stay away. Taita Silvio and Mamita Luz are in Quito, visiting some of their "children" who've grown, and the girls insisted we come on a hike.

They're taking us to a high lookout point, where you can see everything. "Practically the whole world!" Isabel has promised. A day without thinking about Wendell's birth parents will be good. And mountaintop views always give me perspective on things—in this case, what to think about Layla's new TV-viewing habit.

On the way up the hill, we pass some two-story cement houses, unpainted, like islands among corn plants. Dogs live on the roofs, barking and peering over the edges, silhouetted against the expanse of blue above. The higher we go, the bigger the sky grows, spotted with a few clouds like pearls, broken open and melting. You can see far into the distance, across the layers of hills that stretch into the mountains. The earth slopes and curves, rises and falls, joining here, separating there, with the mottled green fabric of leaves draped over it all.

The wind is wild, whipping at our shirts, pushing us this way and that. On the way, Odelia proudly points out eucalyptus trees, and has us smell the cough-drop scent of the leaves torn up in her hand. Isabel plucks tiny edible berries from flowered ground cover, and Eva gathers pale green watercress from streams for us to taste, smiling for the camera as Wendell snaps photos.

Eva motions to a tree whose huge white flowers dangle like

ornaments. "And that's *floripondio*. In the old days, mothers used to put their babies under the branches if they were cranky. It made them sleep." She lowers her voice dramatically. "Thieves use it too. They crush the petals and sprinkle them in your food. And then, you're like a zombie, and they rob you."

On and on the girls chatter, telling us tales and showing us plants and landmarks as they lead us up a hill toward the lookout point. We reach the top of the hill and look around, stunned at the view. On all four sides, rolling hills and valleys surround us, a landscape dripping with sun-drenched green. It's as though a treasure chest has overturned, spilling out gemstones of every possible shade of green—jade and emerald and turquoise, all aglow.

Odelia points toward the next hill over. "Look! Inside that hill are tunnels that lead to a diamond palace," she says. "Secret tunnels."

Isabel widens her eyes. "And the devils try to make a deal with you to make you rich. In return, they take your soul and—"

"So we're not allowed to go there," Odelia breaks in, "because—"

"A bad man lives on that hill," Isabel interrupts. "And he turns into a snake at night and goes into the tunnels with the devils and—"

"Don Faustino." Eva jumps in eagerly. "We're not allowed to go to his house. He made a deal with the devil. That's why he's rich."

"Once," Isabel says, "our cousin's friend's brother went there on a dare and his dogs bit him and Don Faustino just watched and know what he said? He said, 'That'll teach you not to mess around on my property.' The dogs bit him all over, and just when they were going for his neck for the kill, Don Faustino pulled them off."

"And you know the strange thing?" Eva says.

"What?" Of course, I'm taking all this with a giant grain of salt. I've heard these kinds of stories in most small towns we've been to, all over the world. The rich man who made a deal with the devil. An envied outcast.

"He's the brother of the nicest man in town. Taita Silvio."

Chapter 14

In the scant shade of a small tree, Wendell and I wait for the bus. He asks in a strained playful voice, "You think my birth father is a snake man who hangs out with devils?"

I smile. "The guy's probably a harmless hermit."

"What about him siccing his dogs on that kid?"

"Could be a rumor."

Wendell stares at the mountain Imbabura, looming high. "Let's go to his house."

I reconsider. "Well, maybe it's not just a rumor. Obviously Taita Silvio doesn't want you to meet him. Why else would he lie?"

He pulls the crystal from his pocket, rolls it around in his hands. "Either way, I have to know."

The bus comes chugging along, a blue one with a cloud of gray smoke trailing behind. It stops and the doors open. I climb on first, with Wendell right behind me. The door's just closing behind us when, without warning, Wendell grabs my hand and says, "Get off." He pushes open the door and pulls me out after him. We stumble onto the asphalt, and I struggle to regain my balance.

The driver calls out, "You coming?"

Wendell shakes his head vehemently, and the bus pulls away.

Is he crazy? He said there were weird things about him. Apart from his letters, I don't actually know much about him, come to think of it. This is the kind of thing Layla does from time to time, if she has an ominous dream or sees a particular sign. "Three dead bees in a row this morning!" she said a few months ago in Thailand. "One in my dream, one that slammed into our window, and one on the way to the bakery. That's it, I'm not leaving the house for the rest of the day."

Has Wendell had a sign? Or some kind of feeling? Like whatever made him give me the *be careful in the water* warning?

Hands shaking, Wendell takes out his camera and starts fiddling with the knobs, refusing to meet my eyes. "I just— I just saw this thing I wanted to take a picture of."

He's a terrible liar.

"What thing?" I ask.

He looks around and his gaze settles on a crushed plastic Inca Kola bottle in the weeds. "That. It's an artsy shot." He lowers to his knee and snaps a few photos.

Obviously, he's lying. Maybe he saw someone on the bus who he didn't want to see? Maybe he's claustrophobic and the bus felt too crowded?

About twenty minutes later, when the next bus comes, we get on without incident. Wendell tries to act like his regular self. He talks about some landscape photos he wants to take, but he seems distracted, fiddling with the curtain's tassel, eyes darting to the window.

Halfway there, our bus slows. At first I figure it's to pick up or drop off passengers. But then I notice voices rising into a kind of high-pitched frenzy. Something's burning—engine exhaust, rubber, fuel. I turn across the aisle toward the opposite windows, where all the passengers are peering outside, eyes open, mouths dropped. I follow their gaze. First I see the flashing lights of the ambulance and fire trucks, and then the bus, blue and turned on its side like a carcass, the front end smashed into a huge semitrailer. A crowd of dazed people are streaming off the bus, some hunched over, helped by medics, as stretchers are being loaded into three ambulances.

I turn to Wendell. The color has seeped out of his face. He stares like he's seen a ghost.

"That's the bus we didn't take," I say. "Isn't it?"

He nods.

The police direct our bus to keep moving through. I study Wendell. "You knew."

His eyes are glassy. "You think anyone died?"

"You *knew*."

"Maybe you should translate a couple more letters, Z. The two most recent ones."

I race to the corner coffee shop, order chamomile tea and caramel-filled pastries, and shuffle through the unread letters in my bag. I find one from age fifteen, typed, red ink on white paper.

Dear birth mom and dad,

I think I'm going crazy. I think maybe you're the only ones who can understand. Sometimes when I'm zoning out, like listening to music or staring at the wall in class, sometimes I get these feelings, like something's going to happen. Sometimes, something good. Sometimes, something bad.

Like yesterday, I looked at my buddy Aiden in math class and I got this terrible feeling. And then, we were riding bikes home from school and it was raining and his wheel caught on the railroad tracks and he wrecked his bike. He's okay, just pretty bruised and scraped up. But what if I caused it? Or could have stopped it? I don't even believe in this stuff, but it's happening to me.

Will I have to live my whole life like this? What's wrong with me? I haven't told anyone about this. I don't know why, it's too weird.

Please help me make it stop.
Wendell, age 15

There's another recent one, from age sixteen, scribbled on notebook paper with torn edges. The handwriting is fast and furious, written at jagged, desperate angles.

Dear birth mom and dad,

I'm going to find you. I'm going to find you and give you these letters. I need your help. I know you can help me. I can't live with this anymore. It's this big secret that's crushing me.

My girlfriend broke up with me and I think it's because I told her about this stuff. When I begged her not to break up with me (I know, not one of my proudest moments), she said I had abandonment issues and needed to find resolution. (She's taking a psych class this year and thinks she's better than Freud now.) Blah blah blah.

But it's true. I do need resolution. I need you to explain myself to me. I've been writing you these letters and you'll never get them unless I find you. I'm going this summer.

Hasta pronto,
Wendell, age 16

I read the letters three times, and when my hands stop shaking, I translate them.

Then, like I always do when I feel like I'll explode with emotion, I start writing in my notebook. After three lines, I slam it shut, frustrated.

I don't want to write.

I want to talk.

To Layla.

I want to tell her about Wendell, and the accident, and the snake man, and everything else.

When I get home, the door's unlocked. She must be home. But she isn't cross-legged on the floor painting, or staring at a plant on the porch and writing a poem about an unfurling leaf, or kneeling at the crate coffee table and soldering stained-glass mosaics. That crazy energy is missing, the whirlwind that usually sweeps me up. Usually she beams a smile at me, packed with chi, and says something along the lines of, "Hello, my gorgeous daughter. What did the universe shower you with today, love?"

And I always say something like, "Dog shit on my flip-flop." And then she laughs a tinkling laugh, and somehow we get around to talking about whatever we feel like talking about and drink passion fruit juice on the patio. It was a warm, cozy space we created together, Layla and me, now that I think about it.

She's on the sofa, watching TV, her school folders in a neat pile on the crate coffee table. "Hi, love."

"Hey, Layla." I open my mouth to tell her everything,

but then I notice her eyes glued to the screen. I press my lips together.

We watch some *Desperate Housewives* together in silence. During the commercials, she opens the folder marked Lesson Plans and makes some notes. This past week, I popped into one of her afternoon classes and found the classroom silent, the students with their heads bent over textbooks, copying exercises into their notebooks, while she sat behind the desk watching them, her eyes oddly blank. In Thailand and Brazil, whenever I stopped by her classroom, students were dancing on the desks, or impersonating the Simpsons in ridiculous wigs. They were usually laughing so hard the teachers in nearby classrooms complained. But Layla never got in too much trouble. Her students always had the highest test scores of any classes and always gave her the best evaluations.

During an SUV commercial, she looks up from her papers. "Jeff's such a good influence on me, you know?"

"So you really like him?" I say, pushing the Wendell stuff to the side for the moment.

She smiles, a slow smile that manages to reach the corners of her lips but doesn't quite make it to her eyes. "I feel like a grown-up with him. It's weird, but good, you know? And safe. I finally understand your need to be safe."

"Really?"

"Lately, when I'm trying to sleep, my throat feels like it's closing up. It's like I can't breathe, like I'm back in that water, drowning. That's how you feel when you wake up in the middle of the night, isn't it?"

"Try deep belly breathing," I suggest.

Layla looks sad. "It's not too late to give you a piece of a normal childhood, Z."

"Layla, you don't have to do this for me."

She tucks her knees under her chin. "If I'd died in that water, what would have happened to you? I mean, I don't even have a will. Jeff made a whole list of things I need to do. Legal and financial things. Things he did for his daughters."

Desperate Housewives comes on again, and Layla looks back at the TV, the ghostly blue light flickering over her face. "You're happy about Jeff, right, Z?"

"Of course, Layla."

"Because it was pure destiny that dropped him in my path. And he says the same thing about me. He says that his life felt all small and closed up after the divorce, after his girls went to college. And now, he's exploring this whole adventurous side of himself."

"That's great." My voice sounds small and far away.

She turns up the volume and pats my knee. I wonder if that's something she picked up from Jeff. She never used to pat before. I wonder if soon she'll be saying things like, "Oh, my!"

I sink back into the sofa, which isn't so much a sofa as wooden fruit crates with foam cushions, covered by Layla with fabric scraps from her old, holey skirts. What does Jeff think of them? Can he appreciate all the history behind them? One skirt's from Laos, one from Thailand, one from India—flowered silk prints that have frayed and faded in the sun.

We eat a dinner of leftover soup in front of the TV. After washing the dishes, I pick up the worn red book from the crate-table, run my fingers over its soft, old spine. "Want to read Rumi?"

"I'm kind of tired for that, love," she says through a yawn. "Have you noticed that TV has the magical effect of sleeping pills? My insomnia lifesaver. Worlds better than chamomile tea."

I flip to one of Rumi's dog-eared pages, silently read the two underlined words.

Now, fly.

A sign, I decide. Why not? Someone has to be on the look-out for signs. "Layla, I'm going to Wendell's. I might just spend the night there. We'll get an early start tomorrow to Agua Santa for the divination. I'm taking Rumi and the water-colors with me, okay?"

"Okay, love. Enjoy." And she goes back to staring at another rerun of *Frasier,* and you can almost see her soul, like a wisp of smoke, stealing away, little by little.

I half-walk, half-run to Wendell's hotel, almost as if something's chasing me. By the time I get there, it's about eight at night. People are gathered on the streets near the main squares, outside lit-up bars and restaurants.

Upstairs, in his doorway, Wendell greets me in a white T-shirt frayed at the neckline and a pair of basketball shorts.

He doesn't seem surprised to see me; in fact, it's almost as if he's been expecting me. His hair's wet and loose and falling down his back, and he smells fresh, like orange shampoo. He sits on one bed and I sit on the other. "I was wishing you'd come by," he says.

"Did you have a feeling about it? A good one?"

"Actually, I did."

I smile, pleased, and pull the most recent two letters from my bag. "Here you go."

He takes them, sets them carefully on his lap. "And?"

"I think you have an incredible gift."

"So you don't think I'm crazy?"

"No." Then I add, "But I think you should ask Taita Silvio to teach you how to use it."

He leans back and puts a pillow over his face. His voice comes through, muffled. "I want my birth father to teach me."

"Why not Taita Silvio?"

"He's always hiding something. Once you peel off one layer of lies, there's another underneath."

"But if you're so desperate to understand this gift you have—"

"This *curse* I have."

"Silvio can help you."

He tosses the pillow up, catches it, tosses it again. "For years I've had this crazy reunion scene in my head, like the last scene in a sappy movie, you know, with hazy lens filters and tearjerky music. I show my birth parents the crystal and they tell me the secret of how to make these visions go away. It's always them, my birth parents."

He takes a deep breath. "Now I know I'll never meet my birth mom. Never. So at least I want that other piece to be true. The part about my birth dad." He tucks the pillow behind his head. "This sounds incredibly stupid when I say it out loud."

"No, it doesn't. I get it." And I do. He's gotten fixated on this idea of happiness, blinding himself to other possibilities, the way I stubbornly cling to my idea of the Normal Magazine Family.

A motorcycle passes on the street below, and after the engine's roar dissipates, Wendell says, "Hey, Z, want to go to Faustino's house tomorrow? After the divination?"

"Maybe." Honestly, it sounds like a terrible, dangerous idea, but I'm pretty sure if I say no, he'll just go alone. "So," I say, changing the subject. "I was thinking of an evening of watercoloring and Rumi." I toss the Rumi book onto his bed.

He opens to a random page and reads aloud,

"Dance, when you're broken open.
Dance, if you've torn the bandage off.
Dance in the middle of the fighting.
Dance in your blood.
Dance when you're perfectly free."

"Hey, let's go dancing!" As this flies out of my mouth, I realize it's exactly the kind of thing Layla would say. The old Layla, as though a piece of her spirit has crept out and slipped into me. Or maybe it's that I really like dancing and it's not just because Layla drags me out to dance with her.

"I can't dance," he says.

"I'll teach you. Get dressed."

As he changes in the bathroom, I survey his room. It's small, but with high ceilings that make it feel big. The old wooden floors give off a faint smell of pine oil and make our words echo a little. His backpack is stashed neatly against the wall by the door. A Spanish-English phrasebook and a small spiral notebook with verb conjugations copied over and over sits on the nightstand beside a stack of photos. Pictures of the sort-of-ex-girlfriend?

"Can I look at your pictures?" I call through the bathroom door.

"Yeah, they're just pictures of home," he calls back. "Nothing exciting."

The first one is two middle-aged people with light eyes and hair, the man slightly balding, the woman with short grayish-blondish-brownish hair. They're standing in front of a house with a garden of waist-high wildflowers, purple and pink and yellow, spilling out toward the edge of the photo. They look friendly, beaming simple, genuine smiles. The kind of people whose one wish, without a moment's hesitation, would be world peace.

I flip through the rest—a dog with short legs and a long body and its tongue out, huge and close and glistening with saliva, ready to lick you. A picture of light streaming into a blue room with a green bed, a boy's room, with a few band posters and a big framed picture of mountains—the Andes, maybe?

I picture Wendell before I got here tonight, alone on the tight sheets of his hotel bed, repeating Spanish phrases and flipping through photos in a lonely circle of lamplight. I imagine his mother imagining him alone. I imagine his sort-of-ex-girlfriend imagining him alone. But maybe she isn't even thinking of him. Maybe she doesn't care.

The bathroom door opens and Wendell emerges, his hair still loose, but combed now. He's wearing jeans and a slightly wrinkled button-down shirt. He looks good. "Ready, Z?"

"Ready."

Chapter 15

On the way to the *peña*, I tell him about the TV, and how Layla is changing for me, trying to give me a different life.

"Why would she think you'd want a different life?"

"Because I've always begged her for precisely that."

"Why?" He says this in the tone of voice you'd use with someone who'd just dumped money in a shredder.

"I always envied people with normal lives, normal families, normal homes."

He considers this as we walk down the dark street, from one puddle of streetlamp light to another. Most of the stores are closed, their garage-style doors pulled down, only a few pharmacies and tiny convenience stores still lit. Finally he says, "Where'd your idea of normal come from?"

"*Better Homes and Gardens,* 1990 to 1995."

He laughs.

"Seriously. My grandmom's magazines. I read them while I was recovering after nearly dying from malaria."

He stops walking. "When was this?"

"In India. I was twelve. Layla freaked out and her parents paid for our flight to Maryland. We stayed with them for six months. The best months of my life."

My memory of those months in Maryland feels like soaking in a warm bath, and afterward, being wrapped in three giant, fluffy towels that were dried in a real clothes dryer with one of those scented dryer sheets stuck in to make it smell good. It's a floating feeling, an eyes-closed, comfy, blankety feeling, the feeling of not having to worry about anything.

Everyday tasks were impossibly easy. The electricity always worked. Water always came out of the faucet like magic— even hot water. It took me a while to get used to sitting on a toilet seat rather than squatting over a hole. To flushing with a silvery handle rather than dumping down a bucket of water. It thrilled me to stand on the cushy bath mat, watching toilet paper whirl down the shiny, bleached bowl.

After a week, I came out of the bathroom, where I'd spent hours in a reverie, and announced to Layla, "I want to stay here forever."

"Forever's a long time," she said, laughing. "You'd be bored out of your skull, darling."

"I mean it. I want to stay."

"Get better, love. Get better and then we'll see."

"But you'll think about it?

"Sure. But please, please get better, okay?"

Once I was well enough to go out with my grandparents, I was even more seduced. Safe, it was so safe you didn't have to think. You could stroll across the street knowing that cars would actually stop at the stoplight. You didn't have to jostle in and out of crowded buses spitting black exhaust. There was an intense, clean quiet over the neighborhood, a distinct lack of begging children with oozing sores. *This is heaven*, I thought.

Within a few months, Layla was utterly miserable, drinking peppermint tea—which supposedly helped her chronic headaches—all day long. She pitched a tent in the backyard, claiming she couldn't stand the closed-up, frigid house. She slept there, and during the days hung out on the porch sipping tea and cringing at the lawn mower sounds. She refused to go to the giant stores with us, insisted they gave her a stomachache. When I came home with an iPod that my granddad bought me from Best Buy, she threw her arms around me and burst into tears. "What if you turn into one of these kids, Z? All they care about are their cell-phone rings and iPod tunes."

"That's not true." I liked the neighborhood kids, especially the twin girls next door. We hung out at the pool together, spent hours giggling and listening to one another's music on the lounge chairs, sucking on red-white-and-blue Bomb

Pops, reapplying pomegranate lip gloss and icicle-silver eye shadow. "They're my friends."

She wiped her eyes. "Well, your friends should be dropped in the middle of the Brazilian jungle. See what the Yanomami think about those ninety-dollar pants and name-brand shirts."

I should have seen that as a warning, her talking about the Brazilian jungle. And she'd started going online to Latin American ESL job sites, jotting down notes in her note-book. Still, I ignored it.

And then one evening, at the kitchen table, Layla reached for my hand and took a deep breath. That's when I knew. I knew before she opened her mouth.

"I got tickets to Brazil, Z. Supercheap, a last-minute deal. I couldn't pass it up."

Two days later, with my carry on full of Grandmom's old *Better Homes and Gardens*, I sat on the plane to Rio, my iPod blasting, writing page after page of I HATE LAYLA.

Wendell listens, absorbed, as I ramble on about how I was forced to leave the paradise of suburban Maryland. We're passing through the park now, where a few couples cuddle on benches, gazing at each other, kissing, grasping at the other's skin and clothes as though one of them could slip away. I pick up our pace and try not to look at them.

"So, Wendell," I say, feeling suddenly awkward, "what do you and your family do together?"

"What do you mean?"

"Like, do you go to the mall?"

He laughs. "They're morally opposed to the mall. You know, rejecting consumerism and all that."

"Oh. Then what do you all do?"

"Hiking. Biking. Plein air painting."

"Hey, do you go to this restaurant—my grandmom took me there—it was across the mall parking lot, between Best Buy and Old Navy." The air-conditioning in that restaurant was so strong that I broke out in goose bumps within seconds of entering, and the waitress was so unearthly friendly I thought her smile would leap off her face. "Applefleas!" I'm proud that I remember the name, proof I have an insider's scoop on everyday American life.

"Applebee's?" He grins. "Nope. No chains. We go to little hole-in-the-wall ethnic places. Family-owned. Peruvian, Indian, Vietnamese."

"Oh." I try to hide my disappointment.

He elbows me. "If you'd spent your life as a regular at Applebee's, you wouldn't speak a zillion languages. You wouldn't be with me now. I'd still be wandering around the market saying, '¿Mamá? ¿Papá?'"

I laugh. "Someone else would have helped you."

"It was meant to be you," Wendell says. "The second time I saw you, in the market in that orange outfit, I thought, *This girl flies while the rest of us walk*. It's like you don't have the same chains that the rest of us have holding us to earth."

"Not by my choice. It's always been Layla."

"It's you, too. Why would you want to give that up? It

would be like clipping your wings. It would be like going from the life of a bird to the life of, I don't know, a cow or something."

"A cow?"

"Yeah. A cow."

"Hmmm. A cow."

This whole bird thing makes me think of something, a foggy memory. A dream. Actually, a bunch of dreams. Disturbing dreams I had in Maryland while recovering from malaria.

In one dream, I was floating down a river of warm water, so comfortable, when a bird floated by. It was dead. And then I realized I was dead too.

In another, the twins and the other neighborhood kids and I were at someone's house on a fluffy couch. We were watching TV and waiting and waiting. I stuck my hand down between the cushions and found a bone, and then another. Pieces of a bird skeleton.

And another: I was walking on a path with a big crowd of people. My legs were really tired and I looked around and wondered why no one was flying. I wondered if there was a rule against it or if people there just didn't do it or what. So instead of flying, I kept trudging along.

Now it hits me full force, the creepy feeling I had waking up after those dreams. It was like a smoke alarm in the distance, coming through a fog or heard underwater, a warning I tried to ignore.

. . .

Inside the *peña*, it's dark, with spotlights darting around and dry-ice smoke drifting. Onstage, a band plays *cumbias* and people dance, crowded onto a small dance floor. Everyone looks dressed up, the girls in short, flirty skirts or tight jeans and heels, a few girls in indigenous clothes, glittery and elegant.

I wish I'd worn something nicer. My T-shirt is snug, but pretty unsexy—PEE-PEE ISLAND in pink letters over a palm tree. Layla and I bought matching ones in Thailand, mine purple, hers orange. And I'm wearing loose green cotton pants, tailor-made by our neighbor in Phuket in bulk—five pairs for me, five for Layla, at five bucks a pair, in a rainbow of colors. Our practical pants, Layla and I call them. Baggy with a drawstring—more loungewear than going-out wear.

Wendell and I sit down at a table made of thick, dark, worn wood and order drinks.

I expect he'll get a beer since that's what all American teenagers get when they're in countries that don't card. Surprisingly, he orders a bubbly water, so I do the same.

"No beer?" I ask.

"I swore to my mom I wouldn't touch alcohol here."

"Another condition? Along with the babysitter?"

"Yep. You're seeing me in all my mama's-boy glory."

"It's cute," I say.

"Cute?" He looks unsure if he wants to be cute.

"I mean, it's cute your mom cares so much to make you promise. And that you'd actually do it."

When the bubbly waters come, he says, "My treat. For all your help." He opens his wallet, and there, exposed to the world, is Her.

The sort-of-ex-girlfriend. In a worn photo, cloudy behind the plastic. She's all made-up, her blond hair washed and blow-dried and straightened and her eyelashes curled and doll-like. She isn't particularly pretty, more the kind of person you'd assume is pretty because she has all the necessary pretty things—smooth skin and arched eyebrows and glossy hair. But she doesn't look interesting. Or maybe it's just that I don't want her to be interesting.

"So that's Her," I say, tapping my finger over her face, noticing how scraggly my fingernail looks against her perfect, polished face. Her fingernails aren't in the picture, but I'd bet my Pee-Pee Island shirt they're freshly manicured.

"Yeah," he says. "Zeeta—"

"So tell me," I interrupt, embarrassed. "Is She a cow or a bird?"

He laughs. "If I had to choose"—he takes a sip of seltzer—"I'd have to say a cow. But pretty darn good-looking," he adds.

I study the photo. "For a cow," I say, shutting his wallet and clicking my bottle against his. "*Salud.*" I wink, and after a few sips, I grab his hand and drag him onto the dance floor. I teach him how to move his feet and spin me, and surprisingly, he only steps on my foot once. He seems to get the rhythm immediately, and after a couple of songs, he spins me around as if he's been moving to this music all his life.

"How is it," I yell over the music, "that you can't walk through the market without knocking something over, yet you're twirling me around like an expert?"

"We always have music on at our house. My dad wanted me to be in touch with my heritage, which meant blasting Latino music."

We dance and sweat and laugh and grow pink-faced and lose ourselves in the rhythms and darkness and moving spotlights. I'm flying, and Wendell's flying next to me, and it feels good. As I fly, I think about Layla. The old Layla. How she flew through life with me in tow. But maybe I wasn't straggling behind, holding her back. Maybe we were flying through life together, hand in hand. Maybe this is who I am. Maybe this is the life I'd choose for myself, even if Layla weren't around.

And now, because of me, she's turned into a cow.

At one a.m., we walk back to Wendell's hotel, our bodies loose from dancing. "I'm sleeping here if that's okay with you," I say. "I don't want to go home and wake up to more *Frasier* reruns."

Without looking at him or waiting for an answer, I lie down on the bed near the window. After a split-second pause, he settles on the one near the bathroom. The small lamp casts yellow light between us.

"So," I whisper, "what's your earliest memory?"

"Why?"

"For my indigo notebook."

He closes his eyes, and then says slowly, "When I was little, my dad used to sit by my bed at night and play the guitar. Slow, sleepy tunes. Then he'd hold my hand, and when he tried to pull away his hand, I held on, and I said, 'Tell me about how I came to you.' Because I knew when I asked about my adoption, he had to stay. He wasn't allowed to say, 'No that's it, go to sleep.' "

"Tell me the story," I say. "For my notebook."

"I've never told anyone this," he says, embarrassed.

"I'll tell you a story next time."

"Fine, here goes. 'Before you were born,' Dad would say, 'Mom and I wanted a baby more than anything. We cried and prayed and hoped and wished. We went to doctors and herbalists and acupuncturists, but no one could help us. And then, one night, Mom dreamed of a red ribbon that led from her heart to the heart of a baby. And we knew that the red ribbon was stronger than blood. It connected our souls. We felt it pulse with our heartbeats. We felt it whisper that throughout all of time and all of space, that red ribbon is there, linking us together. It tugged us toward you, and you toward us, and finally we found each other.' "

His voice has dropped so low it crackles. "And by this time I was always nearly asleep, and Dad took his hand from mine and put my red ribbon in its place."

The next morning, I wake up to the sound of Wendell in the shower. I open the window and let sunlight and morning air breeze into the room. I study the photo of his parents again. Beside them is the red ribbon that held his letters. I touch the satin, worn and soft.

His cell phone rings and I jump, feeling caught. I consider whether I should answer it. What if it's Her? But maybe it's Layla. I sneak a guilty peek at the phone's screen, hoping it won't say *Love of My Life* or anything. *Sarah* is all it says. No picture. Just the name. Could be Her.

I call through the bathroom door, "Should I get that?"

"Yeah." His voice is muffled over the running water.

"It's Sarah," I warn.

"Go ahead."

I answer it. "Hello. Wendell's room."

"Hi!" A surprised voice. A lady's voice. At least forty. "Is this Zeeta?"

"Yep."

"Zeeta! This is Wendell's mom, Sarah. His dad and I are so, so, so grateful to you. We're so happy to know he has a friend there."

"Well, we're having fun," I say, glad she isn't a stodgy mother who gets freaked out over a girl answering her son's phone early in the morning.

"Zeeta, listen, here's our number and e-mail. Got a pen? If anything happens, call us. If—" And then quiet sniffling.

"Um, are you okay?" I picture her—the smattering of freckles over her nose, her brown-gray hair in disarray— taking off her glasses and wiping her tears with her sleeve.

"It's just that—I mean, I was prepared for him to look for his birth parents, but I always thought we'd be with him. He has high hopes for them. I'm worried they won't be who he— I don't want him to get hurt, Zeeta."

"I'll look out for him," I say in the calm voice I use with Layla when she gets riled up about something. When I was little, sometimes other kids made fun of my accent during my first months in a new place. She'd get in a huff. "How many languages do those little twerps speak, huh? Not half as many as you!" Maybe all mothers do have a certain hyperness in common. Maybe Layla does have some maternal instincts after all; I just overlooked them.

I jot down Sarah's number in my indigo notebook. She wants my contact info too, as backup, which must be a mother thing. I imagine her writing it neatly in a handmade address book. In one of Wendell's letters, written on Mother's Day, he wrote a list of what he liked about his mom, and number four—right after her chocolate chip marshmallow caramel cheesecake—was her talent for making paper with leaves and petals and old newspapers, which she taught him.

Just as I shut my notebook, Wendell comes out of the bathroom, a towel around his waist, his hair loose and dripping around his broad shoulders. He takes the phone with a sheepish half-smile.

"I'll be in the shower while you get dressed," I whisper.

As I go into the bathroom, he mumbles, "Hey, Mom." Out of the corner of my eye, I see him pick up the red ribbon from the bedside table and rub it absently as he talks.

. . .

We eat breakfast together in the hotel café and drink *jugo de tomate de árbol*—a fruit juice that tastes like sweet tomatoes blended with sugar and water—along with croissants and jam and *café con leche*. Dalia the babysitter is swishing around the tables in a lime green polyester skirt suit that clings to her huge hips. She greets us and winks, as if to say, *I know who spent the night together, but don't worry, I won't tell your mom.* Embarrassing. Luckily, the café is busy, and she dashes off to help clear tables.

The TV in the upper corner of the room is blaring the news. It's all about the bus crash. Three people died, one of them a child. I'd nearly forgotten about the accident. After the night of dancing and talking, yesterday afternoon seems like ages ago.

When Wendell hears this, he blinks a lot.

He doesn't touch the rest of his food.

He looks like he wants to dissolve into nothing.

He's quiet all morning, on the bus ride to Agua Santa and the walk up the hill to Taita Silvio's house.

Taita Silvio greets us at the door. "*Buenos días,* Wendell. *Buenos días,* Zeeta. We heard about the crash. *Gracias a Dios* you're all right."

As I translate to Wendell, he nods, his face tight.

Taita Silvio notices his reaction, and says softly, "Follow me, son." He leads us around metal buckets and plastic bowls to a hut, also adobe, across from the main house. Leaning against the walls are rolled-up woven mats and brooms and shovels. Puppies and chickens chase one another in a flurry of ruffled feathers and fur.

Taita Silvio ushers us into the dark curing room. He lights the candles, then settles into a chair behind the altar, looking calmer, his shoulders relaxing, as though this is where he feels most comfortable. He speaks in a slow, gentle voice, motioning to the bench. "Sit, *mis hijos*, sit."

I breathe in the cool, earthy smell of plants and smoke, and a rush of anticipation surges through me. Layla's brought me to plenty of rituals, and as much as I groan to her, I love recording them in my notebooks, noticing the patterns across cultures. The healers I've met haven't stayed inside the box of any one religion. They all believe their powers come directly from some form of God or the Absolute, or whatever you want to call it, but they blend their own mix of native practices with Christianity and Eastern images and New Agey stuff—whatever works for them. If something feels sacred, it feels sacred, no matter which religion box it falls into. They're like chefs, creating their own recipes.

Taita Silvio digs around in a bag behind the altar and pulls out several necklaces of wood and tree nuts, which he drapes around his neck. Then he puts on a hat of feathers, white and yellow and red, with long turquoise feathers rising up and forming a peak.

"So," he sighs. "You want to find your father."

My translation is fast and smooth. Wendell says, *"Sí."*

"Do you have a coin?"

Wendell takes a coin from his pocket, a quarter.

"Rub it between your hands and blow on it," Taita Silvio says.

Wendell rubs it and blows, looking nervous. Then Taita Silvio takes the coin from him. He passes it through the candle flame, again and again, leaving it in the fire for longer each time, until I wonder if his hand is burning. I've put my finger through candle flames before and felt the strange substance of fire surround it for a second, but never for as long as this.

Taita Silvio begins speaking as if in a trance, his voice deep and rhythmic, his eyes fixed on Wendell, but his gaze focused on some place behind Wendell, or inside him. "I see your father. Your real father. He lives in a place with mountains. The top of his head is smooth like an egg. No hair. He's sitting in a place of blue and green. There's music. He's playing music. Sad music."

"That's Dad." Wendell seems to have fallen into a kind of trance himself, talking in an unusually deep voice, his eyes looking at a far-off place inside the candle flame. "He's in my room. Playing guitar. Nick Drake. He plays that when he's sad."

I translate, and Taita Silvio seems to come out of his trance for a moment, looking at Wendell curiously. "Why do you want another father? This one seems good."

"There are some questions he can't answer."

"We all have questions without answers." Taita Silvio

passes the coin through the flame again, and slips back into a trance. His eyes widen. After a moment, his voice emerges, wary. "I see a place of light and dark."

When I translate, Wendell says, "Light and dark?" as though it means something to him.

I nod.

Silvio goes on. "A place of liberation and a prison. I see a betrayal. Danger."

I translate, shivering and rubbing the goose bumps that have sprung up on my arms.

Taita Silvio shakes his head, snapping out of the trance. "Wendell. Please." He pauses. "Go home to your real father, this man who loves you and misses you."

Wendell pulls something from his pocket. The crystal. He places it on the altar next to the four other crystals. "Do you know this crystal?"

Taita Silvio hesitates. "It's a powerful one. For protection. And comfort."

"It's from your brother, isn't it?" Wendell pushes.

No answer.

"It came from some cave near his house, right?"

Silence.

"Did your brother put it in my blankets?"

Taita Silvio rubs his face in his hands.

"We know about Faustino. He's my birth father, isn't he?"

Taita Silvio looks up, surprised. After a moment's silence, he says, "Stay away from him. He's—just stay away from him, all right?"

And as I translate these last words for Wendell, a cold, dark feeling creeps over me, pressing on me until I can hardly breathe. I leap up and run outside into the sunshine, wishing Layla were here, her bag of amulets and charms tinkling.

Chapter 16

"Let's go to Faustino's." These are Wendell's first words after hours of eyebrow-furrowed thought, during which he was probably weighing Silvio's warning.

It's early evening. After the divination, we spent the day in Agua Santa, eating potato soup, collecting fruit, stripping kernels off corncobs, feeding pigs. Wendell was silent the whole time. Now, hearing him mention Faustino's name, I shiver again. We're heading down the dirt street toward the main road, nearly at the intersection. To the left, up the hill, is the route to Faustino's house, and to the right, a cobbled road leads downhill to the bus stop. "Come on, Z! Let's go."

"Uh, Wendell, were you not there with me? Did you not hear Taita Silvio tell us—very clearly—to stay away?"

"I don't care."

"It's late, Wendell. If we're going to the house of someone who might have sold his soul to the devil—who we were warned repeatedly was dangerous—at least let's go in the daylight."

"Fine." He takes one last, reluctant look up at the house on the hill. "Tomorrow."

We turn downhill, toward the highway. I study his face. He looks lost in thought. "Wendell," I say, "did that mean something to you, when Silvio said 'a place of light and dark'?"

He looks at the shadows sliding down the mountains, like streams of dark water. In the sunny spots, the last sunbeams hop over the tips of leaves. Finally, he says, "For a while now I've had these flashes of feelings. And it's true there's darkness, something dangerous. But there's something else, something bright, something really good, Z." He rests his gaze on me, his eyes hopeful. "So bright and good it's worth the risk."

The sun slips completely behind the mountain's peak, leaving a golden halo. "All right," I say, against my better judgment. "I'll go with you tomorrow." I make a mental note to bring my pocketknife and leave a note for Layla, just in case.

On the ride home, the music is so loud it's hard to talk, so we sit side by side in the gathering darkness. When the bus pulls into the stop, we start walking toward the town center. The streetlights have turned on, casting yellow light into the blue dusk.

"Hey, Z," Wendell says. "Let's go to that waterfall tomorrow."

I swerve out of the way of a bunch of Swedish tourists,

nearly falling off the curb. I'm caught off balance. I thought he'd forgotten the waterfall thing. "But we're going to Faustino's house tomorrow."

"Let's go before that. Early in the morning. That's when you and Layla did it, right?"

My fingernails are digging into my palms. "What will you wish for?" I ask finally, because if he's wishing for Her, there's no way I'm waking up at four a.m.

He shrugs, loping along beside me. "Isn't that supposed to stay secret? Like a birthday wish?"

I stare at the orange neon Internet café sign behind his head, suddenly angry.

He stops walking, motions awkwardly to the café. "Listen, I have to catch up on my e-mail."

I slug his shoulder. The slug comes out harder than I expected. "I'll come to your room tonight." I start walking away, and then call over my shoulder, "We'll get an early start. Okay?"

"Thanks, Z!" He grins, rubbing his shoulder. "You owe me a story tonight, remember?"

Walking home to get a change of clothes and a toothbrush, I wonder if he's e-mailing Her. If he'll be wishing for Her tomorrow. The thought makes me a little sick, so I push it out of my mind.

Don Celestino is sitting in his blue chair a block from my apartment, his eyes half closed. It looks like he's dozing, but it's hard to tell since he's blind and it's dusk. I quietly drop a coin into his orange plastic bowl.

"*Gracias,* Señorita Zeeta," he says. And then, "Cheer up."

"How did you know?"

"The birdsongs are heavy today," he says. "Think of happy things."

"Okay." The rest of the way home, I remember last night in Wendell's room, how the sound of our voices moved back and forth in the darkness. It gives me a *pleno* feeling, as if a red ribbon were draped in the space between our beds, each of our hands holding an end, rubbing it smooth.

At home, Layla and Jeff are sitting in front of the TV. He's wearing leather flip-flops and khaki shorts and a bright white T-shirt, with Ray-Bans pushed onto his head—a deliberately casual look. Layla is snuggled next to him in white capris and a buttercup yellow polka-dotted blouse that I've never seen before. It looks like one of the outfits her mother sends her that she immediately gives to the first homeless woman she encounters on the street.

"What this town needs is a good golf course!" Jeff says as a kind of greeting. "Right, Zeeta?"

I bite my tongue. "Hmmm."

"I heard there's one around here, near some lake, but it's only nine holes." He glances at the TV and types something into his BlackBerry—golf stats, I'm guessing.

Layla puts a serious look on her face, like a sitcom mom. "Listen, Z. Jeff and I were talking about what you did last night—sleeping in a boy's hotel room—and we decided I need to start setting boundaries."

I blink, bewildered. *Who's* the one who's been taking along extra sweaters and crackers for her all these years? *Who's* the one who washes the dishes and buys the food and manages the scant bank account?

Jeff offers a sympathetic smile. "We know it's a change from what you're used to, Zeeta." He leans forward on the sofa. "Let me tell you something. I raised two wonderful daughters. And I know Chloe and Camille agree that their success has to do with three things." He raises his manicured fingers, one by one. "Good routines. Reasonable rules. And plenty of love."

Blood's rising to my face now, pure, hot indignance. "Excuse us." I drag Layla onto the balcony, shutting the glass doors so hard they rattle.

"Layla, this is crazy."

"Listen, love, I want to do the right thing for you."

"I'm used to fending for myself."

"I'm just trying to be a good mother. I have a lot to make up for. All the times I could have lost you. Like the malaria thing. We should've stayed in Maryland." Her eyes well up.

I should be feeling grateful that after nearly three years, she's admitted this. Or at least I should hurl an *I told you so* at her. I fiddle with the worn hem of my grubby Pee-Pee Island T-shirt. If we'd stayed in Maryland, I'd probably never even have heard of Phi Phi Island.

I narrow my eyes. "I survived malaria. I think I can survive spending a night with a boy."

"I just want you safe." Layla wipes her tears and sniffs.

"Remember what Jeff said. The transition part is always hard. We're out of our comfort zone." She reaches for my hand. "It's not easy for me, either."

I fold my arms tightly across my chest. "I'm going to Wendell's again tonight." I run inside, grab a new change of clothes, and whiz past Jeff.

"Where're you headed?" he asks with awkward cheer.

Layla says, in a shaky voice, "She's spending the night at Wendell's."

Jeff opens his mouth to say something, but I don't stick around to listen.

I slam the door on the way out.

Just like a normal teenager who's mad at her parents.

It doesn't feel as good as I thought it would.

For a while I wander around the market, distracting myself with its bright rugs and flute music and musty wool smells. The vendors are packing up for the night, and Gaby has already left.

Layla is really, truly changing. I realize I've been waiting for her to throw her arms up and say, *That's it, I'm going back to who I really am.* In the hospital in India, when I was a feverish, vomiting, shaking, shivering, convulsing, aching mess, Layla sat by the bed whispering prayers, holding my hand, crying, saying, *I'll do anything, anything, anything to make you better, love.* Fast-forward six months, past the danger zone, to the kitchen table in Maryland, where, through peppermint steam, Layla announced we were going to Brazil.

What confuses me now is this: we're well past the danger zone of the latest near-death episode. Layla lived through the waterfall, just like we lived through everything else. So why isn't she going back to her old self? What's different about this time?

Maybe it's like the tsunami that hit Southeast Asia before we lived in Phuket. Not just any underwater earthquake turns into a giant tidal wave. It depends on the time, the place, the circumstances, the landscape of the ocean floor, the shape of the coastline, the force of the earthquake.

What are the circumstances with Layla? Her thirty-fifth birthday? The three alleged white hairs? The arrival of Jeff? Or maybe she just hit some random critical number of near-death experiences that put her over the edge. Whatever the reasons, this time seems different.

"Zeeta!" It's Gaby, calling out from a hole-in-the-wall café painted cheery orange. Alfonso and some other vendors are crowded into the booth beside her, eating and chatting. When I duck inside, they make room for me, hand me a *llapingacho*—potato pancake—and beg me to give them an impromptu English lesson.

"We'll pay you!" they insist. I'm not feeling too social, but I accept. I need the pocket money.

The vendors are a rowdy bunch, always ready to make a

joke, giggling hysterically when I hold up a mirror to show them how to put their tongues between their teeth for the *th* sound. I try to laugh with them, but my throat feels so tight I can barely breathe.

An hour later they leave, full and content, while Gaby and I linger behind. From her giant bag, she takes out her latest sewing project, a blouse with embroidered orange butterflies. "So, Zeeta, what's wrong?"

"Nothing," I say. She warned me. I should have wished for general happiness. Or focused on what mattered. Breathing. She knew all along.

She raises an eyebrow, as though she can see right through me. "Where've you been hiding?"

"Hanging out with Wendell." Mentioning him lightens my mood a little.

She nods. "He's very handsome."

"I'm just helping him find his birth parents, that's all."

"That's all?" She flashes a devilish grin.

"He's in love with his ex-girlfriend," I say, my voice bitter.

"Is she here?"

"No!"

"Then what's the problem?" She pokes her needle emphatically into the fabric.

"Gaby, there's nothing more pathetic than chasing after a guy who's in love with someone else. Even if she is on another continent."

Gaby smiles a mysterious smile. "Well, you just enjoy yourself, then, Zeeta."

I sip my bottle of bubbly water. "I don't like him that way, Gaby," I insist. "Anyway, I have my own problems. After Layla's near-death experience, she met this guy. And now she's turning into a different person."

"What kind of person?"

How to describe the new Layla? "Normal," I say finally.

She gives me a wry look. "Your greatest wish, if I remember correctly."

"Fine, fine. You told me so." I glance at the café owner, who is expertly flipping *llapingachos,* a stoic smile on her face, damp with sweat. "But it turns out I like the old Layla better."

"Have you talked to her?"

"She's always with him or watching TV."

"I'm sure you can find time. Why haven't you talked with her?"

I consider this. "She's doing it for me. I've been pleading with her all my life to be normal. I can't just say, 'Oops, I changed my mind. Let's just rewind to how things were before.' " I run my fingers over the smooth ridges of my bottle.

Gaby makes a few more orange stitches. "What do you think will happen now?"

"I don't know. But the way things are headed, I'm worried she'll want to move back to the U.S. to be near him. Turns out he lives near my grandparents."

Gaby thinks. Then she says, "If you're headed down the wrong road, no matter how far you've gone, you can always turn back."

"How?"

"To begin with, tell her how you really feel."

"It's not that easy, Gaby. What if I'm not headed down the wrong road? What if we're finally headed down the right road but I'm so used to the wrong road I don't realize this is the right one?"

Gaby knots the orange thread and tears it with her teeth, then pulls a spool of pink out of her bag. "There's a young man with crazy hair who comes by my booth sometimes. He tells me, *Gaby, I love how you sit here in the flow. You sit here and the universe is a better place because of it.* Now, I think he's as crazy as his hair, but maybe he's right about the flow. Maybe you should think about the flow and whether you're in it, and if not, how you can get back in."

I smile. "What's this guy's name?"

She looks into space, trying to remember. "Who knows. But he speaks Spanish well, only with a different accent." She grins. "He gave me this." From her bag, she pulls out a bouquet of balloon daisies. "Sometimes he's dressed as a clown."

Chapter 17

O n the way to the hotel, I spot Wendell walking out of
the Internet café. He stands outside, dazed, right in
the middle of the sidewalk traffic, getting bumped here and
there as people pass. His face glows orange in the neon light
from the window sign.

"Wendell!" I shout, zipping across the street to meet him.
"I thought you'd be back at the hotel by now."

"She wrote me an e-mail."

"Oh." She with a capital S.

"It was a long one, and kind of, I don't know, sentimental,
I guess."

"Hmmm."

"I tried writing back, but I didn't know what to say exactly,
so I kept writing stuff, then deleting it, and I don't know—"

"How about dinner at the market—fried plantains and potato cakes and supersalty grilled pork bits?"

He looks surprised at the change of subject. "Sure."

On the walk to the food market, he's distracted, probably going over Her e-mail line by line. But once we sit down, he slips into the moment, into the smells of greasy *fritada*— fried pork—and simmering *menestra*—lentil stew—and bubbling chicken soup. It's cozy under the bare lightbulbs of the booths, gazing out over the plastic colored tarps reflecting lights, the people milling around, workers joking with one another as they clean the Plaza de Ponchos.

Back at the hotel, we watercolor by lamplight and talk and lay the drying pictures over the floor, leaving a narrow path to the bathroom. My pictures have geometric designs with pen under the watercolors—a turtle's shell, a flock of birds, ocean waves. I always gravitate toward finding patterns in life's chaos.

Wendell's art has come a long way since his illustrations on the latest letter I translated. As a nine-year-old, he'd done a self-portrait of himself standing on top of a planet, flexing his muscles. Apparently he'd just won an art competition at summer camp. He'd taped on a card from his parents, a recycled-paper one, probably made by his mother, which read, BEST ARTIST IN THE UNIVERSE AWARD. He wrote, *I bet your sorry you gave away the Best Artist in the Univurse!*

His paintings, spread around us, are gorgeous and atmospheric, with a hint of danger. A brilliant blue sky and green hill with a bloodred devil lurking in its center. Golden bread by an ochre oven holding fiery orange coals inside. A silvery waterfall tumbling into a pool full of bones.

"You just might be the best artist in the universe," I tease.

He blushes and says, "I'm an art geek," almost apologetically. "I've taken painting classes, but photography's my main thing. I want to make a book of pictures from this trip. For my portfolio."

"For what?"

"Just this art abroad thing I want to do next summer." He's trying to sound casual, but I can tell it means a lot to him. "It's kind of hard to get chosen, so the portfolio has to be good. I've saved up part of the cost, and the rest I'll make working after school."

"Abroad where?" I ask, trying to sound casual myself. Secretly, I'm thinking that if Layla and I keep traveling, who knows, we might end up down the street from his art school. Coincidentally.

"Not sure yet. The program offers a few different countries. I want to choose somewhere with the best possible light." His face is illuminated just talking about it, the way Layla's face gets when she talks about a new place. I can imagine Wendell traveling the world, always dreaming of a place with light conditions even more spectacular than wherever he happens to be.

When we run out of paper, we crawl into our beds and set the alarm for four a.m.

Wendell turns off the light. "Your turn."

·175·

"My turn?"

"A story."

"Oh." I decide to tell him the first one that comes to mind. It's a memory that's kept popping into my head lately. "Here goes. In Morocco, in Marrakech, Layla and I used to go to the main plaza at night, where people played drums and danced and clapped. It was so crowded you could barely move. It hypnotized you, the rhythm, the lights, the clapping and dancing. Smoke drifted around. Sizzling lamb kebabs and steam from mint tea. At one of those moments, I was looking at Layla's face, all pink and glowing and beaded with sweat. I felt like everything was exactly right, like there was nothing else I'd rather be doing. No other way I'd rather live my life.

"And then, something was moving in my pocket and it was a hand, a little girl's hand. I saw her face for a split second before she lowered her veil and darted off. I checked my pockets. Empty of money, my thirty dirham gone. It was just a few dollars, but it was a lot to me, so I ran after her, racing through the crowds as fast as I could, right on her tail.

"I was indignant. Maybe she thought I was a regular dull-witted tourist, not someone who'd grown up playing in markets. Maybe she thought she'd easily lose me in the crowd. She led me into a maze of narrow streets. They grew more and more deserted, but I kept running. I remember thinking, *It's all Layla's fault! If she gave me a normal life, none of this would be happening.*

"And then, at the end of an alley so narrow you could touch

both walls with your arms spread out, we reached a dead end. The girl turned to face me. A group of other street girls came out from the shadows. Five or six of them. Thin black veils hid their faces. In the distance there was the beating of drums and clapping. No one would have heard me if I'd screamed. My heart was pounding louder than the drums, and I was bending over, my hands on my knees, trying to catch my breath. I was terrified.

"So I stood up straight, and in Arabic, I said to the girl, '*Essalam alikoum.* I'm Zeeta and I'd like to be your friend.'

"She turned to the other girls. One of them was holding a henna tattoo kit and a plastic binder of tattoo designs. I'd seen girls like these wandering the streets, offering tattoos. I'd heard from police that the girls were famous for slipping their little hands into pockets while you were distracted.

" 'Why do you want to be my friend?' the girl asked, suspicious.

" 'Because you're fast and smart and interesting.' I smiled the most open, honest smile I could muster. 'And because you owe me a henna tattoo. Let's see what designs you have.' I walked over to the girl with the binder, who looked about eleven, a couple of years older than me. I flipped through the pages and pointed to a hummingbird. 'How about this one? On my ankle, please.'

"The girl who stole my money slowly lifted her veil. And then, one by one, the other girls lifted theirs. The one who stole from me crouched down and began drawing a hummingbird on my ankle. Meanwhile, another did a flower on my hand for free. Their fingers were quick and nimble. We chatted in Arabic—about where I lived and why I spoke their language and how they got into this line of work, and on and on. A half hour later, when they showed me the finished designs, I gasped, because they were so intricate, so beautiful, and worth so much more than thirty dirham and a run through dark alleys. And there, with my new friends, I thought, *I am exactly where I'm supposed to be.*"

At the end of my story, Wendell says, "So what's the moral?"

"What do you think?"

For a minute, he says nothing, and I think he might have fallen asleep. But then he says, "That sometimes what you thought was bad is good after all. In a way you never expected." He laughs softly. "And that you might even get some cool tattoos out of it if you're lucky." He laughs again. "And that you, Zeeta, are a badass to be reckoned with."

Suddenly, I feel sure that in the darkness, his hand is reaching toward mine, spanning the gap between the beds. I extend my hand into that space and move it around, searching. But his hand isn't there. So I tuck my hand under my chin and fall asleep, dreaming of wandering through a maze alone in the dark.

The next morning, just before dawn, Wendell and I are walking along the trail, through the forest pulsing with insect songs and moist earth smells and rushing river music.

"Almost there," I say.

We round a bend, and the trees open into a giant clearing, with the towering waterfall as its centerpiece, fuzzy through the mist.

"Wow," he says.

"Wow," I say, even though I've already seen it before.

He sets up his expandable tripod and takes a bunch of pictures, some of me alone, and some timer shots with us together.

"Here's where Layla climbed down the first time." I point to the pool at the waterfall's base. "But let's go farther downstream, where the current's not so strong."

We walk along the river's edge, through the underbrush, holding aside branches for each other, until we reach the spot. "Okay, Wendell, take off your clothes, dunk your head under, and think about your wish, exactly what you want."

From my pocket, I pull out the fistful of rose petals I've collected along the way.

"Let me guess." One corner of his mouth turns up. "I rub them all over my nude body?"

"Yep." I smile. "I won't look. But if you're drowning, just scream and I'll rescue you."

"Okay, here goes." He pulls off his T-shirt.

"There's a towel in my pack for you."

"Thanks, Z," he says, taking off his sandals.

I turn away and peer into the trees, the dark forms in the shadows. After a minute, I sneak a furtive peek toward the river, just to make sure he hasn't slipped. The water's up to his hips. His hands are tucked under his armpits, and he's shaking with cold. His hair falls loose, dripping around his face and spotted with rose petals.

I look back to the forest. It's lighter now. In only a few seconds, the spaces between trees look lighter blue and the leaves more distinct, taking shape.

After a while, he calls out, "Okay, ready," and now here he is, dressed, wringing out his hair and looking elated. Together we sit on the rock and watch the blue turn into clear daylight, and soon we can see all the petals of all the flowers on the riverbank and the mossy rocks, and their shades of amber and gold and yellow reflecting sunshine.

"So," I say, "you think you'll get Her back?"

"What?"

"Will your wish come true?"

He pauses. "I didn't wish for her."

Lowercase *her*? I can't tell. "Oh." I falter.

"I was planning on wishing that Faustino was my birth father. And that he was a good man. Then at the last minute I changed my mind and wished for something else." He drapes the damp towel around his neck. "How about you? Got any wishes before we leave?"

"I'm wished out for the moment."

The corner of his mouth turns up. "Thanks, Z."

"For what?"

"For—I don't know, for the towel. For translating. For everything."

"That's what I'm here for, Wendell. Translating and providing towels. And other duties as needed."

He rubs his arms and shivers. In a low voice, a voice that comes from a hidden, tender place, he says, "Then warm me up, Z." He slips his arm around my waist and draws me in, close. We stay like that for a while, long enough for two doves to call back and forth, back and forth.

On the way back through the forest, we walk close, arms around each other, listening to our breath, to the crickets in the trees, to the leaves trembling in the wispy breeze. Sunshine on dew gives the forest a magical, tingling light that makes everything bright and alive.

As we leave the woods, I think I know what he's wished for. And it's very, very *pleno*.

Back in town, we buy pastries at the bakery and sit on a curb to eat them, crumbs and sugar falling in our laps. Then we take a bus to Agua Santa. By the time we get there, a heavy fog has rolled into the valley, hiding the mountaintops. The girls meet us at the crossroads near their house and, singing "Head, Shoulders, Knees, and Toes" at the top of their lungs, lead us to the base of the hill. Above, Faustino's house is perched on the hilltop, barely visible through the mist.

The girls refuse to go any farther. Odelia hugs my waist tightly, as though she's saying goodbye forever. "I told my star friend to watch out for you," she whispers.

"Thanks, *amiga*."

"What about the dogs?" Isabel asks, wary.

"I have my special weapon." I pat the plastic bag of stale bread I bought for a quarter at the bakery. "After a few pieces, those beasts will be my new best friends."

She looks doubtful. "I heard they're really big, mean dogs."

"Even big, mean dogs can't resist stale bread."

The girls perch on a rock by the roadside. "We'll wait for you," Eva says. "And if you're not down in an hour, we'll call Taita Silvio for help."

I laugh uneasily. "Thanks." I turn to go up the hill, and then notice Wendell. He's staring at the girls with a distant yet intense expression.

"Ready, Wendell?"

He blinks fast a few times. "Zeeta, tell the girls—tell them to stay away from their father."

"What?"

"Tell them if they feel scared, even a little, to run straight to Mamita Luz and Taita Silvio's."

I translate for the girls. They don't seem too surprised. They all nod, and Eva says, "We'll be extra-careful."

Isabel studies Wendell's face. "You're like Taita Silvio. You have his same powers, don't you?"

He lets out a long breath. "Except I have no clue how to use them."

"But Wendell," Eva says, "you just did."

Climbing up the hill, I say, "So these feelings you get. Can you actually see the future?"

"It's pretty vague." He pauses. "With your mom in the

waterfall, I kind of felt something bad would happen, something that had to do with water."

"Can you change the future?"

"Sometimes. Sort of. Not always." He tears a leaf from a tree, rips it into tiny pieces. "Like the thing with my ex. We were together for seven months, and then I started to have this feeling she was gonna break up with me. I kept asking her how I could make her happy. She got sick of it. And broke up with me. Ironic, huh?"

I try to muster up some sympathy about the breakup. Not working. "What about the bus accident?" I ask instead.

He tosses his tiny leaf pieces to the wind and picks another leaf. He's nervous talking about this, cautious almost. "I saw the bus and got this terrible feeling. It felt like broken glass and fire and smoke. I had to decide in that second whether to make everyone get off the bus. If they did, and the accident didn't happen, they'd just think I was crazy." He tosses the next handful of shredded leaf. "*Ya no aguanto,* Z. I can't take it anymore."

"Taita Silvio can help you."

"Or maybe Faustino can."

"Maybe."

He touches my hand, lightly at first. Then he holds it. Then I squeeze and he squeezes back. We continue uphill, my heart pounding from happiness and fear. I want to ask him if he has a feeling about us in the future.

I want to, but I don't.

"Thanks for believing me," he says after a while.

"Of course."

"And for not thinking I'm hopelessly weird."

"Trust me, Wendell. I've been around hopelessly weird my whole life. You don't come close." I elbow him. "And maybe hopelessly weird isn't a bad thing, anyway."

Chapter 18

Halfway up, furious barks and growls break the silence around us. Through the fog, four mangy dogs appear. I untie my bread bag. "Any visions of these beasts eating us alive?" I say under my breath.

Luckily, the dogs come no farther. The house's form emerges from the mist—a gray, unfinished concrete structure, two stories, with wrought iron on the windows and door. A huge satellite dish is mounted on the roof and a mammoth black truck looms beside the house. On either side of the doorway are clay pots holding a few tall plants whose leaves form umbrellas, clusters of crimson berries at the base.

A man limps through the doorway. He stands there between the umbrella plants. He's wearing black jeans, a white undershirt, and black boots, and leaning on a thick stick, a cane maybe. I keep a piece of bread clutched in my hand.

As we get closer, the dogs' snarls grow louder until the man kicks them. They whimper and quiet down, except for some guttural rumblings.

"Is that a rifle?" Wendell whispers.

I take another look at what I thought was a cane. "Let's turn back."

After a brief pause, Wendell shakes his head.

From about fifty feet away, I call out, forcing my voice to sound strong and steady. "*¡Buenos días, señor!* We just need to talk with you for a moment."

A few seconds pass before he says, "Who are you?" His words land like cold pebbles tossed through the fog.

"I'm Zeeta. This is Wendell." And since he doesn't seem one for small talk, I get straight to the point. "We think you're his birth father."

He tilts his head, then motions for us to come closer.

Slowly, we make our way toward him, through a crowd of squawking chickens and past a sorry-looking donkey covered with flies and patchy fur. I throw pieces of bread ahead for the dogs. They pounce on it, ravenous.

Up close, I study the man. His hair hangs in a long braid down his back, strands falling out around his face. His face is shaped like Taita Silvio's—a strong jawline and sloping nose—only he looks younger and older at once. Older because his face is more worn, with scars and deep wrinkles. Not like Taita Silvio's wrinkles, all laugh lines fanning out around his eyes and mouth. No, these are heavy wrinkles, pulling at his eyes, furrowing his forehead. Yet younger because of his broad shoulders like Wendell's, and ropy, muscular forearms. His T-shirt is stained with something red, salsa maybe. His snakeskin boots come to sharp points at the toes.

He eyes us with suspicion. "What do you want from me?"

"He just wants to meet you," I say. "That's all."

Almost reluctantly, he extends his hand to Wendell and then to me—a hand not as thick and calloused as Taita Silvio's, not as accustomed to hard labor. "Faustino." He pulls a few stools from the side of the house into a patch of weedy dirt. Now the dogs are sitting by my feet, wagging their tails and drooling, eager for more bread.

He turns back to Wendell.

He stares.

And stares.

And stares.

Is he thinking? Plotting? Trying not to cry? Trying *to* cry? Impossible to tell. His face is expressionless, a mask.

"So," he says finally. "You're my son."

Wendell braces his jaw. "I'm your son."

"Well, at least we think so," I add. "We think Lilia was his birth mother."

He says nothing, and Wendell seems to be in a state of mild shock, so I say, "You two look alike. Don't you think?"

"Yes." And then, in a tight voice, Faustino says, "Did my brother send you here?"

I translate.

Wendell shakes his head.

"The boy doesn't speak Spanish?" Faustino asks me, surprised.

"Speak slowly and he might understand."

He draws out his words, eyeing Wendell. "What did Silvio tell you?"

"He told us about Lilia." I translate Wendell's answer, trying not to look at the gun. "That she lived with you for a while."

He sighs, props the gun against the house, then disappears through the doorway. There's the faint sound of the TV— some elephant squeals and a man narrating in a deep voice. Maybe the Discovery Channel in Spanish, which Layla's taken to watching lately.

More from curiosity than bravery, I peek my head inside the doorway. To the left is a bedroom, where I catch a glimpse of a bed, a big flat-screen TV, and a giant heap of teddy bears. Bizarre. Straight ahead is a hallway with a concrete floor and unpainted walls, and a bare bulb hanging from the ceiling, as though Faustino hasn't quite finished the house. To the right is a doorway to the kitchen, where he's rummaging through a box, his back to me. Quickly, I slip away, outside, past the rifle leaning against the wall. If he planned to hurt us, he wouldn't leave the gun right there, would he?

Wendell, meanwhile, has walked around to the side of the house. "Hey, look at this!"

Behind the house is a high stone wall with a solid black

metal gate. Brilliant leaves and giant flowers cascade over it. I recognize the long, trumpet-shaped blossoms from the *floripondio* tree the girls told us about.

Wendell spots them too. "Aren't those the zombie flowers?"

My mouth is suddenly dry. "Let's leave soon, okay?"

As we sit back down, Faustino emerges from the house with three glasses and a bottle of clear liquid in a beat-up plastic Coke bottle. He pours us each a glass and clinks his against ours in a toast. "To my son."

Wendell raises his glass. "To my father."

Faustino drinks first, all in one gulp.

Wendell sniffs his. "Smells like rubbing alcohol."

"Go ahead, drink," Faustino urges.

Wendell gulps the liquor, then screws up his face. So much for his promise to his mom.

I hold up my glass, examine it. Perfectly clear. Probably just alcohol. No evidence of extra ingredients like poisonous flowers. And he's poured ours from the same bottle. Still, drinking with a possible devil man seems like a terrible idea.

"Toma," Faustino says.

"Thanks, but I don't drink," I say, pasting a polite smile on my face.

"Just one."

I taste a bit with my tongue. It burns. "Sugarcane liquor?" I ask, stalling.

He nods. "Drink up."

I look at him hard. I've been told by people in other Latin

American countries that I have a strong gaze. A gaze with powers to cause good or harm. Of course, I don't believe that, but it's useful for freaking people out in certain situations.

He meets my gaze, looking only amused.

I raise my chin, try another tactic. "If you had one wish, Don Faustino, what would it be?"

He blinks. "Why? You'll make it come true?"

"Just curious," I say, keeping my gaze level.

He looks over the mountains, thinking, and in that moment I casually dump the liquor over my shoulder.

He doesn't notice. "That this piece-of-crap house was a mansion with a hundred rooms. That those chickens were my servants. That the donkey was my private jet. That I could be the richest man alive. That's what we all want, right?" He refills our glasses.

"Don't drink any more," I murmur to Wendell.

"Just one more glass," he whispers.

"What about your promise?"

"I don't want to be rude, Z."

Faustino gulps his, Wendell sips his, and I toss mine discreetly over my shoulder.

"So," Faustino says, leaning back. "Some gringos raised you?"

Wendell nods. "Sarah and Dan Connelly of Colorado."

"Those gringos are all loaded, huh?"

Wendell stares, not getting Spanish slang, until Faustino says slowly, enunciating, *"Mucho dinero."*

"Not really," Wendell says, looking woozy. "I mean, maybe by these standards, but in the U.S. we're just a regular middle-class family."

Reluctantly, I translate.

Faustino nods. "Why'd you come to this crap hole?"

I want to put my arm around Wendell. He looks so unstable wavering on the stool, as though he could fall at any moment.

"To find you," he says in a raw voice.

Something in Faustino's face cracks. A glimpse of emotion shines through, tenderness maybe. "You came all the way here for me?"

For what feels like eternity, but is probably about a half hour, we talk. The conversation stops and starts in fits. Right when I think Faustino might be a decent guy after all—just a little out of touch with his emotions, maybe—something slimy pops out, like his asking how much Wendell's watch costs or how much money his parents make. With every question he asks about Wendell's life in Colorado—even the apparently innocent ones like how he likes school and what sports he plays—I can't help questioning his motives, wondering if he's hatching a devious plan.

But I also wonder how much of my suspicion has been sparked by what we've heard about Faustino. I want to give him a fair shot. I do.

It's not easy. He's as good at evading our questions as

Silvio. He brushes off questions about Lilia, saying it was too long ago. "Some things are best left alone," he says, waving the questions away with his hand.

Wendell seems more patient than me. By now, he has an obvious buzz from the liquor. It's made him relaxed. Too relaxed. His words are slurred, his head wobbly.

I take out my indigo notebook. "Don Faustino, what's your earliest memory?"

"Hiding in a crystal cave."

I jot it down. "Hiding from what?"

"My father, that *hijo de puta*." Grinning, he pours another round of drinks.

When he doesn't elaborate, I open my mouth to ask why.

"Don't ask me why."

Instead I ask, "What matters most to you?"

He shakes his head, laughing. At me or with me? I can't tell with this man. He tilts his head back. "Besides getting rich? Two things." Abruptly, he stands up, stretches, and disappears inside.

I ditch my drink. "Ready to go, Wendell?"

"Just a little more time, Z."

"You're drunk, aren't you?"

"No."

Faustino comes out with two cardboard boxes stacked one on top of the other. One is the size of a shoebox, the other is as big as a fruit crate. Tiny holes have been poked in the sides. "Here, look." He unwinds the twine wrapped around them and opens the larger box a crack.

Wendell and I move our faces close, peer inside. There's a pile of sticks, leaves, and stones, shadowy hues of brown and gray and olive. Now they're moving. No, wait, it's a thick, smooth rope that's moving, and it's huge. Now its head appears, pointed with two beady black eyes.

A snake.

A pit viper of some kind.

Something about the slow undulations and the arrow shape of its head touches a deep, instinctual fear inside me. It's curled up on itself, but it must be a few feet long stretched out. It's staring at me, as if deciding whether to leap from the flimsy cardboard box and sink its fangs into my neck.

My heart freezes.

"Jergón," Faustino announces, closing the box again, securing it with the twine. "Also known as the X snake. See the X pattern? Got three of these fellows from the jungle east of here. A single bite swells the entire arm, turns it blue and black, forms giant blood blisters." He shakes his head, grinning. "Monstrously ugly."

I find words. "This is the part where we leave, Wendell." I stand up, backing away slowly.

But Wendell's captivated. Maybe the alcohol's impaired his judgment. Or maybe he wants so badly to connect with this man that he can overlook the extreme creepiness of the situation.

Faustino lifts up the smaller box, unties the twine slowly.

I can't resist. I peek inside. Some wood chips and sticks and leaves. Faustino pokes at the pile with a stick. Then, a scurrying set of brown legs, fuzzy and spindly, the span of my hand. As fast as the legs appear, they're hidden again.

"Phoneutria," he says proudly. "Armed spider. Got him from the Amazon too. One of the most excruciatingly painful venoms in the world."

"We should be going now," I say. "Thanks for the drinks and everything." I tug on Wendell's arm.

"But I didn't show you the second thing," Faustino says.

"What second thing?"

"The second thing that matters most to me."

For a moment, indignance eclipses my fear. "One, the poisonous snake. Two, the poisonous spider."

"No, that was one thing. My venomous-creature collection. There's a lot more of them inside."

I translate for Wendell. Unbelievably, he says, "Let's see the second thing."

"Wendell, this is really, really messed up."

"Please? After this we can leave."

"What's the second thing?" I ask Faustino flatly.

"Follow me." He heads around the side of the house, toward the wall and the zombie trees.

Chapter 19

Without a moment's hesitation, Wendell follows. And against my better judgment, I follow too. I can't believe I'm doing something so incredibly stupid. At least the girls know we're here. They'll get help if we don't return. "Just for a minute," I say, deliberately adding, "We have friends expecting us at the base of the hill."

Faustino puts his hand on Wendell's shoulder and leads us behind the house and along the stone wall to a thick wooden door with an old metal lock. "Not a word to anyone about this. You swear? I'm only showing you because you're my son." He takes a dull silver key from around his neck and opens the door. "Come in, amigos."

I pause. The walls are high, about seven feet, the tops rimmed with shards of broken glass poking out of concrete.

I've seen this glass-shard technique in cities all over Latin America used to keep out thieves. But now I wonder: what if this wall is meant to keep people *inside*?

"I'll wait outside," I say firmly.

"Whatever." Faustino ushers Wendell inside, leaving the door cracked behind them.

"Wow!" I hear Wendell's muffled voice. "Wow!" It's the same kind of *wow* as the waterfall *wow*.

"Wow," he says a third time. The breeze has blown the mist away, and now the sweet scent of nectar floats out from behind the wall. Leaves make dappled shadows on my side of the wall. My curiosity wins. I take a deep breath and go inside, leaving the door slightly ajar.

It's amazing, the most beautiful garden I've ever seen, even in pictures, even in my imagination. What the Garden of Eden might have been like. Trees dripping with flowers and fruit, giant bushes of blossoms of all colors, all shapes, an explosion of petals and stamens and pistils. It's magical. Bees and insects and hummingbirds buzz through the honeyed air. The smell is intoxicating, jasmine and lily and a symphony of scents I've never smelled before. In places, the foliage is so thick it forms a tunnel of petals and leaves around the path.

I walk farther, hypnotized.

Up ahead, Wendell's just behind Faustino. I follow them at a distance, in case I have to run back out. At least I have a few remnants of common sense left.

Now the trail branches into more paths, a maze, narrow

pathways through the flowers and leaves and branches. *Floripondio* trees abound, their blossoms hanging like stretched-out, upside-down horns, some pure white, some blushing peach, some bloodred seeping into yellow, some strawberry cream–pink melting into vanilla.

Clouds of violet-blue blossoms spill from jacaranda, and magnolias drip white flowers. Brilliant red and orange poppies blanket the sunny spots of ground, their delicate petals dancing in the breeze. Lilies rise in a cluster of smooth, alabaster sculptures. Tall, sunny daisies and candy pink cosmos skim our hips, and orchids peek from damp leaf shadows, clinging to tree branches. Carpets of fruit spread out under lime and grapefruit and orange trees, and still more fruit hangs heavy from the branches. Bougainvillea and honeysuckle crawl up the stone wall. Hummingbirds hover and buzz at the petals, darting here and there.

And then there are hundreds of flowers I have no names for, but their stamens stick out from the petals like long, thin tongues, and their petals burst out like dizzying fireworks. The foliage is so thick it's impossible to tell where one plant ends and another begins, so many leaves tumbling together, shades of silvery sage and vibrant jade and deep forest pools.

Wendell turns to me, his eyelids half-closed in drunken reverie. "Translate for me, Z," he murmurs.

"What is all this?" I ask Faustino.

"My children," he says proudly. "Son, meet your brothers and sisters."

Wendell's gaping. "Did you plant all these?"

"A long time ago, with my father and brother. Some, my father planted before we were born. On his good days, after the work in the fields was done, we'd tend to this garden. Only it felt more like play."

"Why doesn't Silvio come here anymore?" I ask.

He picks a whitish purple flower, tucks it behind my ear. "Beautiful," he murmurs. This man can be charming. In a slightly disturbing way.

But I refuse to let him mesmerize me the way he's mesmerizing Wendell. I fix Faustino with my hardest, most piercing gaze. "You owe it to Wendell to tell him about Lilia."

He takes a long, deep breath and pauses every few seconds as I translate. He doesn't meet our eyes, just looks around at the plants, brushing his fingers along the trunks and leaves and petals, stopping here and there to pull out a weed. "I didn't treat her well. When she was pregnant with you, son. I treated her—I treated her the only way I knew how: the way my father treated my mother."

He pauses to brush a few bugs off some petals. His movements are gentle. "One day she had a black eye. My brother saw. He took her to his house. He and Luz wouldn't let me see her. I wanted to say I was sorry, but he wouldn't let me. I drank half a bottle of *trago* and came after him and threw rocks through his window." Faustino tosses us a meaningful glance. Defensive? Ashamed? Daring? Hard to tell. "I never claimed to be a good person." He pulls another weed from the base of a flowered bush. "Silvio's the one who told Lilia to give you to the gringos, son."

Wendell stares, suddenly sober. "Then what?"

Faustino breathes out, long and forceful. "After she gave birth to you, Silvio and Luz brought her to the family where she used to work as a maid. She didn't have any family, just her employers. She'd lived with them since she was a child, except for the months she lived here in Agua Santa. I went to talk to her, to apologize for hitting her, to swear I wouldn't do it again. She said she'd drive around with me and hear me out."

He whips a switchblade from his pocket, snaps open the knife. "Then we started fighting. I was getting angry and trying not to hit her, but she was provoking me." He slices through a branch blocking the path. "I was drinking, yes, but not that much. We were on a twisty road and I was going faster and faster. Getting angrier and angrier. And then there was a curve, and it was too tight, and the truck went off the edge, into a tree." He cuts another branch, then closes the knife slowly. "At the funeral, Silvio told me, 'My brother no longer exists.' That's the last thing he said to me. Sixteen years ago."

After I translate for Wendell, we stand in the garden, insects humming around us, a surreal sound track. It feels like a strange dream, dark and bright at the same time, slippery and full of contradictions, the way dreams can be sometimes.

"My brother is right," Faustino says. "I'm not a good man.

I'm like my flowers. Maybe on the outside I look good. A nice house, a nice truck. But on the inside . . ."

He takes the flower from behind my ear. "Belladonna. Beautiful, isn't it? Eat a few of its leaves and you'll take a trip to hell, monsters and death everywhere. Eat a few more and you'll die."

I put my hand to my ear, hoping no poison has absorbed through the skin. As I translate for Wendell, the thick scent of flowers becomes suffocating.

"My flowers are like this," he says. "That is why I love them."

I grab Wendell's arm. "Thank you, Don Faustino. This is . . . fascinating." I drag Wendell away as he calls out, "*Gracias,* Faustino."

Faustino shouts after us, "You can call me *Papá,* son. If you'd like."

And then, "Come back soon."

And then, "Please."

Chapter 20

"I think he's jus' lonely." Wendell's zigzagging down the hill, stumbling every few steps.

I roll my eyes.

"He's not so bad, Z." His words slur together. *Eeesnot-sobaaadzeee.*

"He's not? Let's see. There's the gun, the deadly creatures, the poisonous flowers."

"Yeah, but the dogs're nice. An' the garden's wiiicked, duuude. An' he din't try to kill us."

"He told us himself he isn't a good person."

"Ohhh, come ooon."

"Maybe he's waiting for next time. Maybe he wants to get something from us first, like money, before he kills us."

"He's jus' es-es-entric, Z."

"You didn't find him kind of creepy?"

"Duuude, I wanna go back an' take pitchers in that garden."

"I think we should stay away."

And then Odelia and Isabel and Eva run up, arms open, and fly into our arms, nearly knocking Wendell over. "You made it!" Isabel cries. "What happened?"

"Well," I begin, "we just talked and saw his . . . yard and some . . . pets of his."

They look at one another, confused. "He didn't sic the dogs on you?"

"No, *chicas*. But you should still stay away from him, okay?"

"What happened to him?" Odelia whispers, motioning to Wendell, who's sitting on a rock, head between his knees, looking suddenly green.

"Drunk," I say, and then, escorted by the girls, I lead him downhill, my arm around him, tucked under his armpit, holding him steady on the long trek back to the bus. This morning's arm-in-arm walk was much better.

Then he hadn't been stopping to puke every few minutes.

I hold back Wendell's hair as he dry heaves over the toilet in his hotel room. I force him to drink three tall glasses of water before he collapses onto the bed and falls into a slack-jawed sleep. On the adjacent bed, I write about Faustino in my notebook, flicking my eyes to Wendell's chest every few minutes to make sure he hasn't stopped breathing or choked on vomit.

After a few hours, he wakes up, clutching his head and mumbling that he needs to brush his teeth and take a shower.

"Want me to stay?" I ask, embarrassed that he's embarrassed.

"No thanks." With his head down, he disappears into the bathroom, shutting the door firmly.

On the way home I stop by Gaby's. She offers me *tostado*— big salty, greasy kernels of toasted corn—and I realize I'm famished. Between mouthfuls of *tostado,* I tell her everything except the vomit part, to save Wendell's dignity.

She listens like a wide-eyed owl. After turning it all over in her wise mind, she comes up with some possibilities.

One, Faustino is a little *con la luna*—"with the moon," or crazy—and an alcoholic but harmless.

Two, he's "with the moon" and an alcoholic and *not* harmless.

Three, he's not "with the moon" *or* harmless (but maybe an alcoholic), and he's either a criminal, a kidnapper, a drug dealer, or a thief. Or a mix of all of the above.

She leans back in her chair, her hands folded over her belly, like a round, Otavaleña Sherlock Holmes, a knitting needle protruding from the corner of her mouth in place of a pipe. "Somehow he has more money than everyone else. Yet he's not a vendor. And he doesn't have kids working abroad and sending back money. So there must be some other thing, and chances are it's illegal. Take Silvio's advice. Stay away from him."

"But Wendell wants to go back."

She tosses a handful of *tostado* into her mouth, crunching and musing. "You have to let people make their own mistakes, discover the truth for themselves."

"But I'm supposed to protect him. I promised his mother. And I don't want him getting hurt."

She digests that and says finally, "If you think he's in over his head, tell his parents to come get him."

"He'd kill me."

"Better than him getting killed."

Chapter 21

When I get home, Layla's in her bedroom, standing over her small purple suitcase, a hand on her hip, lips slightly pursed, pensive.

"What's up, Layla?"

"Pack your bags, love. We're going away for the weekend."

First, I'm stunned.

And then, upset. I need to fix things with Wendell first.

Layla's flying around the room, in a packing whirlwind. Just the two of us, flitting off like birds for a bit. Maybe a couple of days away could be a good thing. Wendell and I can miss each other and talk on the phone, and then when we see each other again, it will be a warm reunion. And I like the idea of girl bonding time with Layla, away from the TV.

Maybe I'll try talking with her, like Gaby suggested. "Where are we going?"

She drops a strapless top in the suitcase. "A gorgeous hacienda in the mountains. The pictures online are amazing."

I lean against the doorframe. Usually our vacations involve five-dollars-a-night youth hostels, sharing a dorm room with ten scraggly backpackers. Or camping on a beach under a tarp. "We have enough money for that, Layla?"

"Don't worry, love." She throws in her orange bikini. "It's Jeff's treat."

Why is my stomach sinking? "He's coming?"

"It's his idea. We thought you two should get to know each other better."

I dig my fingers into the wooden door. "What about getting your work visa? That should be the priority now. Not taking a vacation. You can't work here much longer with no visa."

"Well"—she hesitates, sizing up a yellow ruffled peasant shirt—"that's something we want to talk to you about on the trip." She tosses the blouse onto the bed, the reject pile.

My heartbeat quickens. "Tell me now."

"Look, love, I told Jeff how much you begged me to stay in Maryland. And he suggested we go back with him. He has some friends who are teachers. They could help me find a job there. He lives less than an hour away from my parents. They'd be ecstatic."

The room starts spinning. "What?" I hear myself squeak, as if I'm outside myself, watching the scene from above.

"It might end up being just a visit, but if we want to, we could stay." She folds a pair of pleated khaki shorts I've never seen before.

I find my voice. "But remember your headaches? Remember how miserable you were there?"

She stares at me, a pair of flip-flops dangling from her fingers. "This is our chance for a normal life, love. I'm excited about it. I really am. This time I can make it work. I know I can. It's what you want, isn't it?"

I open my mouth to let everything spill out, to tell her I miss the old Layla, to tell her I liked our old life. Then the buzzer rings.

"That's Jeff!" she says. "Get packed, Z."

As she goes to let him in, all I can think about are dead birds.

We ride in Jeff's SUV through valleys dwarfed by green mountains spotted with houses, the occasional potato stand and shack selling Coke and snacks on the roadside. It's impossible to tell the outside temperature since the digital thermostat's set to sixty-eight degrees.

During the ride, Jeff comes up with a plan for turning Ecuador into an efficient, well-oiled tourist machine. "Look at this trash burning on the roadside. Now in Virginia—"

Inside his head, he's probably planning out a PowerPoint presentation entitled *What Ecuador Could Learn from Virginia.*

Layla just nods, as though she agrees with him.

I remember conjugating *aguantar* with Wendell. *Ya no aguanto.* I can no longer bear it. I close my eyes and think of what Layla should be saying. *Would* be saying, if she were still herself.

"Jeff," I begin, "the thing is, not every country has enough money to dump their trash in the middle of the ocean. I mean, at least here it's in your face and you realize all the waste you're creating."

Layla's lips purse in disapproval, sitcom-mom style. At *me*.

He forces a personable grin. "Good point." He turns to Layla. "Your spunk runs in the family, honey."

What spunk? Layla's spunk is nowhere to be seen. She's always been the one lamenting how we're trashing Pachamama, Mother Earth, slashing through the river of her veins, gouging deep into her flesh with oil wells and mines.

When Jeff stops at a gas station and goes inside for a pack of chips, I say, "Layla, why aren't you acting like yourself? Why don't you say what you think around Jeff?"

"I'm just being polite, Z. Acting like a grown-up. Maybe you should try it." She puts on her sunglasses and reclines the seat. "Can you grab some peppermints from my bag?"

An hour later, at the hacienda, the concierge carries our suitcases to a suite on the second floor of the enormous, white-pillared, red-roofed mansion surrounded by red bougainvillea and expanses of trimmed grass. Jeff and Layla take the big room, and I take the adjoining one.

The decor's trying a little too hard. Folk art's plastered over the walls: woven rugs featuring chubby indigenous girls hugging baby llamas, dried sugarcane-leaf mats like the ones in Mamita Luz's house, some clay pots dangling from fibrous ropes.

I plop on the bed and call Wendell. After one ring his voice mail picks up. Disappointed, I leave a message with our hotel's phone number.

We eat a bland chicken dinner at the hotel restaurant, and then, while Layla and Jeff drink espressos, I walk back to my room up candlelit stairs and through candlelit hallways.

I flip through some channels on TV and then flick it off. I try writing a little in my notebook, but all that comes out are rambling questions about Wendell, the same ones over and over. *Where are you? Why aren't you calling? Are you okay? Is it something I did?*

I throw down the pen and toss the notebook on the bed. After only one day, the vacation is dragging on for eternity. The place is nice, I have to admit, nicer than anywhere Layla and I've stayed before—giant, fluffy beds, a whirlpool tub in the bathroom, soft mood lighting. Luxurious, but I can't enjoy it.

Finally, I try to sleep, but the mattress feels too pouffy, and anyway, my muscles are all tensed waiting for the phone to ring. Then I remember Wendell's letters, tucked in the pocket of my bag. Just a few left to translate. I pull one out, unfold it. Ink drawings of swords and dragons and knights lace the edges. This must be one of the earlier letters, before he started getting the weird feelings.

In a circle of yellow lamplight, I read slowly, savoring it like a love letter. There's something thrilling about being inside Wendell's head, even if it's his nine-year-old head.

Dear birth mom and dad,

I have it finally figured out! I've been looking at all the clues. Your royalty and you put the rock in my blanket and I think it's really a dimond, the biggest dimond in the world. And it was like those stories where someone said that there was a prophesy where this baby is going to be king and then the bad guy didn't want him to be king and said, kill him, and you tried to hide me but the bad guys found me and they said to the nursemade, take him to the woods and kill him and bring his heart. And she was good, so she wrapped me in a blanket and put your dimond in there so I knew I was royalty, and sent me down the river and then she killed a deer and brought it's heart back to the bad guys.

I just want to tell you guys, don't worry, I'm alive, I still have the dimond, it's hidden in my sock drawer.

DON'T despair. I'll come back to claim
the throne. But just promise mom and
dad can come and work in the cassel
or something, okay? Dad cooks good. He
could be the chef. And mom could be
the royal seamstriss because she sows
my haloween costumes every year. Last
year I was King Arthur.

> sincerely,
> wendell B. connelly,
> age 9

I translate it carefully, considering every word choice, the order of every phrase, drawing it out. Then I stare out the window, into the darkness. There was a time when I, too, thought my father was king and that one day he would find me and take me home to our cozy palace, where he and Layla and I would live in domestic, royal bliss. Over the years, the king evolved into the Normal Father and the palace into the Normal Home.

I tuck the letters in my bag, turn off the light, and thankfully, slip into sleep.

The next morning, Layla and Jeff and I have scrambled eggs and fruit and yogurt at a café table beside a flowering tree, a *floripondio*, of all things. I remember Faustino's proud face as he introduced us to his "children." He truly loves them, you could tell by the way he picked off the insects, careful not to hurt a single petal. Maybe I've been too hard on him. Maybe he's just eccentric, like Wendell said.

I miss Wendell.

And I miss Gaby and Taita Silvio and Mamita Luz and the girls.

It isn't Thailand I miss anymore. It's Otavalo and my new friends there.

Jeff's started calling Layla Pop-Tart. He seems to be half-joking, but it makes me want to punch something. First, Layla is completely against packaged, processed, corn-syrupy foods, and second, Pop-Tart has the word *tart* in it, like she's some kind of gold-digging floozy and he's her sugar daddy.

But when he says it, she smiles, flattered.

On the first day, Jeff takes her golfing near Yaguarcocha Lake. Blood Lake, in Quichua. As they golf, I sit on a cold rock at the edge of Blood Lake. The wind is insane, like an animal trying to rip my clothes to shreds. It actually feels like the air is on a mission to beat me up.

Layla looks absurd on the golf course. Her long wrap-around skirt is whipping around, over her head sometimes, exposing her thighs, her underwear. Thank God she's wearing underwear, at least. She forgot a rubber band, though, and her hair keeps flying in her face, so she can't even see the golf ball.

She's trying hard, I remind myself. She's doing this to give us a better life. And Jeff, honestly, isn't a bad guy, except for the Pop-Tart thing, which is truly annoying. Yet I can't help feeling that things are spinning out of control, taking on a life of their own, like this relentless wind.

If she really wants to change, if she really wants a new life, then isn't it selfish for me to stop her? Jeff's standing behind her now, his arms around her, holding her hands over the golf club. She tilts her head up and moves her face close to his. She kisses him, as though she truly likes him, and likes golf, and likes being this new person.

That evening, I try to call Wendell. No answer. Is he avoiding me? Ignoring me? Has he gone back to his ex-girlfriend? Or worse, what if he's gone back without me to Faustino? What if he's been poisoned by one of the flora or fauna there? What if he's dead in that garden? Buried under one of those zombie trees?

On the second day, we go to San Pablo Lake, where we eat fried fish in a bright yellow restaurant. Then we go out with a guide on a motorboat. He's a friendly middle-aged man with a baseball cap pulled low over his eyes. Squinting in the wind, he tells us a story about the lake—a version of the story the girls in Agua Santa told Wendell and me.

A long time ago, there used to be no water, just a valley. A very rich man who owned a hacienda lived in the valley. Notorious for his greed, he treated all his indigenous workers terribly. One day, a very old man wandered by in tattered clothes and asked for a bite to eat. The rich man turned him away. The old man went around and warned the indigenous workers to gather their things and head to higher ground.

That night, water filled the valley. It drowned the rich man and his hacienda and all his animals and crops, and formed this lake. People say the wandering man was really the god of the mountain Imbabura, in disguise. They say that if you gaze into the water, far, far below you might catch a glimpse of the skeletons and the rich man's house and all his fancy furniture.

As a little girl, I'd ask Layla if we could have our own house someday, and she'd recite,

> "Let my house be drowned in the wave
> that rose last night out of the courtyard
> hidden in the center of my chest."

I peer into the water, below the sparkly surface, deeper and deeper, into the hidden heart of things. I see the sunken three-bedroom house that I wanted to live in. I see the expensive waterlogged sofas that I wanted to sit on. I see the skeleton of the person I wanted to be.

Have you ever noticed that the good guys are the ones who don't have fancy houses or magazine-ad sofas? The good guys are the ones who wander. The ones with the ocean spilling from their chests.

Back at the hotel that afternoon, I try Wendell again. His voice mail picks up after the first ring. I leave another message. Then I check for messages on the hotel phone. Not one.

The next day, we go horseback riding in the mountains.

Afterward, while Jeff and Layla soak in a hot tub, I try Wendell's phone again. The voice-mail box is full. And no messages for me either.

I can't stand it anymore. *Ya no aguanto*. Feeling like a stalker, I call Wendell's hotel. A woman answers. "Hotel Otavalo. How can I help you?"

"Dalia?" I ask, because she's usually hanging around the reception desk. This doesn't sound like her, though. The voice is colder, less personal.

"Señora Dalia's away this week."

"Oh." My muscles tense. The babysitter is gone. "Can I talk to Wendell Connelly?"

"Wendell Connelly," she repeats. A moment's pause. "Sorry, *señorita*. No one by that name is here."

"But he has to be. Room eleven."

"Let me check." Another pause. "It appears the *señor* left."

"What?" I try to collect my thoughts. "Is he with Dalia?"

"No," she says. "Señora Dalia's in Cuenca. Her mother's in the hospital there. Heart attack."

I struggle to find words. "But where did Wendell go? Back to the U.S.? Or to another hotel? Or—"

"I don't know, *señorita*. It just says here that two days ago he checked out. He's gone."

Chapter 22

Most of the ride home, I stare out the window at the rolling mountains, thinking about Wendell and wondering what to do next. I could ask around, try to figure out where he is. Maybe Taita Silvio or Mamita Luz or the girls know something. Or Gaby—she might have seen him. And if they're as clueless as me? I could go to Faustino's again. The thought makes me shiver.

I could call his mother, see if he decided to go home. And if he didn't? They'd panic. What if Wendell fell victim to Faustino's poisonous flora and fauna? I can imagine the scene: Wendell visits Faustino, unable to resist. Faustino demands his watch, forces him to empty his bank account, then pours liquor laced with dried, crushed petals down his throat. Or maybe Faustino's holding Wendell for ransom and his parents are scrambling to send their life savings to him at this moment.

But I can't shake the worry that he's simply avoiding me. Have I annoyed him, spending nights at his hotel room, maybe unwanted? And in the woods—did he reach out to hold me or did I throw myself at him? And on the way up the hill—did he slip his hand in mine or did I grab his?

I wish I could talk to Layla, really talk. Now that her advice is no longer flowing freely, I miss it. She used to give good advice, odd perspectives. Maybe those ancient mystics rubbed off on her. Now, in the SUV, I can't tell if she's awake or asleep. She's sitting in the front seat, her eyes hidden behind new sunglasses, her mouth fixed, her hands folded in her lap.

At home, Layla plops in front of the TV. She's started plopping, plodding, dragging, moving heavily, the way people who think they've finished the exciting part of life do. Already the way she used to float around is fading into memory.

"I'm going out," I say.

"You don't want to hang out with me? Watch TV? Have girl time?"

"No thanks. I'm worried about Wendell."

She nods and flicks her eyes back to the TV. "See you, love." She doesn't ask me why I'm worried about him. If she'd asked, I would have let it all gush out. But I'm on my own now.

I walk to the main square, through angled evening light, all golden and gentle, toward Gaby's booth. I've changed into a long, gauzy sarong that Layla bought me in Thailand, silky swirls of color. It was too *Layla* before and I hardly wore it, but now it seems to hold a little of her old magic.

She gave it to me one sunny, breezy day when I cut school to go surfing. My friends and I were walking across the field toward the beach when I caught sight of Layla with her boyfriend at the time, a shaggy-haired Japanese artist. Layla was flying a kite and wearing a rainbow scarf around her neck that I later discovered was a sarong. She ran up to me and hugged me. I said, "Aren't you supposed to be teaching a class now?"

She laughed and said, "I'm playing hooky."

"Try not to get yourself fired, Layla. Please?" She either didn't notice or care that I was playing hooky too.

She wrapped the sarong around my neck and said, "For you, love." And then, as my friends watched, gaping, she pulled me down to the grass so we were lying on our backs, side by side. Looking at the sky, she shouted,

> "Out beyond ideas of wrongdoing and
> rightdoing,
> There is a field. I'll meet you there.
> When the soul lies down in that grass,
> The world is too full to talk about."

Now, halfway across the world, in that same rainbow sarong, I breeze by scattered tourists, tired stragglers left at the booths. The vendors are packing up, shoulders slumped.

Gaby lights up when she sees me. "Four days, Zeeta! Where have you been hiding?"

"Some hacienda with Jeff and Layla."

She pulls a piece of paper from her bosom. "From your gringo friend."

I take a breath and unfold the note.

Hola, Z,

Staying with Faustino now. Not a bad guy once you get to know him. Spanish is getting mucho mejor. Thanks for your help the past few weeks.

Wendell

I sink into Gaby's folding chair.

He chose Faustino over Taita Silvio and Mamita Luz.

Over me.

And he didn't sign it *Love, Wendell* or *Yours, Wendell* or even *Fondly, Wendell*. Just an impersonal *Wendell*, out of a sense of obligation.

I translate the note for Gaby.

She shakes her head. "What a mess."

Tomorrow is Gaby's day off. It's asking a lot of her, but I try anyway. "Can you come with me tomorrow? Try to convince Wendell to leave?"

"Oh, Zeeta. I would, but I promised my cousin I'd watch

her children all day in Quito." She pats my shoulder. "Why don't you bring your mother?"

"No. Too complicated." If Layla gets involved, then Jeff will too, and for some reason, that seems like a bad idea.

Gaby says firmly, "Go tell the boy's uncle—what's his name, Silvio?—tell him what's going on."

"He doesn't acknowledge his brother's existence."

"From what you've said, this Silvio sounds like a good man. A man who would do anything to protect a person. A man who is more of a father than Faustino could ever be."

On the bus the next morning, the speakers blast cheerful music, *cumbias* that make me think of dancing with Wendell. We pass through the outskirts of town, past tire stores and welding shops and garages, low buildings with dirt lots and cars in various stages of disrepair. And then, outside of town, the rubble gives way to wildflowers and grass and low bushes, and occasional houses with sprays of pink and orange bougainvillea in the yards. I twist my fingers around the plastic bag of fruit I've brought for Mamita Luz.

In most places in the world, especially small-town places, you always bring gifts of food when you visit. A bag of beans or corn or fruit or bread. And your hosts always feed you when you visit. Exchanging food and visiting.

From the time at my grandparents' house in Maryland, I know that suburban Americans don't tote sacks of beans or eggs around on visits. They invite each other to potlucks and barbecues. I try to imagine this Andean landscape stretched out like a tight green sheet of lawns, full of gringo families at their grills and picnic tables, like the Fourth of July in my grandparents' neighborhood. I try to imagine one of these families as me and Layla and Jeff. I try to conjure up a glossy, sunlit magazine ad of Jeff flipping a hamburger, and Layla and me cutting up a fruit salad.

I can't do it. It's like straining to remember a blurry dream that keeps slipping out of focus, and all that's left is a lingering memory of a certain feeling.

At Agua Santa, I get off the bus and walk up the hill alone, watching giant shadow blobs of clouds pass over the mountains. At the turnoff, I keep my eyes open for the girls. They always seem to magically appear, little elves emerging from the foliage.

A sound is rising over the insect songs and rustling leaves, a thin wail growing louder. A frantic, panicked sound.

Then, across the field, they come running, Odelia and Isabel and Eva. Odelia's pumping her little legs as fast as she can, but lagging behind the others. Eva slows and grabs her little sister's hand. A man's running after them with a stick, half-stumbling, obviously drunk, cursing and yelling in a mix of Quichua and Spanish. "I've had it with you brats! You're good for nothing!"

Their father.

My feet freeze. *What to do, what to do?* No one else is around, only a man working in a field far away, out of earshot. I look around for a stick or rock, some kind of weapon. All the rocks and sticks are either too tiny—twigs and pebbles—or too heavy to lift. Last time, when Wendell was here, I knew that the two of us could defend ourselves and the girls if we had to. But I'm alone now. And their father is the worst kind of drunk—not so drunk that he can't stand, but drunk enough to do damage. He's running, each of his strides twice the length of theirs.

The girls whiz by, hair streaming behind them, eyes terrified. They must be making a beeline to Mamita Luz's house, cutting directly through cornfields and yards and pigpens, crawling under fences and skitting around cows and chickens.

At the edge of the road, the man sees me. He slows down and glares beneath heavy eyelids.

I throw back my shoulders and stand tall, trying to appear big, the way you're supposed to do if you encounter a mountain lion. I look at him straight on, and although I can't find any words—my throat feels locked shut—I stare, willing him to back down. Ready to run, I brace myself. He'll have to get past me to get to the girls.

He hangs back, about twenty feet away, and yells something at me in Quichua. Then he turns and staggers in the other direction. Once he's far enough away, I collapse, kneeling in the dirt. Being fifteen years old and confronted with this monster is scary enough. I can't imagine how it feels to a forty-pound five-year-old who only comes up to his waist. Even though they're obviously used to this—running from this man who is supposed to love them—that doesn't make it any less scary.

I force myself to stand and head toward Mamita Luz's. My heart's beating wildly the whole way, along the irrigation ditch, beneath the arc of corn leaves. Wendell must have had a feeling about this, must have felt helpless. All he could do was warn the girls. Now I feel helpless, thinking of a million things I should have said to that terrible man, things I should have done. *How dare you try to hurt a child!* I should have drop-kicked him. Tackled him. Tied him to a tree with a sign reading I HIT INNOCENT CHILDREN and refused to let him go until he swore to never do it again.

When I reach Mamita Luz's house, I knock on the door, my hands and legs still shaking.

"Who is it?" Eva's thin voice calls out.

"Zeeta."

She opens the door, looking worn out, like a very old lady. Wordlessly, she closes the door behind me and heaves a thick wooden bar across it. Mamita Luz is sitting by the oven with Odelia in her lap and one arm wrapped around Isabel. Odelia's sobbing in scratchy gasps and gulps of air. Across Isabel's face, paths of dried tears streak through the grime. Eva's quiet, but beneath her stooped shoulders and crossed arms is a hard ball of anger.

Mamita Luz murmurs in a slow river voice, "You girls are treasures. Your father should treat you like the treasures you are."

A few other kids are in the corner, playing marbles on the dirt floor, talking softly. I stand awkwardly by the wood column, still feeling guilty that I didn't do something to their father, anything.

Mamita Luz nods at me in a sad greeting, then turns back to the girls. "When Taita Silvio gets home, we'll tell him what happened and he'll go talk to your father. You're safe now."

Once Odelia's sobs stop, Mamita Luz says, "Eva, please go cut some *ortiga*. Zeeta, go with her." She hands me a knife. "For the *ortiga*."

I hold the knife tightly, ready to use it on the girls' father if he dares to come here. Eva grabs a bag and leads me to a clump of nettles at the side of the house. The sun's halfway to the top of the sky, the light still fresh, the heat just starting.

Carefully, Eva cuts the stems with the knife, trying to avoid the sharp hairs. Strange how something that can sting you can also heal you.

"Are you okay?" I ask.

She shrugs.

"What happened, Eva?"

"Papi's drunk. He got mad at Odelia. She was playing while he was sleeping and woke him up, and he told her to shut up and started beating her with the stick. But it wasn't fair, it wasn't her fault. She's only five. She was just playing."

Eva's crying now, wiping her tears with her arm as she cuts the *ortiga*. "And he kept hitting her harder and harder and then Isabel tried to grab his arm to stop him and he started hitting her, too, and we told Odelia to run. And I grabbed his arm and told Isabel to run and then he hit me and started chasing after them and I held him back long enough for them to get a head start and then I ran too, and luckily he's drunk enough he kept tripping and couldn't catch us. And last time he did this, Taita Silvio talked to him for a long time and for a while he didn't hit us, but he was in a really bad mood this time and got drunk and . . ." Her voice fades. She straightens up and slings the bag of *ortiga* over her shoulder, sniffing. "Ready?"

On the way back, I ask, "What about your mother?"

"She works as a maid in Otavalo all day to make money for us. She has to, because our father spends all our money getting drunk on *trago*. Mami leaves when we wake up and gets home after we're asleep. And she tells me to look after my *ñañas*. I try, but I can't protect them."

I put my arm around her. "You protected them. You brought them here. To a safe place."

Inside, Mamita Luz boils the *ortiga*, lets it cool, and examines Odelia's legs. They're crisscrossed with red welts and scrapes from her father's stick. How can that man have three daughters when Mamita Luz can't have children of her own?

If Wendell hadn't been adopted, if Faustino had been his father, would his childhood have been like this? In constant fear, running to save himself? Would he have been one of the regulars at Mamita Luz's house?

She sits Odelia on a chair, with her little legs resting on another chair, and lays the damp herbs across her skin, murmuring in Quichua. She heats up lemon balm tea and takes fresh, warm rolls from the oven and gives them to the girls. By the time they finish the food, they're nearly back to their usual selves, playing marbles in the corner with the other kids.

Mamita Luz turns to me, shaking her head. "Nothing makes me sadder than unwanted children," she whispers. "I feel helpless."

"But you're doing so much for them. You give them a safe place to come. You treat them like treasures."

She sighs and takes out a big bowl and scoops a gourdful of flour from a giant sack. She adds water and a pinch of salt, and begins kneading rhythmically, as though she's playing a cello, throwing her entire body into the movements. "Sometimes I wonder, if I'd had children of my own and poured all my attention on them, what would have happened to Odelia and her sisters? Where would they have gone? All these years of wishing for our own children, and now, when I'm comforting these girls, I understand. I know that this is where I need to be. And I feel at peace."

I nod, thinking how badly Wendell wanted to find his birth parents. Now he's found his father, who appears to be a creep. I think how badly I wanted a normal family life, and now that it's within reach, the idea of it makes me want to cry.

"Here," Mamita Luz says. "Want to help?"

I pluck a lump of dough from the bowl and imitate her

movements, trying to make my rhythm match hers. It's tiring. After just a few minutes, my arm muscles feel sore.

"We visited Faustino last week," I say.

"Yes, the girls told us. What happened?"

"Wendell moved in with him."

Her kneading slows and a shadow passes over her face. Her hands rest, buried in the dough. She looks at me, a long, serious gaze. "When one of my children is in danger, I sense it. Even before little Odelia and her sisters came running here today, I felt it. And now I feel it just as strongly. Wendell is in danger."

Chapter 23

I'm determined to protect Wendell. And Gaby's right, I could use Taita Silvio's help.

A half hour later, Taita Silvio comes in, and Odelia leaps into his arms, burying her head in his shoulder. Isabel tells him what happened in a small, serious voice.

"I'll talk to your parents later today, once your father's sober, my daughters." His face looks pained. "Now, why don't you stack the firewood? Small pieces in one pile, big pieces in the other. I'm going back out with Zeeta for more wood."

The girls begin stacking, and we move away. "I think Wendell's in trouble," I whisper. I don't want to panic the girls.

"I know," he says. "Come with me to gather more firewood. We can talk on the way."

I grab a head strap and machete. Machetes at our sides, we walk down a path behind his house, along cornfields and past wildflowers and tall grass, heading toward a piece of his property at the base of the Hill of Tunnels. After a fifteen-minute walk, we're inside the woods, the light dappled through shifting leaves. A few birds flit around. We have to watch our footing on the sloping ground.

"I try to find dead branches and trees," Taita Silvio says, scanning the forest. "This was my father's property, this entire hill. Years ago, I told my brother he could have the hill as long as I could have a small bit of forest on this side to gather firewood."

I sense there's a story behind this, probably related to the fallout Faustino told us about. I wait to see if he'll tell me more.

"I've been coming to this forest for firewood since I was a boy."

"And you saw your star friend?"

He smiles. "Yes. My star friend. He was always there for me, in the same spot, sometimes hidden by clouds, but always there."

I find a fallen log, dry but not rotted, and start chopping.

Meanwhile, Taita Silvio has found a dead tree. He breaks off branches, talking slowly and thoughtfully. "My star friend was predictable. Not like my father. He was like the girls' father in some ways, especially toward the end of his life, when we were teenagers. When he was younger, he was a powerful *curandero*."

I slice my machete blade through dead bark. "How could someone hurt his own children? Especially a healer?"

"Power is a tricky thing, *mija*. It can lift you up high on its wings and up into the sky where you feel invincible. But sometimes you forget the bigger thing that makes you fly. Without God, without love, you fall. You stop being grateful and humble, and you fall.

"And when you try to fly again, you forget how. So you drink liquor because for a moment when you drink you feel that you're flying, but you always fall again. And you drink more and more to try to recapture that, to try to forget your heavy, hard life. And the power leaves you, but still you crave it. You get angry at your family, you hit them, you yell. You cannot bear it. This is what happened to my father."

"I'm sorry," I say, because I have to say something, although *sorry* seems too flimsy a word.

Taita Silvio arranges his pile of wood on the rope, ties the frayed ends together, and heaves the bundle onto his back, secured with his head strap.

I'm almost done with my pile, my shoulders burning from the effort, bits of bark clinging to my sweaty arms.

He helps me finish, and adjusts the bundle on my back. "Tell me if it's more than you can bear, daughter, and I'll put more on mine." On the way home, he motions back to the hill. "That's where my brother and I used to hide from our father. In the tunnels under that hill."

I think of what Faustino said, his earliest memory, hiding

in a crystal cave. And what the girls said about the devil's palace inside. "Any devils in there?" I ask.

He laughs, shifting the wood on his back. "Most of the tunnels are just dark, damp caves. But one of the chambers is special. We crawled through a small hole to get to it. It's made of crystals, the walls and ceilings and floors. You feel like you're flying in there. You can forget the rest of the world and feel safe.

"Usually our father stopped chasing us before the tunnel. But we could find our way to the crystal chamber in the dark. We knew the secret. All right turns, the first right turn every time. We would run through the tunnels and then move the rock aside and scamper in. Even if our father managed to follow us all the way back, he could not touch us in the room. The crystals' powers were too strong. They made the hole smaller so his big belly couldn't fit inside. Sometimes my brother and I slept there. We kept candles and matches there in case we had to spend the night. Back then, we were close."

I'm itching for my indigo notebook, wanting to write all this down. Instead, I try to remember every little detail. Layla would be enthralled. She'd do anything to be inside a crystal cave.

I would, too, I realize.

We pass a fresh spring pouring out of some mossy rocks, making a trickling, gurgling sound. Silvio bends down under all the weight and plucks some watercress. We munch on the tiny, crisp leaves and scoop mouthfuls of water from the spring. He lifts his pant leg and shows me shiny scars up and down the flesh. "I look at what my father did to me and I feel sad. I swear every day that I will stay humble and grateful and always show love to my wife and our children. But my brother, he looks at his scars and feels anger. Our family's blood has power, but one must learn to master it."

"Can Faustino divine the future too?"

"Who knows. Maybe drinking *trago* helps him ignore the visions." He tosses a pebble into the water, making a small splash and widening rings. "That's what my father ended up doing, and what I suspect my brother does."

Is that what Faustino's teaching Wendell? To drink himself into oblivion? I pick a handful of watercress and study the tiny leaves.

"My brother is a man full of anger." He tosses another pebble into the water. "And this is why he is involved with bad people doing illegal things."

I suck in my breath. What am I even doing here? I should be with Wendell. "What things?" I ask warily.

"We don't know exactly. Maybe drugs. Whatever it is, it is dangerous for Wendell."

My stomach clenches. I shift the firewood bundle and adjust the strap across my forehead, ready to keep walking. "What should we do?"

"My brother is dead to me. This is the first time I've spoken of him in sixteen years."

We head back along the path, toward his house. I'm walking fast, despite the twenty-pound load on my back, the strap digging into my forehead. I've already wasted valuable time. Silvio is having trouble keeping up. I don't care. I'm sweating and breathing hard, and suddenly, I'm tired of Silvio's secrets, furious that he'd let a rift with his brother get in the way of Wendell's safety.

"Listen," I say, "Faustino told us why you stopped talking to him. Why didn't you tell us?"

He wipes some sweat from his cheek. "I didn't want Wendell to hate his father. I thought his fantasy would be better than the truth."

"You were wrong, Silvio."

"Perhaps." He sighs. "You know, as boys, we swore to each other that we would never beat our children. Then he beat Lilia while she was pregnant, before the child had even seen the light of day. That angered me. And scared me. It made me wonder if I was capable of doing the same thing. It made me want to never have children, so I would never have to find out."

"Maybe he's changed now," I say. "You could at least talk to him."

He shakes his head. "You can do it. Talk to Wendell. Tell him to leave."

"Wendell needs you. He needs you to teach him how to use his powers for good."

Taita Silvio gives me a strange look. "Tell him to come to me and I will teach him. But I will not go near my brother."

· · ·

Alone, I walk up the hill toward Faustino's house with my bag of stale rolls. It's overcast, the clouds thick and heavy and gray. Fog engulfs the house, the whole hilltop. I can't see the outline of the house until I've nearly reached it. The dogs greet me with their tongues hanging out, drooling for the bread, which I toss to them.

By the door, Faustino and Wendell are standing side by side, watching me. They have a similar way of standing, their weight shifted onto the right foot. It's as though Faustino is Wendell's shadow. As I come closer, I can make out their faces. The features are nearly the same, but something that holds them together is different. Something hard to put your finger on. The aura, Layla would call it. The energy in Faustino's face is all suspicion, making his eyes hard and narrowed. Wendell's energy lights up his face, opening his eyes, softening them.

"Zeeta!" He gives me a hug. It's the kind of hug you might give your girlfriend in front of other people. He sneakily presses up against me a tad longer than if, say, he was hugging a friend or a grandmother. It feels good. It feels good to smell his smell after a week apart. Good to hear his lilting voice, touch his skin. I remember dancing with him in the *peña*. And walking back from the waterfall arm in arm. And lying in the bed next to his and letting our words touch in the darkness.

"Zeeta," he says again. "How's Layla? And Jeff?"

"Lovebirds," I say, eyeing Faustino. He's obviously irritated he can't understand our conversation. "I was forced to spend a hellish vacation with them at some hacienda."

"Oh. I wondered why you hadn't come. I thought you were mad at me."

"Well, maybe I am a little." Looking down, I stroke under the dogs' chins. They're in a blissful daze, not sure what to do with my kindness.

"Sorry. My cell doesn't get reception here. My parents are probably mad at me too, for not calling. Hey, have you finished translating the letters yet?"

"Almost."

"Good. I want to give them to Faustino all at once."

"Okay."

"I don't know what I'd do without you, Z."

I look around, at the donkey swatting its tail at a fly, the chickens pecking around the truck's tires, the dogs sprawled in the dirt. "So, what have you been doing here anyway?"

"Helping Faustino."

"With what?"

He glances at Faustino, who raises an eyebrow. "His work. God, it feels good to speak English. My head was hurting after so much Spanish. Luckily he has a satellite dish, so I can watch TV in English. Those cheesy *Frasier* episodes are keeping me sane." He gives me that sideways smile, tucks a strand of hair behind his ear, and says in a low, secret voice, "I missed you."

Before I can answer, Faustino kicks the dogs out of the way and steps between us. *"Buenas tardes, señorita."*

We sit down on the crates, and that's when I notice, through the fog, a pile of boxes by the door.

"What's in the boxes?" I ask Wendell.

"Teddy bears."

I remember the pile of them I saw when I peeked in Faustino's house last time.

Wendell opens a box. "Look."

Faustino hovers, clearly uncomfortable.

I pick up a bear. It's silky smooth.

"Alpaca fur," Wendell says proudly. "He sells alpaca-fur bears."

"He doesn't seem like the cuddly type."

"He travels around selling them, to Colombia and other countries."

"That's really his job? Selling teddy bears?"

"They're pure alpaca fur. Good quality. Some guys he works with are coming by soon to pick up the shipment."

I turn the bear over. The stitches are sloppy and the stuffing looks lumpy. The eyes sit unevenly over the crooked nose, between lopsided ears. A very sorry-looking creature. A complete rip-off. I can't imagine anyone paying more than a few dollars for it.

Without warning, Faustino grabs the bear. "Maybe you should be on your way. My son and I are expecting visitors soon."

Wendell raises an apologetic shoulder. "Wanna meet downtown for dinner tonight?"

I nod, bewildered. He gives me a hug goodbye, a long, lingering hug, the kind of hug that if She saw, would make her jealous. I breathe in his cinnamon-clove smell. I'm guessing it's from the soap his mom makes as a hobby. Number six on the list of things he loves about her in his Mother's Day letter. Apparently, she blends up special scents for him as random presents.

I want to rest my head there awhile, but instead, I whisper, "I think you're in danger here."

He steps back, half-pushing me away. "What?"

"Taita Silvio thinks so too. You can't trust Faustino."

He sucks in his cheeks. "He's my father."

"Your father is Dan. And he's probably sitting all forlorn on your bed playing Nick Drake songs and wishing you'd call." I can't help it. My words tumble out. "He loves you. Unlike this loser."

Wendell looks away. "Faustino said he'd help me." His voice is tight, a taut guitar string.

"You can learn more from Taita Silvio."

Wendell stares at a place over my shoulder. Then he turns and walks toward the door.

"Wendell," I call after him. "What time do you want to meet downtown?"

He says nothing.

"Wendell! Are we still on for dinner?"

He disappears inside.

Faustino smiles, leaning against the outside wall. *"Adiós, señorita."*

His beady eyes watch me leave. I feel them, smug and victorious, piercing my back.

Chapter 24

As I trudge down the hill, the milky-gray dullness of the sky seeps into my pores. I'm abandoning a failed mission, leaving my sort-of-but-not-really-boyfriend in danger, ruining any chance of him being my real live boyfriend, or even a friend for that matter.

I hear the truck first, and then see it roar through the mist, cloaked in hip-hop salsa that grows louder and closer by the second. I jump off the road, down into the ditch a little ways, barely escaping a wave of mud spray. The driver pokes his head out the window and lets out a shrill whistle. *"¡Ay, mamacita linda!"* The guy in the passenger seat yells, *"¡Que rica bebé!"* even though he has no reason to think my butt looks delicious since it's hidden under my cloak.

Instead of bolting down the hill, I stand still, indignant.

Teddy bear salesmen? No way can I picture these guys selling teddy bears.

And then it hits me.

They're not selling teddy bears. They're selling what's hidden inside the teddy bears. From what Gaby's told me, cocaine is the most likely possibility.

Up the hill, the dogs are barking at the truck. The music stops and the motor turns off. On a sudden impulse, I head back toward the house. Curiosity? Anger? The promise I've made to Wendell's mother to keep him safe? Whatever it is, it makes me reckless and brave. I have to get Wendell far away from those bears and what's inside them. If he gets caught mixed up in this—even innocently—he could spend years in jail. I stick to the side of the road, where the foliage and fog hide me.

From my spot behind a tree trunk, I see the men shake hands with Wendell and Faustino, then survey the boxes by the door. Together, they move the boxes into the back of their truck. I can't make out their words, low and muffled by the damp air. Afterward, they tromp inside the house.

Now's my chance. I run from the bushes, across the clearing to the truck, where I crouch down by the giant tires, my heart pounding. My idea isn't well formed—I just want to find out what's really going on. Find out what's inside the teddy bears, so I can tell Wendell and get him out of here. Wendell doesn't know what's inside, does he? But how can he not suspect something? He must be blinded by how badly he wants Faustino to be good.

I climb onto the tire and lean into the truck bed. The boxes are taped shut. I peel the tape off one, wishing I hadn't just trimmed my fingernails. It takes an agonizingly long time. Every movement makes me jump—a bird flitting from one branch to another, one of the dogs scratching its ear, a fly buzzing past. Finally, I fling open the flaps and pull out a bear and start tearing at the sloppy stitches in back.

The voices inside escalate. "*Cabrón!* You were short on our merchandise last time. We pay you up front, we want our money's worth. What, are you sneaking some for yourself? In this shipment nothing better be missing. And you owe us two thousand from last time."

Then Faustino's voice, "*Tranquilo, tranquilo.*"

Then the men's voices, cursing and yelling some more. A piece of furniture being overturned, something thrown against the wall. I stuff the bear into my bag and jump down to the ground. I should do something. Something, something, something. Maybe the keys are in the truck. Maybe I can go get help. In Morocco, an ex-boyfriend of Layla's taught me to drive his two-stroke motorcycle. How much different can a truck be?

I open the door. A gun's lying on the seat. I know how to shoot a rifle from hunting rabbits in Brazil, but this is a machine gun. I freeze.

Wendell's voice rises in his terrible accent. "*¡Tengo dinero!*" I have money.

"How much?" a voice yells.

"I have it all. *Doscientos.*" I can feel his brain working

frantically to translate the zeros to Spanish. "No, no, no—*dos mil, dos mil*—two thousand. Two thousand dollars."

A pause. Then, so quietly, I can barely hear, "He's lying."

"I have it, I have it! My *dinero* for *arte escuela*. In the *banco*."

He must be talking about the money he's saving for his art abroad program next summer. Silence, then the murmur of voices. The scrape of chairs. Voices growing closer, nearing the entrance. "We're coming tomorrow afternoon for the money. It better be here. All of it."

I close the truck door quietly and run around the side of the house. With wobbly knees, I make my way through the foliage, half running, half tumbling, down the other side of the mountain.

That's when I remember it. The bear in my bag, bouncing against my thigh. Its presence burns and glows and breathes. As though it's a living creature whispering, *You idiot, why didn't you leave me in that box?*

The whole bus ride back, I hug my bag to my chest, thinking about the bear and its illicit guts. Sinking with the realization that I've gotten myself involved in a mammoth mess. I want to toss the thing out the window, but then what will happen when Faustino and those men discover they're short a bear? What if they blame Wendell? No, I'll have to return it somehow. But first I need to see what's inside. Maybe I'm imagining the whole thing. Maybe they're just shoddy stuffed animals after all.

Our apartment is deserted except for fruit flies hovering

over a plate of papaya peels and orange goop spotted with slimy seeds. On the counter next to a half-eaten carton of pineapple yogurt is a note.

Out to dinner with Jeff, love. We'd like to spend tomorrow morning with you, okay?

Layla

The end of her last "a" spirals up and up and off the page, like a bee's path. She's left the kitchen a disaster, as always. At least she hasn't totally transformed into a suburban housewife. That's reassuring. I toss the peels into the trash, tie up the bag, take it outside, put in a new bag, wipe off the counter, do the heap of dishes, and fix some lemon balm tea.

I'm stalling. I'll admit, I'm terrified of opening the bear.

I close the curtains, which are silk scraps hanging from clothespins over the window. Pink-orange light shines through the insubstantial fabric and seeps around its edges. I get our sharpest knife from the kitchen and set it on the crate coffee table. For a moment, I sit on the sofa, sipping the tea, stroking the teddy bear's fur, trying to let its cuddliness do its job. The fur is satiny smooth, but it isn't soft and huggable, not very comforting.

I hold up the steak knife, ready for surgery. Taking a deep breath, I turn the creature over and wedge the blade under the seams.

Gently, I cut the threads. Of course I've seen cocaine in movies, the little plastic bags of white powder. I've never seen it in real life, up close.

I hold my breath as I open the flaps of fur gently, hoping the bags won't tear loose and the powder won't explode in my face. Inside is a small bag, all right, but not a plastic one. The pouch is white cotton, raw like the shirts Gaby sells. I let it sit in my palm, feeling its weight. Its contents aren't soft or powdery. They click against one another, small, hard things, like stones.

I'm vague on the textures of drugs. I've come across marijuana and shrooms in our travels, common among the hippie expat crowds that Layla attracts, but this harder stuff is a mystery.

I peer inside. A small pile of green crystals, like little pieces of lime-flavored ice or sea glass. I pour them into my palm. They're cloudy in places, clear in others, green with hints of blue, bits of ocean. I've never heard of any green crystal-like drugs before. Crystal meth? Would that imply actual crystals? And are they green?

My first instinct is to go to Gaby's for advice. Then I remember the reason she couldn't go with me to Agua Santa today in the first place. She's watching her cousin's kids in Quito all day.

Should I call Wendell's mom and see if she can talk some

sense into him? He'd kill me. But I've already lost him. Or maybe he's never really been mine to begin with. Maybe I've just been his translator, the one he needed to help him. Maybe he always seems so happy to see me just because I speak English. I'm barely a step up from *Frasier* reruns. A companion while She, his true love, is on another continent, absence making her heart grow fonder, making her e-mails mushier by the day. Now that he's found his birth father, he has no use for me anymore.

Of course, I don't completely believe this, but when you're holding a shoddy teddy bear and feeling miserable it's easy to forget all the good moments and just sink into despair. If I call his parents, like I promised, they'll just convince him to go home. And he'll go back to Her and I'll be just a tiny snippet of a memory and soon he'll even forget my name.

But at least he'll be alive. With his art abroad fund intact.

A couple of things I know for sure. I can't get the police involved. They might arrest Wendell, because whatever the green stones are, they're obviously illegal. And I need to sew up the bear and return it, the sooner the better.

I stuff the pouch back inside the bear and search our apartment for a needle and thread. Nothing. It's late now anyway, nearly dark. Too late to go back to Agua Santa. I'll go to Gaby's booth tomorrow, get her advice about Wendell's money mess, borrow a needle and thread, return the bear as discreetly as possible, and beg Wendell to leave Faustino.

With nothing to do now, I walk in circles around the

apartment. I play some CDs, switching restlessly from one to another—Brazilian jazz to Janis Joplin to chanting monks—then finally turn off the stereo. None of the music fits how I feel. I even knock on Giovanni the Taoist surfer clown's door, thinking he might entertain me with flower balloons to make the minutes pass faster. No answer. Now, of all times. And he's almost always hanging out on the balcony doing nothing.

I wish I could fast-forward to tomorrow and get this over with. Then I remember Wendell's last three letters. Maybe they'll make me feel less panicked, less alone. I sprawl on my mattress and unfold the first one, my indigo notebook open, my pen poised for the translation.

Dear birth mom and dad,

Well, it's my birthday again, so I figured I'd write to you, but I don't know what to say because I don't really care that I'm adopted anymore. I mean, I hardly even think about it. I'm just writing out of habit. I had a sleepover and we watched marathon Lord of the Rings. My picture of a chipmunk got first place in the photography show out of all the middle schools. In the whole state. Not to brag. Maybe I get my artisticness from you. I'll never know. Oh well.

Sincerely,
Wendell,
age 13

And the next.

Dear birth mom and dad,
   I did a research project on Otavaleño Indians and
I feel like I know you better now. Do you drink
chicha? Do you celebrate the festival of the
corn? I've started growing my hair out like you.
Dad got me an Andean flute for my birthday and I
can play a little of "El Condor Pasa" on it. I
wonder if I'll ever meet you. I ditched French and
I'm taking Spanish now, so I can talk to you if we
ever meet. If you speak Spanish. You might only
speak Quichua.
   I wonder if you're alive. I wonder if we're like
each other. I wonder if you can read. I wonder if I
have brothers and sisters. I hope so. I've always
wanted some, but Mom can't have kids. Aiden's
older sister got pregnant. She's 16. She's placing
the baby for adoption. I wonder if you were really
young when you had me. I think Aiden's sister is
doing the right thing.
                                          Adiós,
                                          Wendell,
                                          age 14

   Translating the letters isn't cheering me up. It's making me angry. Faustino doesn't deserve these letters. I
stick them back into the bag with the last untranslated

one, still tightly folded. I'm not ready to translate the last one yet. Once it's done, Wendell won't need me anymore.

The next day, at only ten in the morning, the sun's already sneaking its way under the rim of my hat, burning my eyes. The steamy smell of manure saturates everything, clinging to me and my clothes and my bag and probably even the shabby bear and the letters inside my bag.

We're in the middle of a giant field of mud and pig shit. Men and women stand around, bargaining in Quichua, holding frayed ropes with pigs attached, pigs of all sizes. The best are the tiny squeaking piglets with curlicue tails and crazy puppyish energy. I have to admit they make me crack a smile. The bigger pigs are just scary—massive hairy hogs wallowing in the mud, heaps of flesh refusing to budge.

Coming to the pig market was my idea. I was in my pajamas this morning, eating yogurt and translating Wendell's last letter, when Jeff knocked on the door, decked out in a beige shirt and white pants and white sneakers. I opened it and breathed in his cologne, and he said, "So, what would you like to do today? You choose this time, Z."

For some reason, I didn't like him calling me Z, as if he knew me, as if he were a close friend. Layla was in the shower. She'd slept in since she'd gotten in late last night after their date. While she was getting ready, I flipped through the Ecuador guidebook and came across a couple of lines about the Otavalo pig market, a very muddy and smelly affair.

Eyeing Jeff's immaculate white pants and sneakers, I said, "Let's go to the pig market." Kind of immature and spiteful, I know.

"Great!" he said, clapping his hands.

"Layla loves piglets," I said. I wanted him to see her in all her muddy, messy splendor. Most of all, I wanted her to remember who she is—someone who loves kneeling in the mud, cradling a filthy piglet, enjoying the tiny brown prints its feet make on her skin. Plus, Jeff wouldn't want to stay long, so I'd have time to get to Agua Santa by the afternoon.

All morning, through breakfast at the café and on the way to the pig market, I've tried to catch Layla alone, to tell her about the bears and the disaster with Faustino and Wendell. But she looks in another world. Well, she usually looks in another world, but now she seems utterly absent. A distracted gaze and vague, generic comments like, "Oh, those hogs are big all right," and "Look at those wee little piglets."

Jeff's arm stays around her shoulders like a permanent fixture. He's trying to enjoy himself, trying to make us enjoy ourselves. He only briefly mentions that he wishes he'd worn a different outfit, then devotes his attention to the extra-tiny piglets. "Hey, Z, check out that little bacon bit!"

I keep waiting for Layla to bend down and kiss the baby pigs on the snouts, but she stands there, smiling nervously, devoid of chi. We move on, weaving through people and pigs, around piles of manure and patches of mud puddles, past a pig that is—no kidding—the size of a cow.

Further on are a few sheep and cows, less exciting, and that's when Jeff shifts his focus to me. "Layla, honey, did you show Zeeta our itinerary yet?"

The odor of pigs and shit is overpowering. My knees feel weak.

Layla pulls out a folded-up piece of paper from her pocket. "It's official, love. Jeff bought our tickets yesterday. We're heading to Maryland next week."

I force a smile, hoping my watery eyes might seem joyful.

Layla studies my face. "Zeeta, what's wrong?"

I'm staring at a wide-eyed calf and my lip's quivering and my life's flashing before my eyes, like they say it does right before you die. Now my eyes are closed and I see Layla and me hopping across a stream, from one stone to another. Each stone is a country, glowing with the big events of our lives and sparkling with tiny details of day-to-day existence. I want to keep going.

Now the tears are spilling from my eyes and the world's turned blurry and I blurt out, "I can't do this, Layla. I'm sorry. I can't." I turn and run, pig shit and mud splattering my legs, the bear in the bag bouncing against my thigh.

Layla's voice calls after me, "Wait, Z!"

I don't look back.

Chapter 25

Stands for the Saturday market line the streets, ten times the number of booths as the Plaza de Ponchos market where Gaby works. I zoom through crowds of locals and tourists, past booths of bamboo pan flutes, little guitars, CDs of Andean flute music blaring from boom boxes, jewelry made of nuts and seeds and wooden beads, sweaters of llama and alpaca.

I try to keep my sobbing under control to avoid drawing attention to myself, which is the last thing I need with smuggled goods in my bag. I carry the bag carefully, as though it contains a bomb. When I pass two policemen on the corner, I let my hair fall over my teary face. Against all logic, I'm sure the cops will somehow sniff out the teddy bear's contents and throw me in jail.

At her booth, Gaby's chatting with two Korean tourists as the third one films the encounter. She loves the camera on her, speaks right to it, cracking jokes like a late-night-show host. When I reach her booth, she flashes her huge white smile. "Z, sit down! Give me a minute here."

She turns back to the tourists and holds out a scarf. "Three for ten dollars!" she says, careful to put her tongue between her teeth for the *th* sound as I taught her. She holds up her fingers and looks amused as the Koreans translate among themselves. They don't look like they're in any rush to leave.

The man aims the camera at me. I offer him a weak smile, sweat rolling down my sides. I clutch my bag closed in my lap to be sure nothing incriminating is caught on film.

"See you later, alligator," he says in heavily accented English.

"After a while, crocodile," I squeak.

By now, Gaby has registered my tear-blotched face. She strokes my cheek. "What happened?"

I reach my hand into my bag, pull the bag of green stones from the bear's back. I look around to make sure no one's watching us. Carefully, I take a few stones from the bag and then open my palm, letting the sunlight reflect off their facets, liquid underwater light.

Gaby's quick. Within seconds she takes in the torn-open teddy bear, the pouch, the handful of green light. "Emeralds. So that's what the devil's been up to."

"Emeralds?" Emeralds! Of course! One of Layla's ex-boyfriends from Thailand made jewelry and talked nonstop about stones. Emeralds, he said, were one of the most valuable gems, worth more than rubies and diamonds.

"Is that why you've been crying?" Gaby ventures.

I shake my head. "I have to move to Maryland." And the tears ooze out again, but at least this time I don't turn into a sniveling, gasping mess.

"Where's that?" she asks, offering me an embroidered hankie.

"Somewhere in the United States. A little, funny-shaped state near the capital." I blow my nose.

She pats my shoulder. After a moment, she holds an emerald to the light. "Beautiful, aren't they?"

I nod, looking around nervously, convinced that either the police or those thugs or maybe Faustino himself will appear.

"How involved is Wendell?"

"I don't know." I sniff and wipe my tears. "But it's a big operation. There are boxes of these bears up at Faustino's house."

She smooths my hair behind my ear, tenderly. "Colombia's the emerald capital of the world, you know. Green fire is what they call them. Or green gold. For many years there've been emerald-smuggling routes. They're run by a kind of mafia. As ruthless as the drug runners."

"But why to Ecuador?" Talking about the ins and outs of emerald smuggling somehow quiets my crying.

"Here's my guess. Some people either stole the emeralds straight from the mines or they just didn't want to pay the taxes and get the proper documents. So the devil—what's his name? Faustino?—he's a mule, a middleman, carrying them across the border. He probably disguises himself as an innocent Otavaleño Indian going to Colombia to sell his crafts. I bet he crossed the border into Colombia with the bears, then filled them with emeralds. Crossing back over, he slipped the border police a few bills. Claimed the bears were unsold merchandise."

"What do you think he'll do with them now?"

"Probably pass them on to someone else who'll sell them to gem collectors and distributors."

"How do you know all this, Gaby?"

"Sitting around in a market every day for twenty years, you know a little bit about everything." She winks and calls out to a group of tanned hippie backpackers. "Three for ten dollars, *guapo*! Buy one for your gorgeous girlfriend!"

They smile and keep walking. She turns back to me.

"Listen, Zeeta, I'd say put that bear back right away. And get Wendell far away from that devil."

"What about the police?"

"Ha! The police are as corrupt as the rest of them. They're probably already in the pocket of the smugglers. And they might end up pinning something on Wendell to lay the blame elsewhere."

"That's what I figured." I tuck the pouch of emeralds back inside the bear. "Can I borrow a needle and thread, Gaby?"

She insists on sewing it up herself. She's done in about two minutes, although her stitches are smaller and neater than the original ones. Close enough, though.

I stuff the bear back in my bag and stand up. My legs feel wobbly. "Thanks, Gaby."

"And Zeeta?"

"Yes?"

"Bring someone with you. Your mother. Go, drop off the bear, and come straight back, you hear?" She pauses. She hardly ever looks worried, but now her eyebrows have furrows deep as canyons. "These guys kill with no more remorse than stepping on a bug." She kisses me on the cheek. *"Que Dios te bendiga,"* she says, moving her hands in invisible crosses. "God bless you."

As soon as I start to leave, the hippie travelers return. Gaby says, "Ah, you came back, *guapo*. You couldn't resist my treasures! Here, this blue, for your girlfriend's eyes! Three for ten dollars, *guapo*!"

I head home. I want Layla. I want to spill everything out to her. I want her to spritz lavender around the room to calm me. I want her cloud of patchouli to make me feel like everything will be okay. I want her to come with me and charm those thugs and bring Wendell back.

Maybe, all along, she's been looking out for me, too. Yin and yang. Maybe I've taken care of the practical things and she's taken care of the spiritual things—negotiating with spirits and angels to watch our backs.

When I get home, she isn't there. Just a note saying,

*Jeff and I are
looking for you,
love. Please call
Jeff's cell. We need
to talk.
You are the light of
my existence,*

Layla

I brush my fingertips over the letters, a hodgepodge of upper and lowercase, cursive and print, random flourishes and swirls added to letters for no apparent reason. It pays no attention to the lines, crosses them in diagonal waves, curving upward. The words, light and wispy, are butterfly wings, about to fly off the page. I turn over the paper and write a note in my compact, even script.

*Layla, I'm at Faustino's dropping
something off. It's important.*

I hesitate.

*If I'm not back by tonight, call
Gaby. She'll explain.*

I hesitate again. I have the urge to write something sappy, something along the lines of *You're the light of my existence, too.* Instead I write,

Sorry I yelled at you in the pig shit.
Love,
Zeeta

Love. A word I never use with her. She gushes love, but when it comes time for me to reciprocate, the words stop in my throat. Somewhere along the line, I've decided to express my love through cooking and washing dishes. After all, she's gushed enough *you are the light of my existence*s for the both of us. She hasn't seemed to mind. She's always said I have the most beautiful aura she's ever seen and that my heart chakra's pink oozes out everywhere. "Like a big billowing ball of cotton candy!" she said once when I was little.

Sunlight streams through the window, hits the crystal sun catchers, casting spots of rainbows everywhere, even bands of indigo nestled between the blue and violet. Layla's a sun catcher. But settling down with Jeff, she'd be in the shade, just a clear piece of cut glass, nothing special. I miss her spray of rainbows. It isn't flamboyant. It's her.

I walk into her room. Her altar is crowded with pictures of goddesses and Virgins and gods, along with special stones she's found, dried flowers, pieces of driftwood, incense, and a picture I painted as a little kid of me and her together, flying between the earth and the moon and the sun and the stars, holding hands. We're wearing halter tops and long skirts and you can see our belly buttons. Our smiles are perfectly matched half circles. Back then I thought all girls lived with their mothers and traveled the world and found new grandmothers and cousins in every country.

Was I happy then? When did I trick myself into thinking I wasn't happy? When did I get an idea of what happy was? And when did I convince myself that being normal would make me happy?

I take some protective stones from her altar—green jade, red jasper, and a few crystals—what she'd want me to carry.

A few blocks from the bus stop, I pause in front of the phone booths, wondering whether I should call her. I think of Wendell's parents, who haven't heard from him for days. I think of what I've promised Sarah: to call her if Wendell needed her. If I were in Wendell's situation, would I want my mom's help?

I would.

Not that Layla could do anything—in fact, she might create more problems. But I would want her to know. I stare at the orange neon Internet café sign, at my reflection in the window, a girl with her mouth half open, unsure what to do.

Before I can change my mind, I open my indigo notebook to the page with Sarah's phone number and run inside and give the number to the phone girl. I check how much money

I have on me. Two dollars. I put it on the counter. Two dollars' worth of a conversation. About two minutes. Hopefully that will be enough time to explain this mess.

With polished crimson nails, the girl dials quickly. "Booth number two."

The phone rings five times. I clutch the cord, winding it around my fingers. Just when I'm thinking I'll have to either hang up fast or come up with a message, Sarah's voice answers, breathless.

"Hello?"

I try to make my voice breezy, as though I'm just calling about homework. "Hey, Sarah, this is Wendell's friend, Zeeta."

"Zeeta! Thank God! Where's our son? We haven't heard from him for days. We've called the hotel, but they say he isn't there and Dalia isn't there either and we don't have another number for him, and oh God, is he okay?"

"Yes, he's okay."

Silence, little gasps. She's trying to stop crying. But I only have about ninety seconds left, so I cut to the chase. "Actually, Sarah, I'm, uh, a little worried that he's about to make a decision that's maybe . . . not so good."

"What kind of decision?" This is the voice of someone trying desperately to stay calm but secretly hyperventilating.

"Uh, not that it's life or death, not exactly, but—well, financial. I think he might be about to, uh, throw away his art abroad money." I sound like a rambling, incoherent idiot.

"Don't freak out or anything, Sarah. I don't know what he told you about his birth father . . ." I'm guessing I have about sixty seconds left.

"He said he was a nice, regular old guy." Sarah's voice is actually shaking. "Nothing else, no matter how hard we pushed."

"He's—he's a jerk. And I think he's using Wendell. I think—"

"Oh God. We should never have let him go alone. Listen, we're taking the next plane there. I've been wanting to do this all along."

Wendell will kill me. Here and now I am ruining the remotest chance of any future relationship with him. This is like tattling or something, only worse. This is breaking some kind of universal code of conduct, calling someone's mom to come get them. And on a whole different continent.

Thirty seconds left and I don't know what to say. "Sarah, Wendell's gonna kill me—"

"You did the right thing, Zeeta. I won't tell him you called. I'll go online to transfer the money from his account. Then I'll get the plane tickets. For today if I can. I'll tell him it was all my idea."

The gears in my brain are turning and I'm picturing the thugs and how if they don't get their money, they'll use that machine gun, and I'm wondering how many seconds I have left in this phone call—probably about ten—and I'm realizing that before Sarah closes the account, Wendell needs to get far, far away from Faustino. And as I'm trying to form this into some kind of explanation that won't throw Sarah into a total panic, the line goes dead.

I run to the counter where the girl sits staring at the tiny flowers of stick-on rhinestones on her red nails. "I need more time!"

"Your two dollars ran out, *señorita*."

"Can you call back and I'll pay you later?"

She shakes her head, looks back at her nails. "Sorry."

"Please?"

"Sorry."

I race to the ATM. The closest one is broken, the next closest is broken too, and the third closest has a line stretching around the corner. Fifteen minutes wasted.

I stand on the sidewalk, clutching my bag, trying to order my thoughts, which are hard to hear over the pounding of my heart. I need to return the teddy bear. I need to get to Wendell, fast. I need to warn him that his account will be empty. I need to convince him to leave Faustino's house.

The smugglers said they'd come back in the *tarde*, a frustratingly vague word covering anytime between noon and night. The sun's already right overhead. If I'm fast, I might make it there before them.

I run toward the bus stop, unsure how I'll pay for my fare. Usually, you get on the bus and pay later, en route to your destination. I figure I'll sit in the back and hope by the time they get to me, we'll be close enough to Agua Santa that even if they kick me off, I'll be able to run the rest of the way.

A block from the bus stop, I spot Don Celestino on the corner, settled in his blue chair, holding his orange bowl on his lap, greeting passersby. How low can I stoop, begging from a beggar? I slow down in front of him.

"*Buenas tardes*, Señorita Zeeta," he says, smiling.

"*Buenas tardes*, Don Celestino. I have a favor to ask."

His clouded eyes gaze into the distance. "Anything."

"I need to borrow bus fare to Agua Santa."

He reaches out for my hand, holds it open, and drops a fistful of coins in my palm. He closes my hand and pats it. "Enough for bus fare back, too. *Que Dios te bendiga, señorita.*"

"*¡Gracias, señor!*" I take off, reaching the corner just as the bus chugs away. For twenty minutes, which feel like forever, I pace the sidewalk, twirling my finger around a strand of hair in desperation. Once I'm on the bus, my heartbeat calms a little, but my palms are sweating like crazy and no matter how much I wipe them on my jeans, they're wet again within seconds. My sparkly white shirt reflects light through the open window. I feel the opposite of sparkly white. I feel stuck in slimy, pig-shit-laced mud.

By the pink house, I get off, along with a family loaded down with burlap sacks and a little piglet that they've probably bought at the market.

I push the horrible pig-market scene from my mind. *Focus. Feel sorry for yourself later. Wendell needs you now.*

I take off my flip-flops and run up the hill, one hand on the bag slung across my shoulder. Now there's another thing forcing its way into my mind: the gun on the seat of the thugs' truck. If they get there before me, they might kill him.

I have to get there first.

At the top of the hill, I pause to catch my breath. The sky is clear blue, the color of Don Celestino's chair, with just a few clouds gathered at the mountain peaks.

Over the bird and insect songs, girls' voices rise, squealing with excitement. Odelia and Isabel and Eva are running to me, shouting, arms outstretched. "Zeeeta!"

Odelia fixes her huge eyes on mine. "Are you going to Taita Silvio's?"

I shake my head, still catching my breath.

Eva frowns. "You're not going back to Don Faustino's, are you?"

"Yes."

The girls' eyes widen. "Why?"

"I have to get Wendell." I give them quick hugs and take off running up the hill toward Faustino's house, pausing a few times to pluck some stickers from my bare feet. Faustino's truck is there. Wendell and Faustino must be inside.

I haven't brought bread for the dogs, I realize. They're lounging in the dirt patch, licking their fur and snapping at flies. They see me and wag their tails, bounding over with tongues flopping happily.

I let them sniff my hands—luckily that's enough—and head toward the house, taking the bear from the bag, ready to return it to Faustino, wondering what I'll to say to Wendell, how he'll react.

When I'm about twenty feet away, Faustino comes to the door, rifle in hand.

Wendell appears beside him, backpack slung over his shoulder.

He looks confused.

And Faustino looks furious.

He raises the gun and aims it at me.

Chapter 26

I've had guns pointed at me before, when Layla and I crossed the border into Cambodia, and a few times in Northern Africa, but those were just military guys showing off. After Layla smiled and worked her magic, they waved us along without even bribe money.

But this is different. I've taken something valuable from him.

I drop the bear and put my hands up, flip-flops still dangling from my fingers.

Wendell is shouting in broken Spanish, "No! *Ella* Zeeta! She *buena*! She *amiga*!"

Faustino ignores him and moves closer, snatching the bear from the weeds.

"Wendell," I say, "you know what's hidden inside those bears?"

Wendell shakes his head slowly.

"Emeralds."

"But . . ." He turns to Faustino.

Faustino flips over the bear, rips the seams with his switch-blade, and pulls out the bag. He dumps the stones into his palm, weighing and counting them.

"Wendell, he's part of a smuggling ring. We have to—"

"*¡Cállate!*" Faustino sticks his face in mine. His breath smells of hard liquor and onions. "Did you take any?"

"They're all there," I say, my voice unsteady. "Do what you need to do. Just don't let Wendell get involved."

"He's already involved. He's my son."

I swallow hard. "If you think of him as your son, let him go."

He lowers the gun.

Wendell grabs my arm. "What's going on? What's he saying?"

"It's too late," Faustino says, before I have a chance to translate. "I owe these guys—and Wendell's loaning me money to pay them back." He pulls his keys from his pocket and heads toward the truck. "We're on our way to his bank now. We're already running late."

I turn to Wendell. "Don't go with him. Come with me. Say goodbye to him and come with me."

"But I promised him the money, Z."

"Wendell."

"Ask him why he lied to me."

"We don't have time."

"Ask him why, Zeeta. Please."

I turn to Faustino. "He wants to know why you lied to him."

Faustino looks at Wendell, then at the ground. "To protect him. I'll pay him back, I promise. By now they probably noticed a bag is missing, and they won't be in a good mood about that, either."

I translate.

"I don't know," Wendell says. "Maybe I should give him the money."

"No!" I yell, aware of every drawn-out second.

Wendell nods at Faustino. "Come," he says, motioning to the truck. *"Banco. Yo dar dinero tu."* I to give money you.

I brace myself. "Wendell, your account's empty."

"What?"

"I talked to your mom. She transferred all the money from your account."

Wendell says nothing. Insect sounds rise and fall. Dogs bark in the distance. "Tell Faustino, Zeeta," he says coldly.

I turn to Faustino. "Wendell doesn't have any money."

"You're lying."

"His mom emptied his account. And we're leaving now."

The smugness in his squinty eyes gives way to fear. "These guys will put me in the cemetery."

Suddenly, there's the rumble of an engine. A cloud of dust is moving up the hill. The dogs bark and run to the truck.

The big silver truck. The one with the machine gun on the front seat.

They're here.

Faustino drops the bear. "Run!"

"This way!" He heads toward the garden. With one of the two skeleton keys around his neck, he unlocks the door and pushes it open. We run in after him. Cursing, he locks the door behind us.

The truck screeches to a stop. Men's voices start shouting.

Faustino takes off down the path.

We follow him through the scent of flowers, heavy and perfumed, and birds chirping and thousands of insects humming. It's bizarre, racing through this paradise with armed men on our tail. Tree roots and stones trip us, but we regain our balance and keep running. Behind us, fists are pounding on the wooden door, and there's more shouting, and then machine-gun fire on the iron lock, a sharp, staccato sound.

The door creaks open.

"*¡Chuta!*" Faustino cries.

This is farther than we went the last time. It's all downhill, but the path twists and turns here and there. My legs have gained a momentum of their own, and now I'm just trying not to fall or run headlong into a tree. In a couple of minutes, after a sharp curve, the path ends at a wooden door at the base of the hill. To the right of the door, a stone wall topped with glass shards begins and disappears in a tangle of flowering vines. Faustino stops at the door, gasping and fumbling with the keys around his neck.

I spot the men through the foliage, nearing the end of the path. "Hurry, Faustino," I whisper.

He leans over and fits the key in the lock, his hands shaking. He pushes the door open with all his weight. It looks heavy, six inches thick, a solid plank. We stumble inside after him.

In a split second, I take in the details, my eyes straining to adjust to the darkness. The only light comes from the doorway, a dusty golden glow. This part of the cave is small, with three tunnel openings behind us, mine shafts, maybe. They look tall enough for a person to walk through hunched over.

"Quick," Faustino says, just as the men are rounding the last bend, the machine gun raised and ready. "Help me close it."

He leans against the door, and Wendell and I move to help him. There's an inch more to go when the machine-gun barrel forces its way between the door and the frame. Before we can hurl our weight against the door, the men burst inside.

They're silhouetted against the rectangle of light, the same men from yesterday, only now I'm seeing them up close, close enough to smell their stomach-turning hair gel. One's chunky, with a double chin and an XXL Tommy Hilfiger shirt and a fancy gold watch. The other's younger, maybe just a few years older than me and Wendell, and what I notice most about him is a huge zit on his left nostril.

They take a moment to catch their breath, enough time for me to take in how dire our situation is. Frantic, my mind runs through the possible outcomes. They almost all end with us riddled with machine-gun bullets or left to starve to death in the pitch-dark. My one hope is they'll keep us alive for ransom, but even then, Layla has only a few hundred dollars in her bank account.

"We found the missing stones," the Tommy Hilfiger guy says, breathing hard. He holds up the sad-looking bear that Faustino dropped. "But we need that two thousand."

"Give me more time," Faustino says, his palms up. "The boy doesn't have the money."

"We've been more than generous. More than patient."

"*Compadres,* one more chance."

"No more chances."

"Take my truck, *compadres.* It's worth a lot more than two thousand."

"We don't want that piece of *mierda.*"

"And my TV. It's deluxe."

"We want the cash." The Tommy Hilfiger man jabs the machine gun at Faustino's throat.

"Wait! I have some money. It's hidden."

"He's lying, *hermano,*" the zit-nose one says.

So they're brothers. I can see that. Maybe in five years,

after a lot of beer drinking, the zit-nose one will get a gut and another chin like his brother.

"Yeah, he's a bad liar," the Tommy Hilfiger brother agrees.

"Let's give him some *floripondio* and find out the truth. We passed tons of it on the way."

The Tommy Hilfiger brother stays, gun pointed at us, and the other leaves to pick flowers. I glance at Faustino. I'm pretty sure he's lying about the hidden money.

The zit-nose brother returns with a bouquet of huge white blossoms turning rosy pink at the tips. "How much of this stuff do we give him?"

His brother shrugs. "When I use it to rob people, I get it already in a powder."

"The worst is we'd kill him," the zit-nose one points out. "Then we could just kidnap these gringos to get the money."

I'm not a gringo, part of me wants to shout. The other part of me is too scared to talk. My legs feel so weak, I'm sure they'll buckle beneath me. And if my heart beats any faster, I might have a heart attack. Maybe this is a terrible dream, and soon Layla will hear me tossing and turning in distress and wake me up softly with Rumi quotes.

"Give him one." They watch Faustino for a reaction, but he responds with a stony stare.

The guy rubs his double chin. "Make it two, on second thought."

With the machine-gun barrel digging into his neck, Faustino eats the flowers. We wait, and wait, and wait. The guys lean against the wall and talk about a *telenovela* they watch called *The Clone,* and how hot the star Jade is and how they wouldn't mind her doing a little belly dancing for them. Then the conversation turns to whether Leandro or Lucas—who are apparently clones with very different personalities—will end up with Jade. Then they discuss the ethical implications of cloning, punctuated with plenty of cursing.

And as they debate, I feel like I'm falling fast, into a pit with no escape and nothing to hang on to. I'm trying not to let my knees buckle underneath me, trying not to collapse into a hysterical, sobbing heap on the ground.

Then I hear something soft under the men's voices. It's Layla's voice. The echoes of whispers of all the times she's read to me before bed, all the lines of poetry, ribbons of wisdom that slipped inside me.

> They fall, and falling,
> They're given wings.

The lines repeat themselves, a birdsong on a loop. Over and over with my heartbeat and my breath.

Meanwhile, Faustino has sat on the ground and closed his eyes, resigned and waiting. After an eternity of maybe a half hour, he starts saying he's thirsty and clutching his throat. Soon he's mumbling incoherently. I can't tell if it's an act or if he's really drugged. His pupils do look a bit dilated, although it could be because of the cave's darkness. And he is pale and sweating, but that could be because of the angry armed men.

Either way, the thugs seem convinced. "It's working," the zit-nose brother says. "Ask him."

"You got a money stash, *cabrón*?"

Faustino smiles. "I have something more valuable than money." His words are slurred but comprehensible.

"What?" The Tommy Hilfiger brother jabs the gun into his side. He seems oblivious.

"My most precious possessions."

"Bet he's been pilfering emeralds. Bet he has his own private stash, the little snake."

"Where?"

"In a big cardboard box. Tied up with twine. Behind the TV."

"Better be good," the Tommy Hilfiger brother says. Then he raises his gun and bashes Faustino on the head.

Faustino falls sideways, blood dripping from his forehead and making a little glistening puddle on the ground.

Wendell sucks in his breath and kneels over him.

"Why'd you do that?" the zit-nose brother asks.

" 'Cause he's a *cabrón*. I didn't kill him. I won't do that till I make sure we get our money back."

The Tommy Hilfiger brother tears Faustino's keys from his neck. He turns to us. "If nothing's there, we'll kill you. That or we'll kidnap you. Make your family fork over a few hundred thousand for the headache. You better hope we find what we're looking for."

They close the door. The key turns in the lock. I kneel beside Wendell. Now there is nothing but the sound of our breath in total blackness.

Chapter 27

After a moment of shock, I find Wendell's hand. My other hand rests on Faustino's chest. It's moving up and down with his breath. Sticky blood clings to his head, but the wound seems to be clotting.

"I think he's okay," I say. The outside layer of me is talking, but the center of me is reciting, like a prayer, the same lines over and over.

> They fall, and falling,
> They're given wings.

"Breathing okay," I report. "Bleeding controlled. He feels hot, though, and his heart's racing." A few years ago, I signed Layla and me up for a CPR and first aid course in Tanzania, where we lived hours from the nearest hospital. I give Faustino a gentle shake. "Faustino, can you hear me? You okay?"

He moans.

Wendell's hand pulls away from mine and I hear him trying to open the door. "It won't budge, Z. What did those guys say? I caught a few words, but they were talking fast."

I give him a recap. The top layer of me is talking while the deeper layer is wishing my hands would turn into wings, the bones lengthening, the skin stretching into a thin membrane. I picture a bat's skeleton, which I saw in a photograph at Layla's Brazilian ex-boyfriend's art opening. The bones of the wings looked like fingers, as though one day the creature decided, *I'm tired of climbing and falling and climbing and falling.... Why not fly?*

"You know what's in that box, right, Z?"

I nod, willing myself to calm down and think logically. "His poisonous-creature collection."

"Best-case scenario, they get bitten and die." Wendell's voice is scratchy. "But then we'll still be stuck in here. And no one knows where we are. Worst case, they get bitten but not bad enough to die and they come back really angry and kill us."

"We need to hide," I say. "Either that or find a way out."

"This place seems familiar to me, Z."

"Did you have a feeling about it?"

"Sort of." He pauses. "I think this is the place of dark and light."

Dark and light. Where's the light?

It hits me. "Wendell, remember when Faustino said his earliest memory was a room of crystals? Taita Silvio told me about the crystal room. A secret chamber in a cave."

"We'll be safe there." His voice is strangely confident, floating in the darkness. "We just need to find it."

Again, I hear Layla's whisper speaking ancient words, her hand lightly touching my hair. *Darkness is your candle. Your boundaries are your quest.*

"We can find it," I say. "Silvio told me about it." I try to conjure up my conversation with Silvio. It isn't easy, especially under pressure. Five minutes have already passed since the thugs left. By now they might be opening the box. I'm warding off panic and sifting through everything Silvio told me about the chamber.

Right, he said. *All right turns.* "Okay, Wendell," I say, taking a deep breath. "Let's go. The tunnel on the right."

"What about Faustino?"

"We have to leave him here."

"But they'll kill him, Z."

"We have to save ourselves." I find Wendell's hand again.

"*Regresamos,* Faustino," he says in perfect Spanish, even rolling his Rs. *We'll be back.*

I squeeze Wendell's hand. "It's all right turns. That's the secret." I let my other hand brush against the wall to my right. Wendell keeps his left hand outstretched in front, in case of a dead end. We make our way through the tunnel, ducking down. If I let my head rise too high, it hits the ceiling.

The tunnel grows cooler the farther we go. It smells like old rock. Once in a while I hear a flapping, a flutter. "Bats," Wendell says, and I shiver and imagine wings stretching from my fingers.

We walk back even farther, our hands running along the sides and moving in front of us. Even if we'd gone to this chamber dozens of times before, it would still be hard to find in the complete darkness.

How far does this mine go back? We still haven't reached a turnoff. What if Silvio was wrong? Or what if we were supposed to start in one of the other tunnels and then make all the right-hand turns? After all, he wasn't giving me exact directions, just offhandedly mentioning an old childhood memory. Or was he?

Even with directions, the likelihood is that we'll get lost in the dark, or else fall from a drop-off or plunge into a deep hole. Even if, by some miracle, we do survive this, Layla will be making us settle down in Maryland and Wendell will never forgive me once he discovers his parents are coming. Whether we survive or not, I'm doomed. I'm falling. I try to focus on wings spreading, lifting me, a candle of darkness lighting the way. I try to hear Layla's voice.

That's when the tears start pouring out and my nose fills with snot.

When Layla cries—over recent roadkill or a skinny child begging—she quotes Rumi through her tears. *Cry easily, like a child. Keep your grief glistening . . .* The darkness hides my tears, but soon my sniffling gets out of control. Wendell stops. He pulls me close and holds me. "It's okay, Z. We can do this. It'll be okay."

Now I'm shamelessly sobbing and gasping. "A-a-are you mad at me, Wendell?"

"Why would I be mad?"

"That I called your birth father a loser and took the bear."

"I'm glad you're here." He finds my face and wipes the tears with his thumbs. "Let's go. There'll be a turnoff to our right coming up soon. I have a good feeling about this. We're headed toward light."

And that is what I need to feel myself lifting again. About a minute later, my face is dry and the wall curves. "Here it is, Wendell!"

We follow it to the right.

Soon the wall curves again to the right.

A couple minutes later, it curves yet again.

"Stop," Wendell says suddenly, pulling me toward him. "There's stone in front of us." I feel with my hand, and yes, it's a dead end.

"Now what?" he asks.

"There's a hole somewhere. At the base of the wall. Covered by a rock. A pretty small hole. Taita Silvio said his dad couldn't fit through it."

"Let's hope I fit," he says. It's true, his shoulders are so broad they might not. But I don't let myself think about that now. And I don't let myself wonder what happens after we find the chamber, how we'll ever get out of these tunnels. I focus only on surviving the next few hours.

We feel all around the base of the wall, running our hands over the rough stone. The occasional insect scurries away from our hands, which gives me shivers. On instinct, I keep looking back over my shoulder, even though it's too dark to see anything. There's a ruffling sound, and my heart jumps. Footsteps? Bat wings?

"Here it is!" Wendell says, moving my hand over the top of a rock, about a foot or two in diameter, at the base of the wall. With a grunt, he pushes the rock aside. We stick our hands where the rock was. Our hands move in empty space. A hole!

"I'll go in first, Z."

"Let me. It could be a drop-off."

"All the more reason for me to go first."

"I promised your mom I'd take care of you."

"I'll be fine. I told you, I have a good feeling about this." Without waiting for my response, he lowers to the ground and crawls in. I keep my hand on his legs, which go first, and then his hips and back, and then his shoulders, so wide they barely fit. He turns and twists to squeeze them through. His head follows.

And he's in.

"Z, come on in! Careful. There are crystals everywhere."

Again, there's a rustling. I can't tell if it's coming from our tunnel or another tunnel. Or inside or outside the chamber.

I can't tell if it's people walking, trying to stay quiet, or if it's bats, or something else. Don't bears and mountain lions use caves as lairs?

Taking a deep breath, I crawl in, feetfirst, slithering backward, pausing to squeeze my shoulders through. Inside, I stand up slowly. Wendell's hand finds my body—my left boob to be exact.

"Oops, sorry." He lowers his hand to my waist and slips it around my back. I wave my arms around me. Above, my fingers touch crystals of all sizes jutting out from the ceiling, smooth sides and sharp points. I bend down and feel the ground below us, covered with slippery, pointy crystals.

Wendell's voice: "I feel like we've been here before. But where's the light?"

Of course. The candles! "There is light, Wendell! Taita Silvio told me they kept matches and candles here. In a basket. Think they might work after all this time?"

"Maybe Faustino still comes here and restocks the supply."

I can only imagine Faustino coming in here to do something shady, like stashing smuggled jewels. I don't know what Wendell thinks Faustino would do in here, and I don't ask. Even after all that's happened, he's still hoping Faustino's a decent guy. I think, instead, about the task at hand. "If *I* hid candles," I say, "I'd put them right inside the entrance."

We feel around, moving our fingertips over the crystal, all sharp tips and glassy sides. Within seconds, my fingers touch the fibers of a woven basket and then smooth wax and a wick.

"Here!" I pass the candle to Wendell and feel around the basket. There's a small cardboard box. I shake it. Could be matches. I slide it open and my fingers touch dozens of small wooden sticks. "Found the matches!"

I strike a match. Nothing. I try again. *Come on, come on.* After two more tries, a tiny flame appears, an orange glow that lights Wendell's face and the space around us.

I look up and nearly drop the match. I gasp.

It's one thing to hear about a chamber of crystals, and it's another to be inside one. Even from this one flame, the light reflects and refracts thousands of times through thousands of crystals of all shapes and sizes. It's like being inside a heap of snowflakes or icicles, a hollowed-out snowball in sunlight.

Silvio is right. It feels like flying.

Wendell lights a candle. The room is about as big as my and Layla's apartment living room. All the surfaces—the walls and ceilings and floor—are pure crystal. I light another candle. I wish Layla were here.

"My dad used to do some caving," Wendell says finally. "He'd dig this place."

"Layla would, too. She's into crystals."

Somehow, the crystals defy the senses, don't limit themselves to sight or feel. If they had a sound, it would be hammered dulcimer music, notes tinkling off the tips of every tiny crystal. And the big crystals would emit low, mysterious harp sounds, deep and resonant as the calls of whales.

"Let's roll the rock back over the entrance," Wendell says. "Hide out here until they give up looking for us. Then we can go explore and see if there's another exit. It'll be easy now that we have light."

We pull the rock back in front of the hole and tuck my sweater around the edges so that no light can escape through the cracks.

Slowly, we move around, half-crawling, half-climbing, stepping very carefully between the jutting crystals. Some are the width of my pinkie, some the width of my torso. Impulsively, I hug the biggest one—the diameter of an old tree trunk—my fingers barely touching on the other side. Hugging a crystal! What will Layla think when I tell her?

If I can tell her.

If we ever get out of here.

We walk and crawl and climb to the far side of the chamber. In a little natural niche is a cluster of half-melted candles, white, in pools of wax. There are more than a dozen candles, melted down to different heights. They're arranged in a perfect circle around a broken crystal base, about a half inch in diameter. It looks like some kind of altar.

Wendell takes the crystal from his pocket—the one he's had since he was a baby. He presses it to the base. Perfect fit, clean break. He lights the remaining candles. I let my candle drip and press it into the pool of wax, standing it upright. Wendell does the same. Now our hands are free and the room is swimming with reflections and refractions of firelight.

"Who made this altar?" I wonder aloud. "Taita Silvio? Faustino?"

"If we ever get out of here," he says, "I'm gonna bring my mom and dad here."

I do some quick calculations. It would probably take his parents a six-hour plane ride to get here, then a couple of hours by bus from Quito to Otavalo. Less than a day. They could be here by tonight. He might see them tonight.

If we get out of here.

I try not to think of our bodies decomposing and turning to skeletons and being discovered centuries later. Layla says that's a good meditation to do—to imagine yourself dead. It makes you aware of the fleeting quality of life. Makes you live life more deeply. It still feels creepy to me.

"What about Her?" I ask, and as soon as it pops out of my mouth, I wish I could snatch it back.

"Who?"

"That sort-of-ex-girlfriend." I feel pathetic. "Do you want to bring Her here?"

"God, Z, I haven't thought about her since—well, since that e-mail. I wrote her back. Told her I met someone else. Told her I was moving on. And she said okay. Those were our last e-mails."

Lowercase *she*. I can definitely tell the difference.

He stares, his face close and warm in the orange glow.

Suddenly, I understand why Layla cried at dusk at the desert dunes in Morocco and at sunset on the beach at Phi Phi Island. When something is really beautiful, part of you knows it won't last long. And it's almost as if you're an old lady looking back at your life at that amazing moment. *Oh,* old lady Zeeta would say in her old lady voice, *I remember that time in the cave with Wendell when we had our first kiss.*

It's about to happen, I know it.

The space between us is obvious, a magnetic field. And now, almost imperceptibly, the space is growing smaller and closer and I don't know if it's him moving or me moving, but we're closer and closer and now we're touching, my fingers brushing against his fingers and my breasts touching his chest, and now his arms are around my waist and mine around his. In one last movement, my eyes close and our lips touch.

You know how you listen to music sometimes, and it has a certain color and taste and smell and feel? This kiss tastes like cinnamon and caramel, with a hint of minty Altoids. It feels smooth and tender and round. It's warm and golden, like bread or sunshine.

I forget I might move to Maryland.

I forget we're trapped in a mine.

I forget armed men are after us.

I forget everything except this moment.

Layla's right. There's something to be said for candlelight.

Chapter 28

After kissing for a long time, Wendell and I lean back in a kind of seat-nook we've found, where the crystals are smooth and angled enough to sit on. It has to be late. How long have we been in here? Hours? It's hard to tell without any natural light. I tuck my head on his shoulder and close my eyes and drift off.

I'm flying through a dark place. I look down and see the earth below me, all blue and green swirls. And I realize I'm hanging on to something, a small blue chair. And then I see a speck coming closer. Wendell, with his own blue chair. We hold hands and hold on to our blue chairs and head toward a crystal that turns into a star. We sit there together on our blue chairs, and I know that when we want to, we'll fly with our chairs to another star, and another, and another.

. . .

Whenever I tell Layla about my dreams, she says,

> A man goes to sleep in the town
> where he has always lived, and he dreams
>   he's living
> in another town.
>   In the dream, he doesn't remember
> the town he's sleeping in his bed in. He
>   believes
> the reality of the dream town.

> The world is that kind of sleep.

It used to annoy me that she'd mess with my sense of reality. Who tells their kid that life could be one long dream?

But now, half awake, between the dream world and this one, I keep my eyes closed, and ask myself, Why can't your dream become a reality? Why can't you paint your own picture of life? Why do you think Layla has to do it for you? If you want to fly with Wendell on blue chairs, why not make it happen?

Some time later—maybe minutes, maybe hours—I open my eyes. Wendell's staring at me, his face close.

I kiss him. "You know Don Celestino?"

"The blind man?"

"With the blue chair," I say. "He told me once that he never feels scared because his blue chair's always with him."

Wendell considers this. "What made you think of him?"

"His chair was in my dream. Two blue chairs, actually. One for you, one for me. We were flying through space in blue chairs. And I knew that with our chairs, we'd always be at home, no matter where we flew."

Wendell plays with a strand of my hair. "I wouldn't mind flying around with you on blue chairs."

Our faces are so close, I can make out every detail of his face, a small stray hair that he missed shaving, the tiny pulse moving at his neck, a nearly invisible scar on his eyebrow. I'm vaguely aware of hunger and thirst and needing a bathroom soon, but it's easy to ignore all that with his face filling my field of vision. I brush a wispy eyelash from his cheek. "Did you have a feeling about this? Us, together?"

He smiles, almost shyly. "A hundred times, Z. Us, here. But I didn't know if it was just wishful thinking."

He's tracing the contours of my face now. Running his finger to the tip of my nose, up my cheekbone, across my forehead, down my jawline, and back up again.

"Wendell, why did you go off and stay with Faustino? And leave me in the dark?"

"I don't know. I guess I felt stupid about getting drunk and throwing up and everything. And you obviously didn't like Faustino. But I wanted to like him. I wanted to trust him." He cups my chin in his hands. "But Z, even though I tried not to think about you, I couldn't help it. Whenever I closed my eyes, I saw this."

I swallow hard. "Can you see us in the future, too?"

"Actually—" And then he's quiet, his head tilted, eyebrows furrowed. "Hear that?"

I hold my breath and listen. The scraping of rock on rock. The stone we put in front of the entrance is moving. I glance around the chamber, searching for a hiding place. Only glowing light and crystal, no dark corners.

The stone moves aside.

I'm squeezing Wendell's hand so tightly my nails are digging into his palm.

A head of black hair appears.

Black hair laced with silver.

And then a face, Silvio's face, and his shoulders and belly squeezing through.

"Taita Silvio!" we say at the same time.

His eyes take in the situation. *Mis hijos.* He makes his way toward us, nimbly. He knows exactly where to step and which crystals to use as handholds. "What happened?"

We explain, our words tumbling out somewhat incoherently. The emerald smuggling, the thugs, the guns, the zombie flowers, the poisonous creatures, and Faustino unconscious.

He nods, appearing to understand, and then he tells his side of the story, pausing every few sentences so that I can translate for Wendell. "The girls came to me, worried. They said you'd gone to get Wendell, and that the guys in the truck came shortly afterward. I ran up the road and saw a machine gun by the door. A set of keys lay on the ground beside it. I picked up the keys and headed inside. Empty, but their truck was there. Sounds came from the garden, panicked cries. I found the two men there, on their hands and knees, looking for something. They were frantic, shouting about needing to find the keys and go to the hospital. They looked pale and were sweating, in shock.

"I calmed them down and pieced together what had happened. They described the snake that had bitten them, the arrow-shaped head, the Xs on the back. Each of their arms was already swelling, turning blue, blistering. *Jergón* was my guess. Pit vipers from the Amazon. 'Listen,' I told them. 'The venom is very fast and very potent and you've already wasted time. You could lose your arms. I will give you herbs to slow the poison. And then I will take you to the hospital for antivenom.'

" 'Thank you, thank you,' the men said.

" 'First,' I said, 'where are the boy and girl?'

" 'They're fine,' the younger one said. 'We didn't touch them.'

"The older one said, 'They ran off.'

"I couldn't tell if they were lying, but I had a feeling you were safe. Luckily, Faustino had the sense to keep the snakebite remedy *jergón sacha* in a pot beside his door. So I chopped up the root and mixed it with water. I had them drink it, and wrapped more of the root on their arms with a leaf. Then I drove them to the hospital in Otavalo, but they didn't have any antivenom. So I drove them to Quito, just in time to save their arms from amputation. The younger one turned to me and said, '*Señor,* thank you for your help. There's something I must tell you. The kids and Faustino are in the mine, locked in.'

"I suspected you'd found this room, that you were all right. But I guessed you were getting hungry and thirsty and scared. I took the keys to the garden and cave from his neck, and since I already had their truck keys, I drove back here. I wasn't sure whether they had someone else guarding you, so I was quiet coming in. And here I am."

"*Gracias,*" I say.

"*Gracias,*" Wendell echoes, and takes a deep breath. "Did you see Faustino on your way in? Is he okay?"

After I translate, Taita Silvio sighs. "He's alive. His head wound is minor. His eyes are open, but his head is full of terrible visions. Two flowers are usually not enough to kill a person, only enough to drop them into a world of nightmares. Soon he'll be all right."

Silvio takes us on a small tour of the crystal chamber, shows us his favorite crystals, the ones that captivated him since boyhood. Wendell motions to the circle of candlelight. "Who made that?"

Taita Silvio flushes and rubs his hand over his face. "When I told you I never set foot on my brother's property since the situation with Lilia, that wasn't exactly true. I come here every year on November sixth."

"My birthday," Wendell says.

Taita Silvio nods. "The place where I broke off your

crystal. I light a candle every year and wish you well, wish that your life is happy, wish that you learn to use your powers for good."

Wendell's eyes shine in the light from the sixteen candles. "Will you teach me?"

"Nothing would make me happier, *hijo*."

We make our way across the chamber, and again I have the sensation of flying, wings opening and closing in harmony. I can almost hear Layla's voice quoting Rumi.

> "Your deepest presence is in every small
> > contracting
> > And expanding,
> The two as beautifully balanced and
> > coordinated
> As birdwings."

That's what we are, Layla and me, each a wing. We need each other to fly. "I have to talk to Layla," I say.

"And I should call my mom and dad," Wendell says.

I can't suppress my smile. "I have a feeling you won't need to."

We find Faustino leaning against the wall just inside the cave's entrance. The door's open, silvery blue moonlight streaming through.

"Are you okay?" Wendell asks in Spanish, kneeling beside him.

Faustino nods weakly. We walk with him through the garden, stopping at the cistern outside his house to wash the dried blood from his head. After feeding his animals and grabbing our bags, we head down the dirt road.

"We shouldn't leave Faustino alone," Taita Silvio whispers. He turns to his brother. "Come to my house, *hermano*. Eat with us."

Faustino lowers his eyes and shakes his head. "I can't." But he comes anyway.

On the walk through the garden, Faustino says in a gravelly voice, "I thought you swore never to set foot on my land again."

"I also swore never to let harm come to my nephew."

Near the base of the hill, I see people walking toward us at the crossroads. Three people, their moon shadows stretching far behind them. Strange for people to be out at this time of night.

Closer, I notice they're not wearing shawls and ponchos and skirts. They're not Otavaleños. Even closer I see that they're not Ecuadorians, either; I can tell from the way they walk. Two of them walk like Americans, that purposeful swagger. Gringos.

And the third person, she flies along beside them, as though she has wings.

Layla.

Her feet are bare and her white dress is billowing out

around her, holding the moonlight. A braid wraps around her head like a crown. The other two must be Sarah and Dan. Sarah's wearing a sleeveless linen blouse and khaki pants and rubber sandals. She's shivering, hugging her arms around herself. Dan, clad in khakis and a T-shirt, keeps one arm around her, warming her.

I look at Wendell.

He's smiling, raising his hand and waving and then running toward them. Sarah and Dan and Layla start running toward us. Smack in the center of the crossroads, Sarah throws her arms around Wendell. She's crying. And Dan's crying. They hold their son for a long, long time.

Layla's crying too, which doesn't surprise me. What does surprise me is the force with which she hugs me. "I thought I'd lost you, love."

"I thought I'd lost *you*, Layla."

"I don't know what I'd do without you, Z."

"Likewise." Which really means, of course, *I love you, Layla.*

After the hugging and tears, Wendell puts his hand on Taita Silvio's back. "Mom, Dad. This is Taita Silvio, my birth uncle." He motions to Faustino. "And this is Faustino, my birth father."

They all shake hands, and Dan says, in Spanish, "Thank you, Faustino, for helping to bring our son into the world."

Faustino stares at his feet, until Taita Silvio claps his hands. "My wife would like to meet you all. Please come to my house."

"Oh, that's all right," Sarah says. Her Spanish is good too. "We don't want to bother her."

"That won't be a problem," Taita Silvio says, smiling. "She's used to unexpected guests."

The walk to Mamita Luz's house feels surreal with the moonlight on the corn leaves and the strangeness of Wendell's parents being here. It turns out they showed up at our apartment a few hours ago, at around eleven o'clock. Layla answered the door, frantic with worry. She'd read my note and had been using our landlady's cell phone, trying to get ahold of Gaby all evening. Apparently Gaby's cell-phone battery had run down. Finally, around midnight, after it had recharged, they reached her, and she directed them to Faustino's house. They were on their way there when we found them at the crossroads.

We walk single file through the tunnel of corn leaves along the irrigation ditch, Silvio and Faustino leading the way, Wendell in front of me with his parents, and Layla behind me.

Moonlight skips over the narrow channel of flowing water beside us. I hear Layla's footsteps stop.

I turn around.

She's skimming the reflected light with her fingertips, as though she's trying to soak it up.

"You know what's weird, Layla?"

"What?" She glances up.

"You're by a river in moonlight in the middle of the night." I look at her significantly.

"And?"

"And you're not quoting Rumi or anything."

"That's true." She studies the water.

"Don't you have the urge?"

She considers. "I feel an echo of an urge." Her fingertips keep sliding over the water, searching, leaving silvery trails. "I hear echoes of what my old self would say."

"What would she say?"

Layla closes her eyes, offers a small smile. "She'd say she bets the crystals in the cave are a kind of gypsum, maybe selenite. She'd ask if you knew *selenite* comes from Selene, the Greek goddess of the moon. She'd ask if the cave looked like crystallized moonlight."

"Actually, it did." I feel a giant wave of tenderness for her. "What else?"

"She'd say, who knows where the name gypsum came from, but it must have something to do with gypsies, like us, how we used to be, traveling around, chasing moonlight." Her face is almost iridescent.

Quickly, before I can stop myself, I say, "You're the mother I would choose for myself. The old you. The real you."

She takes her hand from the water. Her fingers are dripping moonlight.

I keep talking. "And this is the life I would choose for myself. Traveling and exploring and filling up notebooks."

She stands. We're exactly the same height, something I never noticed until now.

The words pour out. "Layla, I know you like Jeff and you've changed for me and I feel selfish, but I want the real you back."

She grabs my hands. Hers are wet and cool. "I don't know how. I don't know who I am anymore."

I search for something to say to that. Rumi comes out. "There is an inner wakefulness that directs the dream."

She finishes for me. "And that will eventually startle us back to the truth of who we are."

A whistle pierces the night. It must be Silvio or Wendell, wondering what's holding us up. I whistle back, and then we jog through the rest of the corn-leaf tunnel, to Mamita Luz's backyard, where moonlit smoke rises from the chimney.

At the door, Mamita Luz and the girls throw their arms around us and immediately start chattering. Eva tells us they're staying here until their father finishes an alcoholism treatment program. They seem thrilled with this arrangement, and even more thrilled to be awake in the middle of the night with three more foreigners. Odelia keeps bouncing and dancing and skipping in circles like an excited puppy.

Mamita Luz insists on calling Sarah and Dan *cumarita* and *cumbarigo*, literally comother and cofather, but also affectionate terms for friends. Sarah and Dan chat with her easily, talking about their two years in the Peace Corps in Guatemala. Meanwhile, Silvio cleans his brother's head wound with soapy water, applies some herbs, and wraps a bandage around it like a headband. The girls pass around warm rolls as we tell Sarah and Dan and Layla what happened. We leave out the machine guns and the poisonous flora and fauna. We can't get around the emerald smuggling, though.

Layla puts her hand over her heart, while Sarah bites her knuckle. Dan's face turns red. He looks at Faustino and opens his mouth to say something, then shuts it. He puts one hand over the other, in a tightly clenched fist. I'm guessing he wants to yell, *How the hell could you let my son get involved in this?*

Layla fixes Faustino with a hard gaze, a mix of fury and compassion. "What were you thinking, *señor?*"

Faustino answers in slow Spanish. I whisper the translation in Wendell's ear. "In the cave after I ate the flowers, I was a boy again, hiding in the cave from my father. A snake came and turned into my father and he was crying and saying, *Forgive me, son.* And then he left and a white bird came. She turned into Lilia. I said, *Forgive me, mujer.* And she kissed my cheek. Still, I felt full of poison, but then a bee came and I was sure it would sting me, but it thought I was a flower, and it drank and drank and flew off. And then I felt full of nectar and it was a good, golden feeling. And then Wendell came to me, and it was really him, asking, *Are you okay?* And I thought, *Maybe he thinks I am full of nectar. Maybe I am full of nectar after all.*"

No one says anything for a moment, and I feel sure that Sarah and Dan must be thinking *What the—?!,* when Layla takes his hand. "If you were poison in the past and you are nectar now, be nectar." It's as though they have their own language. Crazy mystical-poetry language. Then she looks at me and murmurs in English, "Sometimes the cold and dark of a cave give the opening we most want."

Faustino turns to Silvio. "There's something I don't understand. All those years ago, why didn't you take the boy? Lilia wanted to give him to you and Luz. But you said no. You told her to let him be adopted by foreigners. Why?"

Taita Silvio looks at Dan and Sarah and Wendell, who are still and alert, listening carefully. "I wanted him to be safe. I wanted him far away from you. And also—" He stops.

"What?" Faustino leans forward.

"I was afraid I would turn into our father. I wanted the boy far from me, too. I didn't know if I was strong enough."

"But look at all these kids around you." Faustino sweeps his arm over the room. "You two are the father and mother of the town. Everyone knows that."

"Now I know." Taita Silvio pauses. "There's something else. After Lilia asked us to take him, I did a divination. I saw something. Something like a string—a red one—stretching from the baby to a gringo couple. And I saw that this was good, that they belonged together."

"*Gracias,*" Sarah says, wiping her eyes, putting her hand over Wendell's.

Faustino stands up. "I'm taking off for a while. In case those guys come looking for me."

"I don't think they will," Taita Silvio says.

Faustino shrugs. "You never know. I'll stay in Colombia for a few months until this blows over."

Taita Silvio lifts the leather string with the two skeleton keys from his neck. "Your keys, *hermano.*"

Faustino puts up his hand. "Give them to the boy. The cave is his now."

Silvio reaches out, grasps his brother's hand. "It was wrong of me to hold a grudge for so long, *hermano.* I hope you visit us when you come back. You are welcome in our home."

Faustino nods and starts out the door.

Wendell stands up. "*¡Espérate!* I have something for you." He reaches into his backpack and pulls out the small bundle of translated letters. I take the remaining translations from my bag and tuck them into the red ribbon.

Faustino hesitates.

"He started writing these letters when he was eight years old," I say. "They're important to him."

Faustino shakes his head. "Give them to my brother."

A shadow of disappointment passes over Wendell's face. Then he nods and glances at Taita Silvio, managing a halfway smile. "All right."

Faustino takes a last look at Wendell. "Forgive me."

And he's gone.

Chapter 29

Once Mamita Luz puts the girls to bed, Taita Silvio opens the letter in Spanish on top. It's the last translation I did, before the pig market, which seems like years ago. "May I read it out loud?" he asks Wendell.

Wendell nods.

Taita Silvio reads word by word, in a drawn-out, labored rhythm, pausing to take a deep breath between sentences. He's only had up to a third-grade education, I remember. But the nice thing is that when he reads so slowly, every word feels weighty with importance. And this way, Wendell and his mom and dad can understand the Spanish more easily.

Dear birth mom and dad,

Thank you for making me and giving me to mom and dad. I know you're probably poor and maybe now you're even starving and begging for scraps on the street. If I saw you begging I would give you money. Sometimes I cry and feel sad for you. Sometimes I feel bad that I get to go to Bojo's on my birthday and eat pizza and Coke and cake until my stomach sticks out like a soccer ball and meanwhile you're all dressed in rags and you can see your ribs and everything. I think you did a good thing to give me to mom and dad. You made us happy, me, mom, and dad.

Thank you,
Wendell B. Connelly,
age 12

Mamita Luz chuckles and pats her husband's belly, soft and round. "No ribs in sight with my bread nearby."

Taita Silvio reads a few more letters out loud and we laugh a lot and cry a little and eat bread and sip lemon balm tea. Afterward, the kitchen feels so cozy and warm that even though it has to be nearly dawn, we don't want to leave. Dan finds the guitar in the corner and strums some tunes, humming lightly. Then Taita Silvio picks up a reed flute and starts playing along with him. Together, they create a spontaneous melody.

Wendell's watching them while Sarah and I are watching

Wendell. He's their music. His dad is the reed and Silvio's family's genes are the carefully placed holes, and some mysterious force like the Absolute is the breath, and they've all come together to create this beautiful boy.

This boy who kissed me in a crystal cave.

This boy who chose me as his She.

After a while, Sarah and Dan start yawning and saying they're ready to head back to the hotel with Wendell. I'm ready to go home too, but Layla's discovered that Taita Silvio's a healer. Now, of course, she's in the middle of a passionate conversation with him. You'd never guess it was five a.m. by the amount of energy she suddenly has.

We say goodbye to Wendell and his parents, agreeing to meet at the market for dinner that evening. Once they leave, Layla jumps right back into her conversation, detailing her near drowning in the waterfall with dramatic flair. She's standing up, twirling her arms around, demonstrating how the water sucked her under, as though it's a modern dance routine.

Silvio nods gravely. "You have fright, *cumarita*," he says. "At the moment you were drowning, your spirit left your body. You need to get it back." He sips his tea. "You haven't been yourself lately, have you?"

I answer for her. "No, she hasn't!"

Mamita Luz pats Layla's shoulder sympathetically. "Would you like my husband to give you a *limpieza, cumarita*?"

Magical words for Layla. An invitation to a spiritual

cleaning. Her secret life goal, I've deduced, is to have her spirit cleaned in every country in the world.

This time, she really needs it.

"Oh yes! Thank you!" She hugs Mamita Luz. "Thank you for having such a lovely husband and making such delicious bread. Thank you for everything!"

In the candlelit curing room, I sit on the bench at the wall, while Mamita Luz and Taita Silvio prepare for the *limpieza*. As instructed, Layla starts to undress, first unwinding her wraparound skirt.

In a cotton spaghetti-strap tank and hipsters, she stands in perfect yoga posture, with a hint of a belly poking out. She's always refused to do crunches—they might block her golden belly chakra. She's entering a trance state now, eyes closed, belly expanding and contracting with her breath.

Meanwhile, Taita Silvio is arranging the altar with Mamita Luz's help. They put the huge feather headdress on his head and the strands of beads around his neck. The framed saints on the walls stare down at us. The gaze of the Virgin of Agua Santa is especially tender. Sacred water. I know that makes Layla happy. She loves water goddesses in any form.

On the altar, candlelight reflects off the laughing Buddha with all the happy bald babies crawling over him. It makes me think of Mamita Luz and Taita Silvio and all their children. It makes me think of all the different ways to be a mother or a father, or a daughter or a son. Of all the different ways to feel at home in this world.

Mamita Luz spreads a plastic doormat under Layla's feet

so that the dirt floor won't get muddy. Then she holds a glass goblet of water before Layla. "Sacred water, *cumarita*. From a melting glacier. Drink."

Layla sips.

Mamita Luz sits down and Taita Silvio begins chanting in Quichua and whistling, meandering melodies that make me think of the flute music he played earlier. He blesses a green bottle of liquid. Mamita Luz whispers something to Layla, and Layla closes her eyes, and Taita Silvio spits all over her, forceful gusts like ocean mist in a storm. He's at least five feet away from her but easily soaks her. Again and again he blows away the bad air, calling her spirit back.

He takes two stones from his altar. "*Cumarita*, think about who you really are." He rubs them over her, patting her flesh rhythmically and chanting, as though her body's a musical instrument. A smile to rival the Buddha's lights up her face. This is the kind of thing she lives for.

Taita Silvio grabs a bundle of leaves.

"*Chilca*," Mamita Luz whispers.

With the *chilca*, Taita Silvio taps Layla in a regular rhythm, making circles around her stomach, back, and neck, chanting in Quichua and whistling all the while. Now he's focusing on her chest, just over her heart.

Layla's shivering, and if there were more light in the room, I bet we could see her turning blue. Next, Taita Silvio puts a handful of rose petals cut into tiny pieces in his mouth, then takes a sip from the green bottle. He spits on her. "Rub the petals into your skin." Then he gives her white stones to rub over herself. "Think of what you want, *cumarita*," he says. "What you truly want."

Layla smiles and concentrates.

Then Taita Silvio takes another swig and blows the liquid on her. This time, he lights a lighter as he spits. When the alcohol spray passes through the flame, a fireball forms and shoots across the room. I jump a foot off the bench. Just before it reaches Layla, it goes out.

Not much surprises me in healing ceremonies, but fireballs are a new one. One fireball after another, and each time I jump. All the fireballs make Layla stop shivering and bathe her in an orange glow. She looks like an angel.

My heart racing, I think, *This is my mother.*

And then I think, *She's back.*

The fireballs stop. Layla opens her eyes and smiles at me. Mamita Luz comes to her with a pink towel and her clothes. Taita Silvio sits down, looking worn out but satisfied. "We're finished. Your spirit is back, as strong as ever, *cumarita.*"

In the fresh early morning air, we head toward the bus stop, Layla and me, side by side, our strides synchronized. In my left palm, I'm clicking together the amulets I've brought: jade, jasper, and crystals. I'm tired, a happy tired, a tired that lets down my usual defenses and gives me the courage to say, in a raw, simple voice, "I missed you, Layla."

"I missed me, too." She laughs a sleepy laugh and throws her arm around my shoulders.

We walk down the road, a ribbon through masses of green,

as though a sea of leaves has parted just enough for us to pass through. All this green feels delicious, painted with angled lemony light, dripping with tree shadows. Power lines criss-cross the hills like silvery spiderwebs, and tiny, faraway people walk along their own narrow ribbons of road, curving here and there.

I lean into her. "What now, Layla?"

"Now, fly!" she says with another laugh.

"Seriously, Layla."

She throws her head back and gazes at the sky. "Okay, how about this? Jeff will head back to Virginia, and maybe we'll e-mail a little, and then after a while, he'll fade into our memories." She unbraids her hair, still damp, and runs her fingers through it, letting it tumble over her shoulders. "A couple of years from now, when we're in another country, and we pass a handsome older fatherly type, or flip through a magazine and see a well-dressed man playing golf, we'll say, *Hey, remember that Jeff guy? Remember how we almost moved to Maryland?*"

"Really?"

"Yes."

I click the stones around in my hand. "And," I say, "we'll feel a little sad, maybe, but then we'll blast Moroccan music and you'll shout, *Dance with me, Z!*"

Layla snakes her hands up in a quick belly dancing move. "And you'll roll your eyes, and groan, *It's the middle of the night, Layla! What about the neighbors?* But you'll join me anyway."

I breathe in the mist rising off the shiny green cornfields in the valley, the luxurious gown of Pachamama—Mother Earth—embroidered with emerald leaves and crystal lace, trimmed with the silk ribbons of rivers, fringed with petals and leaves. "And secretly, I'll love it." I raise a calculated eyebrow at her. "On the condition, of course, that we establish some rules."

"Hmm." She lifts her hair, twirls it, and ties it in a loose knot. "No rules. How about agreements?"

"Okay. Agreements."

By the time the bus arrives, we've agreed that we'll put ten percent of our money away for my college fund, ten percent for her retirement, ten percent in investments, and ten percent for emergencies. I've agreed to complain less about her boyfriends. And she's agreed—very reluctantly—to take turns doing the dishes.

Finally, the most important agreement: I get to choose what country we go to next. I just need to figure out where that will be. Which involves, of course, Wendell.

A few days later, at six a.m., Jeff and Layla and I are standing in a drizzle in our courtyard. He's stopped by on his way to the airport, left his SUV, engine running, on the street. He's particularly handsome in the rain, his skin damp, his eyes the same iron gray as the sky, looking wistful. I feel a little stab of regret that we'll probably never see him again.

He launches into a speech. "Thank you for everything, ladies. You're looking at a different man from the one you met on the plane." He even sounds like a Handsome

Magazine Dad, sturdy and sentimental. "I've got it all planned out, thanks to you. I'll take Spanish night classes. I'll go on a weeklong trip to a different country every year. And I'll always order the daily special."

"But will you eat it?" I ask.

"At least a bite." He grins. "Even if it's snake or iguana."

I look away as Layla gives him a long kiss goodbye and whispers in his ear.

Before he climbs into the SUV, I give him a copy of Rumi.

Inside the apartment, Layla and I watch a few minutes of golf with the volume turned down so we can hear the rain on the roof. We list a few things we like about Jeff, sort of a memorial service to their failed relationship. Layla tears up a little as we stick the TV back in its box. Later that morning, we'll sell it at a pawnshop and put the money in our brand-new money market account.

A week later, I come home from the market to find Wendell and Layla drinking foamy papaya juice on the sofa. They look excited. Before I can ask what's going on, Layla leaps up and announces, "Wendell has a surprise for you, Z!"

She runs behind me and covers my eyes with her hands. They're warm and sticky and smell like papaya, like a little kid's hands.

"Uh, Wendell," I say, "care to enlighten me?"

"You'll see," he says.

Layla leads me to my bedroom, sits me down on my mattress, and removes her hands. "Open your eyes, love!"

I open my eyes. My room feels different. It's no longer empty. And in a split second, I figure out why. Nine prints hang on the previously bare wall. They're photos, Wendell's photos, some color, some black and white, some sepia, and they fill the wall, floor to ceiling.

The center photo is of steaming bread in a shaft of sunlight. Then there's the crystal cave in warm candlelight. The mountain Imbabura, towering and shrouded in mist. A close-up of watercress by a trickling stream. Wendell on the floor with drying watercolors surrounding his face (I took that one). Me in the café, the first day we met, when he talked about the light hitting my hair (and yes, you can actually see red highlights). Gaby sitting like a queen at her booth, among scarves and clothes of all colors. The waterfall at sunrise, all silver spray. A portrait of Mamita Luz and Taita Silvio and the girls, standing proudly in front of their house, smoke rising from the chimney like a child's drawing of a happy home.

Wendell sits next to me on the mattress. "Like it?"

I'm speechless for a moment. *"Que pleno,"* I say finally. "I love it, Wendell."

"Good!" Layla says. "Now I'm off to my class. Late as usual." She kisses me on the forehead and breezes away.

I stand up and look at the pictures closely, noticing the shapes, the color contrasts, the composition of light and dark. "Wendell, remember in the cave, when I asked if you saw us together in the future?"

He stands behind me, wrapping his arms around my waist. "I didn't get a chance to answer."

"Well, what is it you see?" Asking this scares me. What if he doesn't see us? Or sees us far away from each other? Sees us lonely? Or sees us with other people?

He presses his face into my hair. "We're together. In a place with amazing light conditions. And lots of fountains."

Chapter 30

I'm sitting in the shade of a *floripondio* tree in Faustino's garden, jotting down impressions on the last page of my indigo notebook, glancing up once in a while to watch leaf shadows shift on Wendell's face. It's the day before he has to leave, and we're having a farewell picnic. We've just eaten avocado-and-cheese sandwiches and watermelon slices and caramel-filled pastries. I'm full and content, tingling with the thrill of filling another notebook, relishing the breeze moving over my skin.

A few feet away, Giovanni is perched on a boulder, blowing up a pink balloon, his curls dancing wildly around his face. He's teaching the girls and Mamita Luz and Taita Silvio and Gaby how to make balloon pigs. Layla—who's already mastered balloon-creation from a previous clown boyfriend—is wandering around the garden, watercoloring petals and bugs and stones.

I close my notebook and slip my hand into Wendell's. He's spent the past month living with Mamita Luz and Taita Silvio, learning about healing and divining. Every day, I stop by their place, and Wendell and I walk to Faustino's house with the girls to feed the donkey and chickens and dogs. Sometimes we hang out in this garden, sometimes in the crystal chamber, which mesmerizes the girls. Their father is making some progress with his treatment, and their mother comes by to visit when she can.

I glance at the impromptu balloon-animal-making class. Gaby is forming the balloon pig's snout, with Giovanni's guidance. She twists with so much vigor, the balloon pops. She jumps and, in English, shrieks, "Holy cow!" which sends the girls into giggle fits. Her English is getting better by the day, and I've been making enough money from our tutoring sessions with the other vendors to put some into savings.

Layla meanders over to me and Wendell, crouches across from us, and opens to a fresh page of her sketchbook. Things with Layla have been good. She's been doing her half of the dishes—or at least convincing Giovanni to do them for her. And I haven't complained once about how our apartment's been invaded by exotic balloon creatures—dinosaurs, armadillos, potato bugs.

"You know, Z," Layla says, dipping her brush into the green, "if you'd been a boy I was going to name you Wendell."

"Really?"

"Yep." With broad, impulsive strokes, she starts painting a picture of what I can only assume is an abstract representation of Wendell and me. She glances up at Wendell. "It means wanderer, right?"

He nods. "My parents named me after my grandfather."

"When I was pregnant, I knew my child and I would be wanderers together." Layla slathers deep green onto the page, forming our cheekbones, noses, the curve of the leaves surrounding us. "And I loved this idea. But you were a girl, so I named you Zeeta."

"What's that mean?" Wendell asks.

"Seeker. Because we're not just wandering the world." She swishes her brush in the glass of cloudy green water and dabs it in the red. She splashes the red among the leaves, bright flowers. "We're seeking."

"Seeking what?" he asks.

I'm curious how she'll distill all her searches. Seeking enlightenment? The ultimate spiritual high? The Absolute? Ourselves?

"Who knows," she says. "Maybe whatever we're seeking, we've had it all along."

I think of the blue chair.

She rinses the red from her brush and dips it in the blue. She makes the sky in a few quick strokes. "But that doesn't mean we stop seeking." She tears off the finished portrait and hangs it from a tree branch with a clothespin. It looks like a strange flag, this sketch of Wendell and me blending into the leaves, flapping there in the breeze. "See, you two are perfect for each other, the wanderer and the seeker. Soul mates."

I'm more than a little embarrassed, grateful everyone else is out of earshot. I decide to change the subject, fast, before she starts talking about past lives and karma and how her soul mate keeps eluding her, which I've heard many times before. "Hey, Layla, maybe our next country could be one with really good light conditions."

She doesn't blink at the strangeness of this suggestion. "That would be nice. Inspire me to paint more."

"It could be a place with lots of fountains, too," Wendell adds.

"Fountains and light," Layla murmurs, nodding. Suddenly, her eyes widen. "I know just the place!"

I squeeze Wendell's hand, and he squeezes back, and everything feels right, the perfect mix of chance and choice and fate and wishes. And as Layla draws in a breath to name our next home, the ground beneath us transforms into the worn, comfortable wood of a blue chair, already lifting us into a watercolor sky.

Glossary and Pronunciation Guide

adiós	ah-dee-OHS	goodbye
¿Algo más?	AL-go MAS?	Anything else?
¿Algo para tomar?	AL-go PA-ra to-MARRR?	Something to drink?
alli punlla*	AH-lee POON-zha	hello/good day
amiga	ah-MEE-gah	friend (female)
amigo	ah-MEE-goh	friend (male)
anaco*	ah-NAH-coh	wraparound skirt
banco	BAHN-coh	bank
buena	BWAY-nah	good
buenas tardes	BWAY-nas TAHRRR-days	hello/good afternoon
bueno	BWAY-noh	good, all right, okay
buenos días	BWAY-nos DEE-ahs	hello/good morning
cabrón	cahb-RRROHN	very offensive insult along the lines of "asshole"
café con leche	cah-FAY con LAY-chay	coffee with milk

cállate	CAH-ya-tay	shut up
canguil*	cahn-GEEL	popcorn
chicas	CHEE-cahs	girls
chicha*	CHEE-chah	traditional fermented corn drink
chilca*	CHEEL-cah	medicinal herb
¡Chuta!	CHOO-tah	Shoot! or Darn!
compadres	com-PAH-drays	coparents or slang for friends
con la luna	cohn la LOO-nah	"with the moon" or crazy
cumarita*	coo-mah-REE-tah	comother or slang for female friend
cumbarigo*	coom-bah-REE-goh	cofather or slang for male friend
curandero	coo-rahn-DAY-ro	healer
cuy*	coo-EE	guinea pig
Don	Dohn	Mr.
Doña	DON-yah	Mrs.
dos mil	DOHS MEEL	two thousand
ella	AY-ah	she
espérate	ays-PAY-rah-tay	wait
floripondio	floh-ree-POHN-dee-oh	flowering plant native to South America
fritada*	free-TAH-dah	fried pork
gracias	GRAH-see-ahs	thank you
gracias a Dios	GRAH-see-ahs ah dee-OHS	thanks to God
gringa	GREEN-gah	female from the U.S.
gringo	GREEN-goh	male from the U.S.
guapa	GWAH-pah	beautiful
hacienda	ah-see-AYN-dah	large estate
hermano	err-MAH-noh	brother

hijo de puta	EE-ho day POO-tah	son of a bitch (very offensive insult)
Imbabura*	eem-bah-BOO-rah	huge mountain near Otavalo
jergón*	hayrr-GOHN	kind of pit viper
jergón sacha*	hayrr-GOHN SAH-chah	medicinal herb used for treating snake bites
jugo de tomate de árbol*	HOO-goh day toh-MAH-tay day ARR-bohl	sweet juice made from a "tree tomato" fruit
limpieza	leem-pee-AY-sah	spiritual cleansing
llapingacho*	yah-peen-GAH-cho	traditional potato pancake
mamá	mah-MAH	mom
mamacita linda	mah-mah-SEE-tah LEEN-dah	pretty little mama
mamita*	mah-MEE-tah	mom
menestra*	may-NAYS-trah	traditional lentil stew
mestiza	mays-TEE-sah	female of mixed ethnic heritage—indigenous and white
mestizo	mays-TEE-soh	male of mixed ethnic heritage—indigenous and white
mierda	mee-AYRR-dah	shit (offensive)
mija	MEE-hah	my daughter
mijo	MEE-ho	my son
mire	MEE-ray	look
mis hijos	mees EE-hohs	my children
mucho gusto	MOO-choh GOOS-toh	nice to meet you
mucho mejor	MOO-choh may-HOHRR	much better
mujer	moo-HAYRR	woman

ñaña*	NYAH-nyah	sister
ortiga	ohrr-TEE-gah	medicinal herb (nettle)
Otavaleña	oh-tah-vah-LAYN-yah	female from Otavalo (may refer to indigenous Quichua speakers)
Otavaleño	oh-tah-vah-LAYN-yo	male from Otavalo (may refer to indigenous Quichua speakers)
Otavalo	oh-tah-VAH-loh	a small city in the Ecuadorian Andes
Pachamama	PAH-chah-MAH-mah	Mother Earth (Quichua goddess)
papá	pah-PAH	dad
Parque Bolívar	PARR-kay boh-LEE-varr	Bolívar Park, a plaza in Otavalo
peña	PAYN-yah	live music club or bar
perdón	payrr-DOHN	Excuse me
phoneutria	foh-nay-OO-trree-ah	highly venomous South American spider
Plaza de Ponchos	PLAH-sah de POHN-chohs	Ponchos Plaza, location of the outdoor crafts market in Otavalo
que rica bébé	kay RREE-cah bay-BAY	A possibly offensive catcall
que Dios te bendiga	kay dee-OHS tay bayn-DEE-gah	God bless you
¡Que pleno!	kay PLAY-noh	Cool!
Quichua	KEECH-wah	indigenous language of Otavaleños in the Ecuadorian Andes

quiero	kee-AY-roh	I want
Regresamos	rray-grray-SAH-mohs	We'll be back
señor	sayn-YOHRR	sir or Mr.
señora	sayn-YOH-ra	ma'am or Mrs.
señorita	sayn-yoh-REE-tah	Miss
sí	SEE	yes
taita*	tah-EE-tah	father
telenovela	TAY-lay-noh-VAY-lah	soap opera
Tengo dinero	TAYN-goh dee-NAY-roh	I have money
toma	TOH-mah	drink
tostado*	tos-TAH-doh	toasted corn
trago*	TRAH-goh	liquor
tranquilo	tran-KEE-loh	calm
Ya no aguanto	YA noh ah-WAHN-toh	I can't bear it anymore
Yaguarcocha	yah-wahrr-COH-chah	"Blood Lake" in Quichua

* Word that is either indigenous Quichua or Andean Spanish

Author's Note

Several years ago, in the Ecuadorian Andes, my Otavaleño friend told me a fascinating true story. One day, a teenage boy traveled from Europe to my friend's indigenous community, searching for his birth parents. The boy looked just like my friend, yet spoke no Spanish or Quichua. After a lot of digging (with the help of his translator girlfriend), he discovered he was my friend's half brother, and was embraced by their family. I loved this story, and started weaving it into a novel.

More than a year later, I returned to Ecuador. One evening, I found myself in an adobe curing room with a *curandero* spitting fireballs at me (sound familiar?). When he asked me to imagine what I truly wanted, I was prepared to envision a successful pregnancy, which was what I'd spent the last five years wishing for. My husband and I desperately wanted a baby, but had struggled with infertility. As I stood there in the darkness, soaking wet, wrapped in the hum of Quichua chants, it occurred to me: Maybe a successful pregnancy isn't the key to my happiness. Maybe my baby is growing inside someone else, waiting for me. Maybe our spirits are connected. Maybe, somehow, they've been connected all along.

After returning from Ecuador, I began the adoption paperwork. Three months later, my husband and I saw a picture of our beautiful one-week-old baby. Over the next nine months, as the paperwork was processed, I wrote a draft of my novel and traveled twice to Guatemala to visit our son. He finally came home with us in December. For the past year, I've been finishing this novel, loving my son with every particle of my being, and feeling tired . . . but happy!

As I wrote Wendell's story, I thought about the search my son might someday make for his birth parents. Maybe it will be a journey in his imagination, or maybe it will be a physical journey. I hope what he finds at the core of his journey is love, in all its surprising forms.

Follow Layla and Zeeta to their next home in

The Ruby Notebook,

on sale in September 2010!

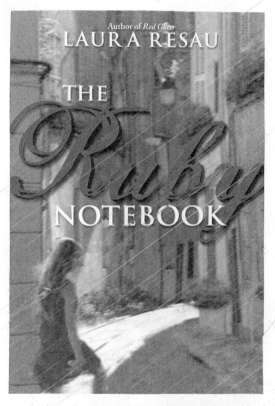

As I rummage through my bag, I call out, "Layla, did you put a CD in my bag at the café today?"

"Nope."

"Well, whoever put it there stole your motto." I plug in the c and read from the case, "Make every day a song."

" kind of guy."

I open our ancient clock-radio-CD player, hoping it will rk. Layla bought it at a flea market in Chile, and we've agged it around six countries since then. It's on its l leg ut we can't afford any new music-playing devices. cu last year, we vowed to save nearly half of our in- e fo lege, investments, retirement, and emergencies— h lea little money for luxuries. I put in the CD and play.

The music starts out slowly, one delicate guitar note plucked after another. Behind my eyelids emerges a single star, then another, then another. Each note is pure and bright, each as huge as a sun and as tiny as a snowflake all at once. And then comes a cascade of crystalline notes, and then the chords, deep and wide and resonant. The crescendos send me flying, weaving through galaxies, spinning like planets.

It's only one song, no words, but at the end of it, I realize my eyes have closed and I'm holding my breath. In the silence after the song, I press pause and look at Layla.

She's leaning against the kitchen doorframe, a far-off look in her eyes. "Whoever gave you that must be completely smitten."

"What?"

"That music exudes love. It's made of love. Someone's got it bad for you, Z."

"I don't think so."

Layla looks skeptical.

"I have a boyfriend, Layla, in case you've forgotten. I haven't even looked at another guy." As I say this, I realize I'm not being entirely truthful. There was that unusually handsome accordionist. But everyone was looking at the band, not just me. He'd have no reason to think I noticed him.

"When did you find it?" She spins the pastry roller thoughtfully.

"In Nirvana Internet Café. But someone could've put it in

my bag on the square." I flip the case open and closed, frowning. "I don't think it's an admirer."

"Then who?"

I search for a more logical explanation and, giving up, say with a wry grin, "A *fantôme*."

"A ghost?" Layla spreads another thin sheet of pastry on the *mille-feuilles* and shoots me a mischievous smile. "Then Monsieur le Fantôme chose the perfect music to reach right into your heart."